SCYTHE

Published AD 2013
Genre: Spiritual Fantasy

SCYTHE

II

SCYTHE

DEMON HUNTER

By
Caleb and Tommy Davis

ISBN # 978-0-9825522-4-7
Genre: Spiritual Fantasy

SCYTHE

SCYTHE

Rejoice not against me, O my enemy; when I fall, I shall arise.

-Micah, and Bunyan's Christian

SCYTHE

VI

SCYTHE

Tommy's Dedication:
For my parents, Majorie and Gene Davis

Caleb's Dedication:
For my beautiful wife, Lauren

SCYTHE

VIII

SCYTHE

Chapter One
Ogdognals

For two days and two nights we had tracked the three Ogdognals, and pressed them hotly for all of the third day. And now, through the third night we chased them, a night quickly disappearing into the misty light of a new dawn.

Our gargoyles kept to the scent well, bearing us on their muscle-ripped backs, their huge nostrils sucking in the stench-wake lustily as they ran.

It had been near dusk three days before, at that time of day when one can barely distinguish between colours, when I and my three fellow hunters had come to the edge of a wide, open field. We paused to look across it.

There, on the far side of the hundred-acres, we caught a glimpse of the three, our prey, perched on the thick low limbs of an ancient oak that somehow supported their massive weight.

Our prey was a trio of infleshed demons, Ogdognals by type and rank. Despite their huge size, they could really move. But our gargoyle mounts could run for hours without growing weary and I felt mine bristle underneath me when it also caught sight of our prey, though sharp eyesight was only one of our gargoyle's tools for tracking. Their sense of smell is keen indeed, and they hunt as well by scent as by sight.

Taking note of us, the Ogdognals made their move quickly, as we had suspected they would. We also knew we would have to be ready, that the dangerous enemies across that field would either take or give ground; they would either run from us to try to prolong the hunt and wear us down further, or else they would charge towards us to end it quickly.

I held a half-breath, weapon in hand, awaiting their choice.

They chose the former, and I exhaled a sigh of disappointment. Even though a pitched battle across open ground was to their decided advantage due to their size, my hunt-mates and I preferred to settle the matter without the delay of a long and indefinite chase.

Yet our quarry left us little choice.

But before they could sink into the dark labyrinth of the thick, green forest, I chanced a volley of arrows from my crossbow. Crokow, the senior demon holding rank among the trio, laughed deeply and loudly enough that I could hear the chunky, evil laughter even at that great distance when my arrow only grazed its heel, doing no more apparent damage than to knock off a few scales and leave a small scratch on the thick under-hide.

It was not the first time I had heard that mocking laughter. Crokow and I had a history.

This was actually our fourth meeting. We had both hunted one another and fled from one another several times before, and each time we had parted it had laughed a deep,echoing belly laugh in mockery of me and my cause.

But a few hours later, it wasn't laughing. It was running--and it was leaking.

I had dipped the tips of my arrows in globluscyn, a paste made from the crushed roots of the globus bush, which had the effect of a loosener, a stomach turner, in Ogdognals.

For the unlearned, Ogdognals are the fourth class of demons, and it was their under-lord Crokow and a brace of underlings that we now pursued.

We sometimes referred to their class as A-minus-Four, meaning that if you begin at the top with Apollyon himself and count down four tiers, or classes, there you will find this particularly disgusting type of demon.

Unlike higher-level demons, Ogdognals cannot take on human form, but rather take brutal, grotesque animalistic forms so strange they almost defy description.

A demon-hunter in training is told that there is no perfect description of an Ogdognal; they will know one when they see it. One might posses the body of a bull but the head of a ravenous wolf. Another might resemble a bear with a crockadile's head, but with the huge hind legs of tiger.

Fanged and clawed, an Ogdognal is always big, many times the size and weight of a man, usually well over a thousand pounds. Yet they can move with frightening speed. Evil, filthy, and smelly, they are fairly cunning yet with a demonality of sorts. They can communicate with fellow demons but rarely try to speak to humans and then only with threatening hisses or hideous laughter.

The globluscyn drug was very potent and it took only a short time for it to work its way through the thing's dense double-muscle, into the blood stream, and from there into the digestive system.

SCYTHE

Once there, it churned everything Crokow had eaten into a thick brown, syrup-like mucus that emitted itself slowly from whatever orifice it found most convenient.

It was this reeking waste the thing involuntarily trailed behind it that left an odor so pungent our mounts easily kept the scent. So acidic was the waste that a vapor rolled fog-like from the puddled substance and burned my eyes and nose, mocking the thick bandana I used to cover my face.

But our gargoyles, brazen and audacious beasts that they are, seemed to thrive upon the stench. They even lapped with forked tongues at the small puddles of it that Crokow left along the trail when our pace slowed. Nasty creatures these gargoyles, but very useful when hunting a demon, serving as both mount and hound.

Especially handy are they in pursuing earthbound demons like Ogdognals, which do not possess the ability to take flight, as other, higher-level demons do. I was glad that at least these things we pressed after were earth-bound; a demon that could take to the sky posed a whole other set of problems. But that was not my worry, at least not for the moment.

While pursuing the scent trail, even as pungent as was the waste-stench, our mounts suddenly caught a new scent on the wind. The gargoyles suddenly became wild, as if possessed themselves, and broke into a mad and uncontrolled dash, ignoring the reins that we pulled hard against their forward thrusting heads.

This pace was too fast, too erratic, but there was no turning the beasts. I could barely stay aboard my mount, even though the boney, fan-like outgrowths at the forward and rear portions of its back served as a natural saddle. We had to slow them and regain control, or risk losing control and losing our prey.

I quickly whip-wrapped the heavy leather reins around my forearms and gauntleted, clinched fists, pulling now against my mount's large head with all my strength. Even though I leveraged my weight by pressing my feet against the horn-like barbs that grew out of either side of the beast's upper shoulders, still I could not slow it down.

Without warning, as suddenly as it had begun its mad charge, my gargoyle mount dug its hoof-claws into the ground and came to a vigorous halt, sending me flying over its head and bouncing along the trail.

SCYTHE

If the mad dash had angered me, the sudden stop on the hardened trail infuriated me. My fellow huntsmen had not fared much better.

When I had regained my feet, I reached for my whip to teach the beast to obey the reins. It was then that I realized why our gargoyles had charged. The new scent that the morning breeze carried was the scent of Ogdognal blood.

There beside me, in the middle of the path, lay one of our enemies. At least what was left of it.

Chapter Two
The Dreadlock

I am called Scythe, and I lead the Dreadlock, and the Dreadlock hunts demons.

Each member of the Dreadlock has earned the title of Dreadknaught, a demon hunter who has sworn to live and, if the need arise, to die tracking, hunting and killing the infleshed creatures of Apollyon's under-horde. Each and every one of the enemy that has broken the mouth of the pit will be found and destroyed; this is our oath, our creed, our word, our duty and our cause.

The Dreadlock is a four-man team that consists of me, the tracker Kae-san and two other volunteers who have joined us in the fray.

Kae-san and I have worked together the longest. In that time, Kae-san has proved his value as a tracker a thousand times over.

Though two years my junior and somewhat short of stature, he can pick up an enemy's cold trail that I would have overlooked and passed by. Though he is most valuable as a tracker, Kae-san is more than able when it comes to sword-work. He has a pleasant-enough face though he rarely smiles, and the crystal-green orbs of a hawkish trailsman. Hailing from the sea coast, he usually keeps a two-day stubble on his chin. When we chance to pass through a village, Kae-san gets more than his share of glances from the fair maidens.

Then there is Rag-dan, the beast-master who introduced us to our gargoyle mounts some three years ago. Before Rag-dan, we had always ridden a horses into battle, but he changed all that.

Rag-dan trains and looks after our gargoyle mounts, mounts that lend a powerful advantage to our cause. Equal to me in years, Rag-dan is two inches taller than my six feet. Broad of shoulder, narrow of waist, Rag-dan wears his hair long and in all seasons save mid-summer he keeps a thick beard and mustache.

Finally, there is Invictus, the newest and youngest member of our band of brothers. While an excellent swordsman to have seen only eighteen summers, Invictus is so free-spirited that he is prone to over-enthusiasm at precisely the wrong time. He has a boyish face with high cheek bones that are framed by a jaw line so square some would call it angelic. Angelic face or not, Invictus is as fierce in battle as any infleshed demon you might care to meet.

The young man wears a care-free attitude lightly on his muscular frame and practices daily with his sword. His company I find pleasant and encouraging, as he possesses the natural temperament of one who takes his duty seriously but himself lightly. And though he comes from the region of Flatland Farms, where honourable men work hard every day tilling ground their fathers left to them, the life of a farmer did not appeal to him. Neither did he adjust to his mother's gentle plans for him. And so Invictus looked to other interests, and that is how we found him.

Presently, each man was drawing a weapon and scanning the surrounding brush in case the other two of our prey lie in ambush. We first made sure our gargoyle mounts were tied off around the perimeter as sentries, and then approached with caution to more carefully examine the carcass on the ground before us.

Gathering around the sight, we looked with disgusted delight upon the mangled mound of blood puddled, bone splintered mess of Ogdognal, freshly killed. Thick, coarse, needle-like barbs of pork-u-pine fur were mixed with its scale-coated skin and other shreds of flesh in a blood-soaked meatpie there in the middle of the trail.

"The other two turned on this one," said Kae-san, after a moment of contemplation. He then pulled a short but heavy-headed hatchet from his belt and whacked a stump from the carcass.

With a gauntleted hand he reached down and picked up by a toe-claw the thick, scale covered foot he had hacked off. It was a hind foot, probably two feet long from heel to claw, heavy enough that Kae-san strained to hold it up with one hand. Leather-like skin, thickly padded underneath, covered the sole of the foot from heel to ball. The ball of the foot itself was covered with more pork-u-pine barbs, these thicker but shorter than the ones on the other parts of the body, and slanted back at an angle towards the heel. These barbs could dig into the ground, tree bark, or whatever surface the Ogdognal crossed, giving the thing traction, agility and speed, and leverage in a fight.

The toe claws were just over six inches in length, serrated along the edges, and ending in sharp points. Some of the other claws had been broken off bluntly, probably in the short fight that had been this one's last. Kae-san tossed the foot aside to examine the whole of the Ogdognal carcass.

"Obviously the work of a double team," he pointed out as he used his hatchet blade to trace the various jagged cuts and tears that ran across the torso and back of the carcass. "Look at how this set of gashes runs from the sternum towards the back. Then notice that on the other side the gashes are wider and run in the opposite direction."

SCYTHE

I nodded my head in agreement with Kae-san's evaluation, admiring his ability to discern such things from a quick examination.

This level of hunt-craft was invaluable in a Dreadknaught, and I felt a tug of shame for having fewer of these skills than my comrade.

Sure, in demon-combat some say I have few equals. But you cannot kill what you cannot find, and I was thankful to have Kae-san at my side as we tracked these hell-lungers. But now Kae-san had a question for me.

"Why do you think the two others would have turned on this one?" Yet, I had already been pondering that very thing.

"Well, this is obviously not Crokow. Crokow probably weighs three thousand pounds. This one is no more than a ton, I would estimate. My guess is that either this one had injured itself and was slowing the trio down, or perhaps it had made the mistake of pointing out that it was Crokow's crapp-trail that allowed us to track them so readily. They have not been able to shake us, even in the thick of these woods. Indeed, we were gaining on them. Crokow, upon hearing this challenge, would no doubt have turned with vengeance on this one. And, to prove its loyalty, although we all know demons really posses none, the third one apparently joined his senior officer in mauling this one." I looked up to see Kae-san nodding his head in agreement with my deduction.

"But," Kae-san wondered further, "though this creature is quite mangled and his innards laid bare, I see no sign that the other two dined on his flesh as we have known these Ogdognals to do."

"I'm sure, Kae-san, if there would have been more distance between them and us that Crokow and the other one would have enjoyed cannibalizing their recent comrade. But remember, once an Ogdognal chooses to run and not make a stand of it, it is their normal habit to keep running until in the clear. Yes, we must keep watch of an ambush, for anything is possible with these curs, but it would be out of the ordinary for them to do aught but continue their flight. They are on the run, and since their momentum is tilted in that direction, we should remount and press them. With any favor of Providence at all, by day-break tomorrow our gargoyles will be nipping at their scaly heels! That is when they will turn to fight, and that is when we slay them both."

The sight of our immediate foes reduced by one-third, and that with neither scythe blade nor sword yet bloodied, had emboldened me, and I uttered that last sentence with particular relish and confidence.

Until I heard it.

Rather, I felt the vibration from the pounding of something moving towards us that shook the very ground, even before our ears caught any sound. We waited in stunned silence for a few seconds more as the rumble grew louder... and closer. Kae-san then looked wide eyed at me and I at him as we both yelled together....

"THEY CHARGE!"

SCYTHE

Chapter Three
Land Thunder

The sound of the charge quickly built to a subterranean echo-thunder that we felt under our boots, and heard the sounds of snapping tree limbs as something massive tore through the forest towards us.

Kae-san dove to his left and me to my right, off of the path and into the bush. Our brothers-at-arms, Invictus and Rag-dan, must have run to collect and steady our gargoyles, for when I looked around these men were nowhere to be seen.

Spotting Kae-san in the woods across the path, I quickly tossed a spool of razor wire in his direction while holding to one end myself. When I felt the wire tense, I knew my partner had remembered his training and had secured his end to the base of some trees he had fallen among.

I found myself near the base of a large water-oak and wanted to anchor my wire to it, but the charging thing was almost on us now. I tried to whip my end around the tree trunk, but it was too short to go all the way around and so, fell limp.

In my rush to throw the spool across the path to Kae-san, I had failed to keep enough slack on my end to tie around the big oak. My eye caught a glimpse of the leaves on the forest floor as they were being jostled about by the vibrations of the land-thunder. I had only a couple of seconds left to secure my end of the razor wire. If it was still in my grasp when the charging wretch snagged it, my hands would instantly become fingerless nubs.

As I reached for the silver strand of wire, I felt against my face and body the spray of rocks being kicked up by the charging Ogdognal—hundreds of small rocks and pebbles were flying off the path, ripping through leaf, vine and twig. There was only one other tree close enough to tie too, a small pine about ten inches in diameter. With the wire in my gloved hands I dove towards the pine, slinging the wire at the tree in a way that I hoped would whip-wrap around. The wire buried itself deeply in the pine bark just as the ground-thunder reached a deafening roar.

I rolled away from the lethal wire but caught a glimpse of it snapping taught as something large and menacing flashed across the pathway. Rolling over again, I was half buried now in the decaying leaf-bed of the forest floor. I looked again and saw that the pine tree was slowly tipping over and falling towards me. Rolling once more, I sensed the trunk of the water oak against my back and I braced myself against it for whatever might come next.

Then I realized what had happened. The wire had indeed been snagged by the charging demon, but must have caught it at just the wrong body-point, its hard, boney-shell covered knee cap. As sharp as it was, the wire still could not sever the cap to take off the leg, and the weight of the beast had simply pulled my end of the wire clean through the relatively soft meat of the pine, felling it nearly on top of my head, missing me by inches!

Kae-san and I both jumped back onto the path, he with his sword drawn, me with twin hand sickles ready for action. The ground thunder was quickly subsiding, the sound drifting away from us. We had not even slowed the beast down.

"How many came by us, Kae-san?" He was breathing heavily in the stress of the moment.

"I saw only one," he replied. "I only caught a glimpse, but it looked to be no bigger than the dead one there." He motioned towards the carcass with his drawn sword.

"Makes sense, in a way," I replied. "Crokow is too smart to be the lead on an ambush charge. That means he may still be around." The other two members of our band had taken cover somewhere near the gargoyles in the woods. They needed to be warned of a possible sneak attack by the unaccounted-for demon.

"Rag-dan! Invictus!" I yelled into the forest, "be on your guard for the big one...Crokow may lurk near!" But I felt Kae-san's hand on my shoulder, trying to quiet me.

"Listen," he said, putting an index finger to his lips. And there it was, more distant thunder, rolling in on us from up-trail, from the same direction it had come before. But this time we would be ready.

"Re-wire!" I ordered, pulling a fresh spool of the flexible razor wire from my heavy leather waist-pouch. This second beast was moving towards us at a terrible pace, yet we had an extra few seconds to locate big oaks on either side of the path to which we might anchor.

That done, we waited with weapons drawn, crouching low inside the wood-line along the path.

It appeared out of a dust cloud some thirty yards away, but something was wrong. It was only twenty yards away when I realized what I was seeing. I raised a weapon and dropped it with heavy thrust onto the taught razor wire. Kae-san had obviously done the same thing because the wire fell limply to the path, the charging creature galloping harmlessly over it.

The creature pulled to a halt near the bloody mound of spent Ogdognal. This second charger was no demon, but rather a mighty black stallion, the largest horse I had ever laid eyes upon.

Its coat was so deeply jet-black that it reflected a sheen of jade in the morning sunlight that was now peeking over the tree tops. So long in leg was this animal that a child could have walked under its belly without having to crouch. Across the horse's back an upright rider sat erect in a massive leather saddle, his spine as straight as a ship's mast. The handles and hilts of two short-swords were visible as they hung on either of his hips. A third weapon, a long-sword, was strapped across his back, the cross of its hilt clearly visible over the man's left shoulder.

The rider looked battle-ready, yet he was not panicked, a rare quality for one engaged in such a dangerous trade as ours. Even the bravest Knights I've fought alongside have always shown at least some nervousness when on the hunt, but not this rider.

There was also something remarkable about the way he sat the horse. It was as if the massive horse did not carry him, but he carried himself, and that with the confidence of a man utterly convinced that he held to truth and was not afraid to die for it.

Presently, three more horsemen galloped down the trail. Their mounts were fine and strong looking, yet not as exquisite as the stallion, whose rider I correctly assumed to be the captain of the lot. I was impressed with the fact that he was willing to lead his men in battle, as I myself am want to do, instead of just ordering them into it.

These three formed about their leader, and I noted that all were dressed more or less alike. Each wore a long black lapel riding coat that hung down past their spurred boots when sitting astride. Under these coats they wore neatly cut, black leather vests with black-pearl buttons, and under the vests were tailored shirts dyed charcoal grey. Their boots were also of heavy, black leather with pointed toes, which were also capped in black pearl. They wore black pants, sharply creased and made of heavy indigo clothe with few noticeable tears. A black silk stripe ran down the side of the pants legs, giving the four the look of a military order.

Atop their heads they wore crisp leather broad-brims, tasseled in pale gold. Above all of this, the feature that stood out the most was their eyes, especially those of their captain. Intense eyes, yet without a trace of worry. Wide, but not awkwardly so, and as deeply blue as the Pool of Eden before the Fall.

Kae-san and I came out of our hides, moving up the slight banks of earth onto the path. Appraising the group, we realized who they were, and we looked at each other with a degree of wariness. In unison again we said to one another...

"Baptines!"

Chapter Four
Baptines

It was only then that the riders noticed us. Instinctively they reached for their swords, each of them being armed with at the least two. All of them reached for arms, that is, except the captain. He merely looked us over with a plain blank stare, as if he had grown bored waiting for us to appear from the woods.

He watched indifferently as Kae-san dutifully began to re-roll the limp razor wire onto a spool. With that done we walked down the trail to where the four horsemen remained near the carcass, where they cast similarly disrespectful glances over both it and us. Their captain spoke first, nodding as he did to Kae-san's spool of wire.

"That wire would not do my mount's forelegs much good," he said smoothly with a thick accent that must have tasted of molasses. Kae-san, who is usually very level headed, but on the other hand easily riled if he feels his honour trifled with, tensed beside me. I knew he had been offended at the mild rebuke offered by the long rider.

"That's why we cut it limp and *allowed* you to ride over it unmolested," replied Kae-san with more than a hint of challenge in his voice. One of the horseman lieutenants must have himself taken offense for his captain, for he replied as he wheeled his steed nearer to us with sword still in hand,

"If that wire had crippled one of our mounts, you bush-hiders would have paid a high price!"

Kae-san took a step towards the horseman before my hand pressed his shoulder, urging restraint. Discretion being proportionate to valour, I knew I had to turn this conversation to a more constructive direction if possible. After all, if these Baptines were not on the same Team as us, at least they were on the same Side. So I tried to clarify the situation.

"We were expecting another Ogdognal. One had just charged past. We hoped to cut the next one down to a more manageable size with our slice-wire. When we saw your steed's snout, we released the tension on the wire."

"The demon that ran past you was not charging. It was in retreat," said the Baptine captain, knowingly. "We met two of them in a clearing not a mile hence. When they saw us they offered no battle, but turned instead to the south. They split up and we pursued the smaller of the two because he stayed to the path. Our mounts make much better time on a path than off. It was that one who ran by you. The larger one took to the south-east woods."

"The larger one is called Crokow, an Ogdognal leader," I replied. "We have trailed a trio of them for three days and were pressing them hard from the south when we came upon this mangled corpse." If the Baptine was impressed with my knowledge of our common foe, his face showed it not a whit.

"I care not what it is called," he replied sharply, "I only wish you could have proven useful in stopping it, or at least slowing it. Too much to ask for I suppose." Now I felt *my* face grow warm with anger as my honour was being called into question.

Baptines! I thought, frustrated. Their talent is outweighed only by their arrogance. Known for excellent horsemanship and sword play, as well as exceptional zeal in the demon-hunt, they are yet so full of stifling legalism that they would not dare even speak the name of a demon, much less study the various classes with their attendant abilities and special evils.

And though I had never actually seen the Baptines in combat, I've heard from others who have that these flaws put them at a disadvantage by not knowing the range of their enemies' ability. For this lack of knowledge, it is also said, the Baptines compensated with faith, and went on. This I find not totally without merit, for faith is vital. But we Dreadknaughts chose to handle things in a more tactical way, and I would not be belittled for it!

I made my way over to the stallion that the Baptine captain sat upon and took hold of its reins near the mouth-bit. This caused the other riders to tense, but Kae-san now had his own weapon drawn, and none struck out. The steed would have turned its head but I held firm the leather reins and spoke to its master.

"Sir, we came into this forest in pursuit of our prey. We came here to kill demons and dispatch them forever from this realm. Before today I've never met you, but from what I've heard, we share a common goal."

At this time Invictus and Rag-dan came up the trail leading our four gargoyles. The presence of the gargoyles made the horses jittery, but they did not bolt as any normal horse would have at the sight of our mounts, beasts that most reckoned to be from hell themselves. But I had no time to take admiration in the horses' superb training, for I was not finished addressing the captain.

SCYTHE

"If you came here for the same purpose, then let us count one another, if not friends, then as least allies, and if you cannot stomach even that arrangement, then let us agree to hunt the hell-spawn as disjointed units. But either way, know this, stern Baptine: The Dreadlock lives by a code of honour no less noble than your own, and we will not be looked down upon, neither will we be belittled. I dare say we have slain our share of hellions, with a few more to spare!"

I watched the captain closely, hoping that my face reflected the stone gaze that I saw in his. He sat stoic upon his steed, hand still at hilt, for some seconds longer. I thought I caught the shadow of an almost-smile brush over his face. Whether the grin was born of sarcasm or just plain disgust I could not tell. And then he spoke, not in answer to me, but rather to his horsemen, as if I were not even present.

"I heard that these Dreadfuls were riding hell-beasts," said he.

"That's 'Dreadknaughts,'" I said aloud, "and as for our mounts, these gargoyles have proven doubly useful--can your horse track a three day old trail?" The Baptine captain looked me in the eye while giving a sharp order to his men.

"South, men, we ride south down this woods-trail; regular formation with swords at the ready. Don't bunch together now, and keep a sharp eye out. A demon needs to die before the sun falls into the west." With this last phrase he drew the long-sword from the sling across his back.

Backing his horse sharply a few feet before wheeling the stud on its hind feet, his eyes continued to hold mine, yet unable to penetrate my own steely gaze. He turned the spirited stallion south and led down the trail, his men following according to his instructions, each one with sword drawn. In seconds, the last of the four had disappeared behind the deep green foliage of the forest, a large and drifting dust trail the only sign of their leaving.

The Dreadlock gathered round me as if to hear whatever summary wisdom I could conjure concerning the Baptines, but I had little to say of them. They were what they were, just as we all are. They had no doubts about what they believed, holding neither trust nor confidence for those unlike them. This held contradiction for me, though I myself had often said that in the demon-hunt, one could trust only those of one's closest circle.

Perhaps we are all guilty of contradiction, I thought to myself, guilty of hypocrisy, carrying out our blood-thirsty deeds in what we deemed a righteous cause. At the end of the day we should not demand trust from other men, but respect only.

Yet I doubted that we had earned any from the Baptines this day. Either way, there was no time to ponder that now. Kae-san asked me,

"What now Scythe? The path would be clogged with us and the horsemen on it."

"We take to the woods. A southward octagon will be our pattern men; run the pattern of the eighth digit across these woods and let your beast howl up hell itself when it picks up Crokow's scent! Make your gargoyles ignore any other scent, for we hunt the stink-trail! Kae-san, start a fire in that pile of demon flesh. And men, mind your mounts; they are tough but not indestructible, and hobbled gargoyles will do us precious little good when the chase ends at the fight! Be watchful over one another as brothers-in-arms, and always watch for the ambush. We ride!"

And with that the four of us mounted and lurched into the thick of the trees, Rag-dan and Invictus to the left of the path, Kae-san and me to the right, running the crisscrossing figure of an 8, with the forest path splitting where the two circles meet. I hoped that in our circular pattern we would cross ground where Crokow had recently been. I could only pray that he was still leaking from the drug-potion that my arrow had carried through his scaly flesh.

SCYTHE

Chapter Five
To Dread It Not

For nearly four hours we pushed on through forest and glade, around lagoons, through swamps and over rocky outcroppings that we encountered deep in the beautiful woods as we re-covered the same ground which we had so recently hunted. It was then that I saw Kae-san approaching on his mount, waving a gauntleted hand at me as if he needed to stop and talk. As he approached I called out,

"What is it Kae-san?"

"My mount is slowing. We have driven them hard for days now. These beasts will hunt till they drop dead of exhaustion, as will the Dreadlock if you ask it of us, but-"

"But you are right, Kae-san, we must rest soon, for the gargoyles' sake and for our own. Do you know of a good place we could take a few hours rest?"

"Indeed I do Scythe. Last night when we paused to water our beasts, I scouted about the woods a little."

"A brave thing to do with angry demons nearby."

"Brave or foolish, I needed to stretch my legs. And when are demons not angry? Nonetheless, as I walked I found myself seeing a spot in the dark that was darker than the dark around it, a black hole in the night forest. I drew my sword and inched closer to it, for heaven only knows what evils these precincts hold. When nothing emerged from the place, I struck flint to a pinecone and tossed it at the hole. The light revealed the mouth of a cave of some type. I called my mount to the place and let him sniff about the entrance but it discovered no trace of anything foul. And, if I judge properly, at the rate we now travel we will be near the place again within half an hour. From the look I gained of it, I would say that the shaft of the cave itself is wider than the mouth, and a narrow mouth is easily guarded."

"True, Kae-san, it is, though I must admit I had trouble guarding my own with the horsemen back on the path a few hours ago." Kae-san laughed at my play on his words, and continued explaining his plan to find us a resting place.

"What's more, the mouth of this cave is situated at the base of a rise in the forest floor, and sitting astride the cave itself is a broad elm tree, its roots growing down around the rock walls of the cave. With our mounts sleeping at the mouth of the cave, we could enjoy a few unworried hours of rest."

"Say no more, Kae-san. Once again I am made to envy your woods craft and your sharp eye, finding cave holes in the dark. We will hold out for another half hour then, and find this—"

My words were cut short as the blistering howl of a gargoyle screeched through the trees in such a tone as to make us nearly cover our ears. We listened for several seconds, but the unmistakable howling of a gargoyle did not stop.

"One of our mounts, raising-Cain on your order, Scythe!" said Kae-san, with an expectant look on his smiling face. At that moment I was reminded that men like Kae-san are easy to work with, approaching even such grim work with a hearty attitude.

I turned my mount and we rode hard towards the sound, riding, for all we knew, into battle and death. Yet we were too exhausted to fear death, as our veins glutted themselves with the juice of excitement, and our souls with anticipation.

We soon found Rag-dan and Invictus waiting on the main path the Baptines had trod, their gargoyle mounts pitching about nervously. I wondered aloud if they had scented the trail of the smaller demon that the horsemen were after.

"Men, I asked you to avoid this path, it is Crokow that we want," said I.

"Scythe," replied Invictus, "my beast has picked up another odor, and if I mistake not, it is that of the blood of some earth-beast."

For the unlearned, an earth-beast could not be a demon, for demon flesh is unearthy, alien, generated by otherworldly forces that go unnamed among common men.

We put our noses to the air and caught a whiff riding on a breeze.

"Smells like the blood of a mammal," said Rag-dan.

"Smells like the blood of a horse," I replied. "Draw weapons men! Invictus, take the right wood-flank, and the left for you Rag-dan. Kae-san and I will ride this middle path. On the double-quick men, let us see what mischief our Baptine friends have stirred up!"

Kae-san and I kicked sharply at the hair-less hard-ribbed sides of our mounts, and they took the freedom we offered with loose reins. Ears peeled back tight against their huge, leathery skulls, their snarling mouths with razor fangs snapped at the air before them as if to tear a hole in the wind through which to run.

Onward they bore us with utter enthusiasm for a fight with whatever awful hellish thing that awaited.

SCYTHE

I and the other three bladesmen are called Dreadknaughts because, some say, we do not dread facing down one such as Crokow. But if any of our party had no fear of demons whatsoever, it was not the men who rode but the beasts that bore us into battle, for they are the truly fearless.

The gargoyles were able to run with us astride them as fast as we cared for them to. If we could have stayed atop them, they could out-distance a horse, even a stallion like that of the Baptine Captain, and that on straight-away runs. But none of us, not even Rag-dan their original master-trainer, could hold on to them at such speeds.

The problem was that they were overly fleet of foot and of such a wild nature as to be very much unpredictable at high rates of speed. They might, if allowed enough rein, dig-sprint at incredible speeds, only to stop or make a quick turn of sharp angle without any warning whatsoever. Such erratic movements were more likely to lead to the death of the rider, slung head first into the trunk of a tree, rather than the slaying of a demon.

And so the gargoyles had to be let-to-run with good speed, but never at a full sprint. This was the only advantage, I must say, that the more compliant and domesticated horse enjoyed over the gargoyle as a battle mount. The horse, being of a more tame and predictable nature than the gargoyle, could be given all the reins to run at its top speed, for rarely would a well trained horse surprise you in its movements.

But in that respect only was the horse superior. Take that same horse into the wild forest, or across the craggy split-rock face of a mountainous region and it could merely pick its way laboriously along, and would not cover in a day the distance that a gargoyle would cover in an hour over that same terrain. Flexible and strong, our mounts are agile on hoof-n-claw feet and always straining to find the fight. The secret is that they *want* the fight, and ride to it with a kind of beast-joy.

That is why riding these creatures into demon-battle gave us the great confidence that we presently enjoyed, even as worn-out as we were. I have never known another Hunter to ride anything but the traditional horse. More than once have our mounts been mistaken by other Hunters as hell-prey, but that is of small matter to us. Reputation among friends may be desirable, but reputation among enemies is ten times desirable.

SCYTHE

We rode hard but did not have to ride far to find the trouble. Ahead of us we first saw one of the horsemen, still mounted and standing in the path. His sword was in-hand, his face turned upward as if to behold the sun now high in the sky. As we rounded the bend in the path, the low-limb tree canopy covering the path gave way to the high boughs of taller trees, and my eyes followed the track of the horseman's gaze up into one.

I found myself looking to the top of a huge poplar that must have been nearly one hundred feet high. There, about halfway up, holding on with one forepaw to the sturdy mast of the tree's central shank was the demon whose leg we earlier failed to cut with slice-wire. With its other massive paw it held the limp body of a headless, though still saddled horse. A steady stream of horse blood ran down the limbs and trunk of the tree, looking black against the deep green of the leaves.

I looked around to see what had become of the dead horse's rider. He lay on his back at the edge of the path about thirty feet from the base of the bloody poplar. One side of his face and upper torso had been torn clean of both clothing and skin, revealing patches of dark red muscle and bloody tissue. Two other horsemen had taken positions farther down the path, one of which I noticed was the Baptine captain. All of them had swords drawn and were looking up into the tree, but other than that they seemed at a loss for what to do next. I rode past the first horseman and made my way to the captain.

"Looks like you lost a man. I'm sorry to see it," I said to the captain, not knowing how he might take the simple offer of sympathy. To my surprise he was somewhat receptive to it, although his sternness was now agitated by the anger and sorrow he felt at his loss of the soldier.

"He was a good man, but he knew the risk of this business and died doing his duty."

"From the way his flesh was scrapped away, I'd guess he got a hard brush from that devil's porcupine fur." The captain would neither confirm nor deny the accuracy of my deduction.

"I'll mourn him later," he replied irritably. "Right now I must find a way to kill that thing up there." His eyes watched intensely as the treed demon held tight, still chewing away on horse flesh.

"I see its making a meal of the horse. Do you have a plan on how to get it down?" I asked.

"The dead one there was our only bowman, and his bow and quiver were tied to his saddle. The rest of us carry swords only. I'll have to wait for the thing to come down."

All of this he said in a cold and factual way, as if he were talking more to himself than to me. It was clear that he wasn't going to ask for our help. About this time, the demon took another bite out of the dead horse, snapping the saddle's belly-cinch in the process. Away fell the saddle, bouncing from limb to limb on its way to the ground.

The bow and arrows that the captain just spoke of were shaken free of the falling saddle. Most of the arrows were smashed to toothpicks as they struck against the tree's limbs, floating in splinters to the ground below. The bow itself lodged in a bough about twenty feet below where the Ogdognal held to its perch.

Kae-san rode up to where the captain and I sat mounted. The Baptine captain rubbed his horse's neck to keep it calm in the presence of our gargoyles.

"Scythe," Kae-san said to me, "Rag-dan has taken a position about three hundred feet behind that poplar to the north-west. Invictus will go further south and cross the path, holding at a south-westerly position. They will hold the back door shut and wait for our play."

The Baptine Captain heard Kae-san's report but showed neither approval nor disapproval. I knew that the demon, even as massively powerful as it was, would not be able to hold itself and the weight of the dead horse much longer. But we needed to flush it out of the tree on our own terms.

"Well, Baptine captain," I said, addressing the tall horseman formally, not knowing his given name, "I believe that we can un-tree the beast for you, unless you harbor objections."

I was hoping that this captain might be ready to accept our offer of help and work together with us, but he only wheeled his stallion and trotted over to where another horseman sat further down the path, offering not a word in reply. Kae-san took the slight.

"This is no time for him to stand aloof from us Scythe!"

"I know, Kae-san, I know. Pride is the downfall of all men. These horsemen may never warm to us as allies, but we can't worry about that now. What say we stick this demon and show it that the tree tops are to be reserved for birds?" Kae-san smiled a smile so cheerful he might have been at a dance where young people pranced to the music of a fiddle.

SCYTHE

I reached for my unique, multi-load crossbow and tossed it to him. As Kae-san wound the strings back to the trigger-catches, I unsnapped my cape and prepared for action. Taking my scythe in one hand and the leather reins in the other, I let out a high pitched battle-cry, and kicked my mount hard in the ribs.

The beast dug its hoof-claws into the ground and charged toward the huge poplar tree. Just before we reached the tree I swerved the gargoyle to the left of the tree trunk and held the blade of my scythe high in the air so as to catch the lowest hanging limb. The blade caught hold to the limb and I held on, allowing my momentum to sling me up and onto the limb as my mount kept running.

Having gained purchase on that limb, I looked up to see that the next highest limb was too far for me to reach with my scythe in hand. So I took the scythe in both hands and slung it so that it made one complete rotation, end over end, burying its blade into the meat of the limb above me. Pulling my two hand sickles from their leather sheaths at my sides, I began to climb the tree trunk by sticking one sickle blade-point into the trunk, pulling myself upward, then sticking the other sickle into the trunk and repeating the motion. By the time I had climbed to the second limb, the front of my clothes was matted with the horses' blood that had drained from above.

Now that I had reached the second limb, I sheathed my hand sickles and pulled my scythe from where it was stuck in the limb. I looked down at Kae-san and nodded.

Kae-san, still mounted, let go with an arrow from the cross-bow, and behind that one followed four more in quick and deadly succession. I knew that at least one arrow had found its mark when I heard the demon shriek in pain.

But from my vantage point, I could not tell exactly what else was happening at the top of the tree. Then I heard Kae-san yell out a warning. A rain of horse blood and intestines began to fall all around me and I grabbed hold of my limb with my free hand, hoping not to get knocked to the ground by what I knew was coming next.

What was left of the horse's body came bouncing down from the top of the poplar, banging from limb to limb, lifeless and limp legs flailing disjointedly.

I heard the thwok-thwok of another volley from the cross-bow and the demon let out another piercing screech. As tree bark, leaves and branches began to fall around me, I knew that the beast was coming down the tree. I knew I would get only one try, so I took my scythe in both hands, balancing myself on the sturdy limb below my feet. And then it was there, a flash of claws, fangs and huge, blood-red eyeballs. As I ducked I felt the air-rush off a heavy claw as it whip above my head. The stinking scent of Ogdognal invaded my nostrils. The blade of my scythe flashed, and demon blood splattered black across the green branches.

With that whack I had severed its fore-leg, which fell away and hit the ground just before the now dismembered Ogdognal itself landed hard.

An awful devil-shriek filled the air, the thing having realized that I had dismembered it.

Thwok-Thwok. Two more of Kae-san's arrows buried themselves into demon flesh as it yelped and screamed all the louder now, scrambling at the base of the tree in an insane rage. I knew that the Ogdognal would either attempt to break out of the man-circle which now began to enclose it, or else would come back up the tree to avenge its lost paw. The scratch of claws against tree-bark told me it would be the later.

It was coming back up the tree towards me, but with only one fore-paw, the thing was slowed considerably. This gave me an extra few seconds to react.

I looked down at the limb I balanced on. I whacked down hard with the big blade of my scythe, making a clean cut in the limb between the tree trunk and the part I stood on. I rode the dropping limb down towards the ground as the demon tried to move up the tree trunk with my scythe blade lifted high for a down-stroke. Spotting it just below me, I saw the Ogdognal release its hold on the tree trunk to claw at me. I came down hard with scythe, the point of which caught the beast at the sternum just below its neck and sliced downward, opening up its mid-section as if it had been held together by a zipper.

Its scream was agonizing, and the roar of it blasted my ears as the limb I road downward landed on the ground. Holding my scythe in one hand, I used my free hand to do a round-off away from the limb, and came up running towards Kae-san. My gargoyle mount had returned to Kae-san, who handed me its reins as I leapt astride it. Invictus and Rag-dan had come up out of the forest and were closing cautiously on the Ogdognal, who now struggled mightily in a quagmire of its own spilt internals.

We knew it would make one last, crazed charge at us and we knew that this was when a wounded Ogdognal was most dangerous.

SCYTHE

It had managed to stand up on its hinds. As we prepared to receive and counter the charge, something big and black swept past us at a terrific speed. We saw the brilliant flash of a broad-sword, and then the severed head of the Ogdognal was spinning bloody circles in the air. The headless corpse fell in a heap to the ground as we watched.

The Baptine captain circled his stallion and then trotted back near the carcass he had just beheaded. Leaning over in his saddle, he thrust the tip of his now bloody sword into the severed head, raising it to the level of his eyes. Surveying it for a few seconds, he jerked his sword and flipped the head over towards us where it rolled near the feet of our gargoyles.

I looked up and saw the captain pull a white fleece from his saddle bag. He pulled the blade of his sword through the fleece, restoring its shine. Re-sheathing the weapon, he spurred the stallion and rode away, southward down the path without a word. His two remaining men had strapped the body of their fallen comrade across one of their mounts and now followed in their captain's wake.

Invictus and Rag-dan joined Kae-san and me on the path.

"Scythe, I had crept close enough to see you take the fore-paw off the hellion. It was a tremendous cut, but I dare say I have never seen such a demon-beheading as that the horseman just now displayed before us," said Invictus with forced admiration.

"Aye Invictus, a more forceful sword-blow I have rarely seen, if ever." But Kae-san was less generous with his praise of the Baptine's sword play.

"True, gentlemen," pointed out Kae-san, "but the thing had already lost a fore-paw and most of its guts to Scythe's weapon."

"True enough, Kae-san," I said, "but the fact that I had maimed the beast made it more dangerous in my mind, not less. Let us give credit where it is due."

"No doubt you are right about that Scythe," said Rag-dan, who had dismounted to check the hooves of our gargoyle mounts, "but I have yet to see one of those horsemen climb a tree as you did!" We all laughed together at Rag-dan's remark.

After Rag-dan finished checking our mounts, we reunited the severed head with its pile of corpse and set it afire. We took up our figure-eight search again, riding back through the forest for a few hours. But finding neither scent nor trace of Crokow, we concluded that he had gotten away from us for the time being, and we made our way back down the path.

SCYTHE

Night was falling around us and a chill was on the air when we came upon a village.

There was an inn at its center with yellow light glowing from its windows in a warm and inviting fashion. It looked like a place that a weary hunter could get his belly full as well as find a soft bed.

We tied our gargoyles off in the woods just outside of town, allowing them to feed on a wild boar we had killed for them an hour before.

Making our way to the inn, we noticed a horse stable next door. Tied up inside were three fine horses who were being brushed down by a stable-boy. There was also a carpenter wood-working just inside the stable doorway. He looked to be cobbling boards together in the shape of a coffin.

SCYTHE

SCYTHE

Chapter Six
Hell's Revenge

"Well, at least we know where the horsemen are at," stated Kae-san blankly.

"Yes, it is obvious that they are reclining at the inn, and since it is the only place to get a warm, home-cooked meal around here, so must we," I answered, adding, "It may be best not to engage them in conversation. They mourn the loss of one of their own, just as we would had one of us been lost back there. Let us respect their need to be left alone in their thoughts, as they must respect our right to get a bite to eat and some needed rest." So saying, I led the Dreadlock up on the inn's front porch and made our entrance.

As we entered, the warmth from a massive hearth wherein large chunks of oak were being consumed by an orange fire hit us full in the face. A welcome relief from the cold it was, indeed.

There looked to be about thirty noisy men seated around various tables spread about the dining area that looked only large enough to seat about half that number. A man whose age and dirty apron identified him as the innkeeper made his way through the maze of tables that sat at less-than-comfortable distances from one another. He was moving towards us, a towel over his left arm and four frosty mugs in each large fist. Without looking up at us, he spouted in our direction,

"Table for four'll be ready directly, shut the door to the wind and stand at the bar till yer seated. Remove your hats in my place, sirs," and then in the direction of the barkeep, "four fresh mugs to the bar!" That comment about hats I thought uncalled for, until I looked and noticed Invictus, the youngest of our crew, was the only one who had yet uncovered, which he did immediately by taking his leather skullcap in hand.

"Guess we'll make our way over there gentlemen," I said, and we attempted to negotiate our way through the tightly packed crowd of men. As we did, I looked the crowd over to see if any took special notice of our entrance.

None seemed to, and for that I was thankful. If a Dreadknaught desires anything it is anonymity. To never draw attention to oneself is our firm rule.

I also looked the crowd over to see how many went armed. Any wise man is armed when he goes out, and I did not expect any trouble, but if any trouble were to come I wanted to know from which quarter to expect it. And, in a pinch, I certainly would not hesitate to ask good armed men, even strangers, for their help in a fight with Ogdognals. Further, I know that if Hell is to be defeated, the people would have to rise against it—The Order itself cannot accomplish the task, though we might hold the demons at bay until the people are ready.

This reminded me of another rule of the Dreadlock: always be aware of your surroundings--never get caught off guard. Some of the men at the tables, I noticed, kept daggers in their belts. Others kept a sword in a sheath, but only a few. Most looked to be unarmed, save for fork and spoon. We ourselves had agreed to leave our heavy weapons, scythe and swords, tied safely to our gargoyles, carrying only small weapons such as daggers and hand-sickles on our persons, well concealed. If something went seriously wrong, we figured that we could make due with our small arms until Rag-dan could call forth our mounts, which would come quickly at his call.

I should here mention that, though our prey and primary enemy is the incarnate demon, it is known that there exists men who have allied themselves to the hell-horde, and its master Apollyon.

Called Guilelocks, these men are betrayers of their own kin and give aide to the monsters when they can, in exchange for some earthly treasure. They must be looked out for, though in truth they look no different from you and me. Why they would sell their souls to such a one as that I know not, yet we know that they are in the world and must be accounted for.

But on this night all the patrons seemed to be heavily involved in their plates. This was a doubly good sign; it meant that these men were here to fill their bellies foremost, not to cause trouble for strangers like us. And just as importantly, it meant that we had picked an inn that had good food, hardly a given when on the road.

About that time a door behind the bar, opening to the kitchen, swung open and a table-boy came rushing through with plates of steaming food. The springs on the door were creaky, old and worn, and their lack of tension allowed the door to remain open for a moment, affording us a look into the kitchen.

There we spied three apron clad women, stout and plump, working slavishly over hot stoves. Their faces were spotted with brown wheat flour, their hair done up in buns, and their foreheads moist with droplets of sweat and steam. Fat, stubby fingers held large cooking forks that worked furiously, here at turning battered chops frying in a skillet of hog lard, there at poking holes in the crust of a large apple pie to allow it breath to cool.

I looked smiling at Invictus, whom I noticed had also spied the busy cooks. Invictus grinned back at me and said,

"The food should be tasty tonight boys. Heaven be praised for fat lady cooks!"

With that remark all four of us broke out into the heavy joyful laughter that every man needs at the end of a long and stressful day. What made Invictus' comment amusing was that all of us had at some time endured the offerings of skinny male cooks who knew little of the arts of spicing and flavoring food.

But the bustle of the room hushed and the enjoyment of our laughter suddenly ended when we realized that the crowd of rugged looking men had hushed and together turned to look at the four of us standing at the bar. We wondered for a moment if the lady cooks were the wives or mothers of some in the crowd and that we had somehow given offense, their husbands and sons thinking we had made a joke of their loved ones, although that was not the intent of our laughter at all. But our worries were unfounded, for just as quickly as the crowd had paused to observe us, they went right back to their plates of food and hearty conversation, as if we had been four flies on the wall.

"Don't be so nervous, lads," Rag-dan said, putting his arms good-naturedly around the shoulders of Invictus and Kae-san, "you are safe and among friends tonight. Hot biscuits and warm beds for us all!"

With that remark we laughed again, though not as loudly as the first time, and drained our mugs that the attendant had set out for us.

"Table for four!" yelled the innkeeper in our general direction, at last, and we again made our way through the crowd. As we did, Invictus asked me,

"Any sign of the horsemen?" Before I could answer him, my eye caught a glimpse of another small dinning room that opened off the great room, its entrance partially hidden by two large, leafy potted plants and a curtain.

Through an opening in the curtain I could see the form of a tall man sitting in a chair, dressed from head to toe in fine black garments and pointy boots. Behind him, leaning against the wall was a long sheathed sword whose silver-wire hilt and handle formed a large cross. For a reason that I know not, that cross struck me at that moment so beautifully as to weaken me in my knees. I stumbled, bumping into a bearded man who was negotiating a large fried beef-rib. He looked up at me, his beard and mustache caked thick with a burgundy colored sauce and bits of meat. His harsh, accusing gaze brought me out of my daze, and had me begging an apology.

"Forgive me, sir, how clumsy of me. Beg your pardon." The bearded man, beef-rib still in hand, surveyed me another few seconds without a change of expression. He then grunted, either his forgiveness or contempt, and returned to gnawing his rib.

We found our seats and were informed by the innkeeper that our menu choices were either beef or pork. He then told us that he was out of beef and had no intention of butchering another cow this late in the evening and that our pork would be out shortly. He further informed us that we had to pay for the food upfront, as well as a room if we planned on staying the night.

All forked over silver coins which disappeared into the folds of the innkeeper's gravy-stained apron. Before leaving us, he set four fresh mugs before us, having charged us for three drinks apiece, whether we wanted them or not.

"You've got one more mug apiece coming, so make these last unless you want to pay more. Coffee is available, black, strong and extra." With that remark the innkeeper left us. Now that he was gone, I answered Invictus' question about the horsemen.

"Invictus, I believe our Baptine friends are enjoying their dinner in the small, curtained room behind those potted greens." Invictus and the others made casual glances towards the rear of the dining room.

"Yes," replied Invictus, "I think I see their captain sitting with his back to the wall, and it looks like his broad-sword is resting behind him."

"Wiser than I thought," said Kae-san. "He's taken up a safe position. In that small room no enemy can approach him from behind, and he has a good view of the only doorway, which is easily guarded. Tactically sound. Not at all like four men sitting in open space, surrounded by strangers, many of them possibly armed and in league with who knows what scion of hell."

When we realized Kae-san was mocking our own poorly chosen dinning position, we all burst out fresh with laughter, caring not whether it drew hard looks, and fairly spraying our table down with drink.

SCYTHE

"Kae-san," I said merrily as I wiped at the table top with my napkin, "do you remember that time in the Wilderness of Amoriscia that we found that little inn, and you wanted to—"

My next words were shoved back into my mouth by an explosion of violent force that shook the whole building on its foundations.

We felt the floorboards quiver underneath our feet at the blow the building had just taken. I turned quickly to look to the back of the room. Shards of what had been the outer wall of the inn were flying through the curtain that veiled the little room where the Baptines dined. The curtain fell and I watched as the two horrific claws that had punched holes clean through the building's outer wall now wrapped about the mid-section of the Baptine captain, snatching him right back through the wall, bringing a portion of the now splintered and shattered wall with him.

An act of such astounding violence naturally leaves one in a state of shock, yet even in shock I did not have to guess at what I was seeing.

I fell back on my training: when you are under attack, there is but one thing to do, attack back.

"Crokow is attacking!" I yelled to my men as I got up and ran towards the small room that now had a gaping, jagged hole in its exterior wall. As I charged I pulled both my hand-sickles, making my way through the tables around which men still sat, aghast.

Some of those who had caught a glimpse of Crokow's attack sat frozen to their chairs, jaws hanging open with half-chewed food spilling from their mouths.

Those who did not see the attack had only heard the crash of the crumbling wall and felt the whole building quiver on its foundations. Most of them sat in stunned silence, their minds refusing to form an opinion as to what had just taken place. I heard one manage the word 'bear.' I knew that it was no mere forest animal that had made this attack, though for the horse-captain's sake I wish it had been.

I continued to make my way quickly around the tables, holding my sickles high above my head in an effort to avoid cutting one of the patrons.

My hand sickles I keep razor sharp at both the outer and inner edges. With a double edged weapon I can cut an enemy with either a fore-stroke or back-stroke, slinging or hacking, pushing or pulling the blade. This makes my weapons doubly dangerous, to foes in a moment of wrath, to friends in a moment of carelessness.

SCYTHE

Making it through the doorway where the curtain had been, I crossed a dozen feet of floor to the wall and leapt through the dark hole. Even though Crockow could have already killed the horse-captain and have been waiting for the next fool to follow through the broken wall, it was a chance I had to take. My mind and my instincts told me to move forward; this attack out in the open with so many people around was out of character for an infleshed demon.

The demons are well trained by their Master to work as inconspicuously as possible, their greatest effectiveness being among those who believe the myth that they don't even exist, and continue to believe it right up to the moment that they are devoured.

This being the case, I felt sure Crokow would immediately flee, giving few people the chance to get a good look at him.

Besides that, one of the Dreadknaught's chief rules of engagement is; when attacked, the counterattack must be without delay to be effective. And though you be frightened nearly out of your skin, show no fear of death, for a holy-warrior is as-dead already, having sworn a life-oath to die daily, and finally, for the cause which we gladly embrace.

Landing on my feet, it took a moment for my eyes to adjust to the darkness of the night. In that brief span, Rag-dan and Invictus had followed my lead, as had the now leader-less Baptine riders, though still befuddled over the taking of their master with no warning at all.

With great presence-of-mind, Kae-san had exited through the front door and circled around the building to upset any ambush that our enemy might have planned from around a corner. He had grabbed up four torches along the way, reminding us that a thinking warrior is the best kind.

It quickly became clear that Crokow had fled, and there was no sign of the captain. The moon was coming up now, and would soon be high in the night sky. We followed Crokows' tracks to where they entered the forest not far from the village edge. Here it was that I formed my plan and issued my instructions.

"Rag-dan, bring the gargoyles up, quickly. Invictus, take your mount along the other side of the road, opposite of where it entered, in case the cur crosses back over the beaten path. The rest of the Dreadlock will hunt the hot trail. Let us hurry men. It's likely too late to save the captain. Just being pulled through that thick outer wall is enough to kill the average man. But at least we can take hot vengeance on Crokow for the deed!"

SCYTHE

The two remaining horsemen stood with us as I gave my orders. Now leaderless, they seemed to be waiting to be told what to do, but would not ask. As is often the case, men who are never given much responsibility are quite lost without their leader. Since I still did not know if they desired to work with us, I did not feel the right to instruct them as to their actions, nor could I know how they might react. But this was no time to consider feelings.

"Baptines, your horses cannot follow through this thick forest. Do what you will, but if you want a chance to save your captain, or if he be dead, to kill the one that robbed you of him, then ride down the beaten path and listen for the scream of our gargoyle mounts. They will set to howling if battle is joined. You should know that your Captain is probably already dead. If you don't hear the signal within a couple of hours, then you can know it for certain. If we find the body, we will return it to the village if possible."

The horsemen were downhearted and that with good reason, yet it was but a few moments and they had their steeds saddled and were thundering down the road, swords at the ready.

Mounted they sped away, and Rag-dan came up with our beasts. I noticed in the moonlight that he held an extra weapon in his hand. It was the mighty broad-sword of the Baptist captain.

"Found this on the ground outside the hole in the wall."

"Thank you Rag-dan," I replied, taking the weapon in hand and feeling its heft and quality. "This is as fine a sword as I've ever held." I handed the sword to Invictus. "Invictus, you wield a fine blade, perhaps you can return this to its rightful owner, or at least stain it with demon-blood!" There was now among us a general feeling of sympathy for the Baptine captain, though only a few hours ago we were all embittered towards him, another warning as to fickleness of the hearts of men.

"I will try, Scythe," replied Invictus. "And let us pray that his hands will still have the strength to grasp it."

"Yes, pray as hard as you can, but pray as you hunt!" With that we mounted and were off.

SCYTHE

SCYTHE

Chapter Seven
Hell Hath No Fury...

Though our gargoyles had rested but little, their bellies were full of fresh hog's flesh, and once they struck Crokows' trail we could tell they still had a few hours of hunt left in them.

Nostrils flaring and red eyes bulging, they pulled hard against the reins in pursuit of the pray. My globluscyn had run its course and Crokow no longer left such an easy trail to follow, yet our mounts had the thing's natural scent to chase, which for now was potent enough.

Why does the scent of demon flesh enrage the gargoyles so, I wondered? Even Rag-dan, their trainer, has never been able to answer that question. Was this passion born of repulsion, or of familiarity? I had seen either become reasons for hatred in the hearts of men.

For whatever reason, our mounts were hungry for the chase and for battle, so we set them to it and let them run hard through these woods. Their night vision is almost as good as their day, and we held on for dear life, not knowing when or how the night might end.

No member of the Dreadlock wanted to be the first to complain, but we all knew that even though our gargoyles would hunt until they dropped dead if we required it of them, the men mounted on them couldn't last through the night without more rest. We had hunted almost constantly for nearly four whole days. The Master-Hunter who trained me had forced me, during the trials of hunt-camp, to complete a five day hunt with almost no sleep. But no one wanted to fight Crokow at the end of a five day rest-less hunt.

As we hurried after our quarry, I tried to think through the events of the past hours and get a handle on what part we were playing in the greater scheme of things. Did Crokow have a plan it was following, or was it now alone in these woods and fighting merely by rage and instinct? Perhaps, but something told me there was more to it.

Crokow had earlier lost two of his companions, one by our doing and one by its own. Then, both parties that hunted it, the Dreadlock and the Baptines, had called off the chase by the time we reached the village inn. Crokow could have been long gone, so why had it doubled back? And why had it taken the chance of an attack that would likely net it one enemy, the Baptine captain, but would put the rest of us hot on his trail again.

SCYTHE

My weary mind could conceive of only two possible explanations. The first, and most ominous, was that Crokows' attack at the village inn was an intentional ply to draw us into a trap. But that would mean Crockow had already received Ogdognal reinforcements, which seemed unlikely. Long had we hunted the Ogdognal class to near-extinction. Our sources told us that there were only a few surviving, and those were being pursued by other crews in other regions. It seemed unlikely that Crokow could have found help while on the run. A perchance meeting with hellish comrades in the forest? Perhaps, but unlikely.

The second explanation of Crokow's strange behavior was that when it had doubled back to the village inn, it had done so with a specific target in mind. That specific target was obviously the Baptine captain. But why would he take such a chance with his own life just to kill a single Hunter? Or did the horse-captain hold more value, more significance than I knew?

As I pondered the mystery, my questions only gave rise to more questions. Was there also a history between Crokow and the captain; had they met in battle before? Did Crokow hold a personal grudge against him? Like all demons, they hated the Great Ruler we served much more than they hated the Hunters who served Him. If they could kill us all they would, but only because they desire to harm the cause of our King. All of this was very intriguing, but there was little time to think on it further.

An hour had already elapsed since we had left the village inn. We could definitely hunt for another hour and a half or so. At that point I would have to call the Dreadlock together and come to a decision on whether we could physically hold out any longer. I hated to see Crokow escape again, especially after having snatched the horse-captain, but I had to be reasonable about the safety of the Dreadlock. We had already witnessed the death of two Ogdognals during the past few days. If we had to content ourselves with that for now, then so be it. My men would live to hunt another day, and Crokow would still be in the world. Another chance would come.

Then something happened that told me I wouldn't have to wait for another day to face Crokow. As we toppled a gentle rise in the forest floor, we spotted something up ahead in a small clearing about fifty yards distant.

At first we could see only slight movement among the moon-made shadows. But drawing nearer we saw a huge figure as it moved to the middle of the clearing. It was definitely Crokow, hideous, huge and bare-fanged in the moon light.

In the shadows at the edge of the clearing we could also see the outlines of what appeared to be the horseman's body, which looked to be lashed with vines to the trunk of a large acorn tree. We held no hope that the man was alive, for one of his legs was missing, with just a bloody stump hanging below his hip. Crokow sat in the middle of the clearing, gnawing on something, likely the man's missing leg.

I froze still, trying to hear the warning that was going off deep in my mind, and at the same time striving to hold my mount back from charging ahead into the clearing.

Something was amiss here. Crokow would never stop in the middle of the hunt just to snack on a man's leg. With the Dreadlock pressing him on gargoyle mounts, he would have eaten it on the run. This had to be some kind of trap, my heart told me. I motioned for Rag-dan and Kae-san to regroup to my position.

"Kae-san," I said, "we cannot risk a full attack. This has all the signs of a trap."

"I was thinking the same thing, Scythe. Crokow's behavior is very strange. That means it has plans for us," replied Kae-san.

"Quickly, Kae-san, what options do you suggest?" I asked.

"If Crokow has some friends waiting to ambush us then our options are limited. One of us can charge him, leaving the other two of us to sniff out the ambush. Our second option is to send the gargoyles in unmounted to draw out the ambush, which we will deal with on foot. But we may loose our mounts to Crokow's claws in the doing, and these mounts would be hard to replace," he answered.

"Impossible to replace, but we must act now," I decided, "so we'll take the second option. I hate to lose one of our mounts, but our enemy is desperately wicked, and we must be equally audacious for the Kingdom's sake!" Working quickly, Kae-san made ready with a huge battle axe that he kept in his pack for special occasions. Rag-dan gathered our three gargoyles, whispered some mysterious language in their pealed-back ears, and set them off. Away from us they tore through the brush of the forest towards the clearing just ahead, their eyes fixed on the enemy in the small clearing, howling like furies as they charged.

We hoped that Invictus would hear their howling and come to our aide against whatever devilry we were about to encounter. But there was no time to wait--it was time to move. There being no time to spread out, we double-paced toward the enemy more or less as a group.

Terrible shrieks echoing through the trees told us that our gargoyles had made contact with Crokow. We had to time our attack so as to come just behind the demon-ambush, if there was one. Or, if Crokow proved to be alone, we had to arrive in time to help finish him off before he had a chance to do serious harm to our mounts.

We arrived at the edge of the clearing just in time to see some large object twisting through the air awkwardly towards us. We dove to the ground as the object sailed overhead. My stomach turned gut-in when I realized that the flying object was one of our mounts.

It weighed probably nine hundred pounds, but Crokow had flung it twenty feet in the air as if a toy. A second later, another gargoyle rolled towards us, bleeding heavily, with what looked to be a human leg bone stuck in its neck.

This was not the start I had hoped for. Crokow had dismantled two of our mounts, and was probably about to do the same to the third. That would leave three of us to face him on foot, and we still didn't know if others waited in the forest to help finish us off. At the same time, I knew there was no retreating from this fight. We had to enter the fray, and enter it now.

"ATTACK!" I yelled at the top of my lungs and rushed headlong into the clearing.

Crokow turned to receive the attack, but he was jerked around suddenly as the third gargoyle caught it from behind, sinking its fangs deeply into the demon's hind leg.

As Crokow turned to fend off the gargoyle, I sliced the heavy blade of my scythe across its back.

Even though my blade struck where his back was protected by heavy porcupine fur, it penetrated to bite deeply, opening a gash in the flesh that revealed the beast's vertebrate. It screamed a great devil-screech across the forest in response.

I knew my blade had swung true and cut hard, and hope soared within me. Yet my blade had not penetrated the thing's spine, and therefore had done little enough permanent damage.

Suddenly, a human voice sang out a warning. I turned in time to see two more Ogdognals emerge from the forest. It had been a trap all along!

These two new threats emerging from the woods were not quite as large as Crokow, but they were plenty big enough, and with fangs bared they were digging fast towards me. My heart sank as quickly as it had lifted a moment before.

Thinking this might be my end, I determined to fight manfully to the death, as I knew my brethren would do. I screamed what I thought might be my last battle cry.

"To the death! Vengeance on demons!"

At that precise second, Rag-dan entered the fray, sword flashing. He engaged one of the demons, halting its progress, while Kae-san did as well with the other.

Their swords immediately went red, cutting deadly arcs in the air. But the Ogdognals came on hard, trading blood for ground.

The clearing was small, and within seconds both men were fighting retreating actions, doing all they could not to be overwhelmed by the massive weight of the enemy. The enemy was paying for every foot of ground, but the ground was small and growing smaller.

I trained all my attention on Crokow, who had thrown the biting gargoyle away and into the base of a nearby black-gum tree. Then it turned back towards me, snapping at me with dagger-fangs as I tried to cut it with my blade.

We fought desperately, but it was only a moment and the three Ogdognals, by use of their sheer weight and size, had the three of us backed into a circle. We were back to back now, fighting for our lives.

The enemy was crafty, and saw their advantage and began to press us even closer, gladly suffering a few wounds from our weapons to get close enough to kill us.

Their mass was their main advantage, along with hide, scale and fur that was hard for our blades to deeply penetrate. At this point it seemed there was little we could do but prepare to die with our honour, if not our bodies, intact.

Crokow had moved within striking distance of me. It lashed out with a heavy paw and I swiveled my body to make him miss. I avoided the full force of the blow, but not all of it. Claw found flesh, and I felt fire in my left thigh.

Three claws, in fact, had sliced deeply into the muscle, drawing a gush of crimson. I parried with my scythe, hacking a downward blow, hoping to catch him with the point of my blade. But Crokow had anticipated the counter and swept my scythe from my hand with its other paw. Instantly my hands dropped to my belt, retrieving twin hand sickles from leather pouches.

SCYTHE

It would be hard work to fight a three thousand pound grunt from hell with light weaponry, yet what other choice had I? From the sounds of human groans coming from behind me, I feared that my comrades fared little better. If one of us didn't clear a breakout path within seconds, this fight would be over and that horse-captain wouldn't be the only one on the menu tonight.

Then my ears picked up the sound of more ground thunder. It was foolish to take my eyes off Crokow to see the source of the sound, but I had to know.

As soon as I realized that yet another hell-beast, an Ogdognal every bit as huge as Crokow, was rushing from the tree-line towards us, I knew that my life was about to end. Crokow and his crew already had the better of us and we could barely hold them off as things stood. There was just no way we could physically withstand the added weight of another Ogdognal. I knew it was my time, so I summoned my last ounce of courage to finish well, to die fighting ripped open and bloody, to die like a Dreadknaught!

I expected the charging Ogdognal to make right for our center, the center that could not hold, in order to bust-up our fighting formation. Crokow had kept pressing me, forcing me to focus on it. But, out of the corner of my eye, I sensed the charging devil take a path running just behind Crokow.

I thought delirium must have been attacking my brain, because I thought I saw this new demon extend claws as he approached Crokow as if to strike him.

Then Crokow's head suddenly jerked upward in reaction to unseen pain, reinforcing what I had indeed witnessed.

The demon had torn a large chunk of scaly flesh, splintered with bone, out of Crokow's shoulder as he passed behind, and without stopping rushed headlong into the woods on the other side of the clearing.

At that instant Crokow's belly was fully exposed. It was a target so inviting that it overcame my wonder at this strange good-fortune. Totally confused, I somehow still had the presence of mind to seize this my only chance of survival.

I threw one hand-sickle with all my remaining strength and watched its rotating blade sink full into the beast's belly, the handle only remaining exposed.

Emboldened now, I rushed the demon as it sought to ward me off. Down came his forepaw towards me but, with a two-handed grip, I brought my second hand-sickle to meet it, the blade slicing through the bones of the paw as blood and dismembered claws flew through the air.

Having made this blow, I rolled to my left, in case the new Ogdognal tried to flank me from the woods into which he had disappeared, yet it was nowhere to be seen.

Crokow was now in severe pain, and with another awful hell-shriek it raised its undamaged claw high, preparing to drop it ripping towards my head. But a sword flashed behind him, and all that swept towards me was a blood-spraying half of its fore-leg.

Who was hacking at him from the rear? All Crokow could do now was fight the air with his two bloody stumps. If he could still manage to win, Crokow knew that he would be restored, for it is said that Old Scratch is willing to regenerate any limb lost in battle to one of the King's Hunters.

Nonetheless, it was hard-going for him now. I rolled over bloody grass to retrieve the long scythe that he had knocked from my hands earlier. Then I rushed my old foe one last time, knowing it would be the end for one of us.

I came in low with the scythe, swinging side-armed, and cut deeply into the devil's thigh. This enraged it even more, but without its fore-paws and weakened by his wounds, he was a slow moving target.

Again I saw another sword-flash behind Crokow, which must have pierced the spine, for he wheeled and then fell sprawling to the ground, his legs twisting grotesquely underneath.

I snuck a quick peak behind me to see how Rag-dan and Kae-san were making it. That's when I saw Invictus emerge from the woods into the clearing, riding his red-eyed gargoyle. He attacked the Ogdognals from the rear with powerful, sweeping strikes from his own broad-sword, giving much needed relief to our nearly overwhelmed brothers-at-arms.

I wanted to join that part of the battle, but I first had to dispatch Crokow. It was then that I realized what human help I had enjoyed in my fight with it: the Baptine lieutenants! I had forgotten about them, but they had been true to their friend.

Between the bleeding Crokow and the horse-captain that was lashed to the tree stood a tall steed with rider abreast, his now-bloody sword held at the ready. And another Baptine was at the acorn tree, hacking away at the vines that held the body of their captain. Crokow then made his last move, but he only had strength remaining to crawl on hinds and bloody fore-stumps towards me. The horseman behind him saw this and was not shy.

He nimbly rode his mount right up and onto Crokow's back, the warhorse's hooves stomping and flaying wildly at the demon. The weight of the horse and rider forced Crokow face down in the grass with a thump, his head not six feet from my boots.

I grasped my scythe with a two fisted grip. The scythe blade began its swing from the ground behind me, arching high over my head in a smooth semi-circle, building momentum as it swept point-first through the air.

The fire-hardened tip entered Crokow's head at the base of the skull, piercing the skull and lower brain, and exiting through his mouth, sticking into the turf below.

I had killed many times before in the heat of battle, when vicious battle-rage becomes mixed with the cause that drives me. Yet I had always considered that battle-rage different from an actual heart-hatred, and I had vowed to never enjoy killing, or to kill out of pure spite, for, as does all hate, even the hatred of an evil enemy becomes a cancer in one's soul.

Even so, I must admit that dispatching Crokow gave me a deep sense of satisfaction. Whether this is a fact that I should be proud of or not is difficult to judge.

The battle having turned our way, Dreadknaught and Baptine together now turned all on the two remaining demons, circling them, closing on them with measured blows, and finally slaughtering them together.

Our gargoyles had shaken off their injuries enough to help us finish off the wretches. They died falling one atop the other, a convenient pile of filth ready for the flame. We removed the Horse captain's femur from the gargoyle's neck and treated the wounded.

The gargoyle would live to hunt another day, as would each man involved in the fight, though none of us were sure of the life of the Baptine captain.

Chapter Eight
Quest for Honour

Somehow, by some unseen grace, the horse-captain was still alive!

Unbelievably to me, he had managed not to bleed to death after the dismemberment. Later we noticed that the dangling ends of his leg's cut and torn blood vessels had been for the most part seared closed, apparently by the acidic nature of Crokow's saliva. This had slowed the bleeding enough to keep the captain's strong heart beating. Just.

Like him or not, I had to admit that he possessed a physical constitution as tough as any I'd seen. Drenched in sweat, the fever had set in. He drifted in and out of consciousness as we carried him back towards the village inn, mumbling words and phrases I could not make out. The only time I understood anything he said was when I remarked that I could hardly believe he still drew breath.

"Oh ye of little faith," he said softly, his face looking pale-battered and swollen in the moonlight. I was glad to see him alive, even though I still could not call him my friend.

Even if he never hunted again, at least this last battle had robbed Hell of one more boast. And this was all that mattered, the reputation and honour of our Prince. The lives of Hunters are penultimate, and we count them as nothing when measured against the larger goal.

We had to take it slowly on the way back to the inn so as to keep the injured man as stable as possible. Two long poles had been formed from saplings, and together with a thick wool blanket they served as an ample litter on which to carry the horseman.

As we plodded along, my mind now returned to that which was most baffling, even more baffling than Crokow's strange attack at the inn. I speak of the mystery Ogdognal who charged unexpected into the battle *against* its own kind, the one who ripped into Crokow's shoulder at the pivotal point of battle, allowing me the opportunity to counter Crokow and turn the tide against it. Not only could I not account for this Ogdognal that was every bit as large as the overlord Crokow, (in the demon world, size often equates to authority, which is attained through intimidation and fear) but it also had the nerve to attack its natural ally, effectually dooming it.

Something was going on in the Realm of the Devils. If there was a scism amongst them, was it limited to their lower classes, or had it spread to their hierarchy? Was their infighting more significant than the occasional turning on one another while on the run, as we had seen earlier that same day?

Was this attack on Crokow a sign of some deeper division, some failure of discipline in the house of Apollyon, or just mere payback for the killing of the underling we had found earlier on the trail?

And if so, what did it mean for the future, and how could we exploit it to our own advantage?

These questions and attempts to reconcile fact with strategy began to so weary my mind. I had to deny myself these thoughts for awhile, at least until we could take food and rest.

We made it out of the woods, back onto the smooth beaten path. To hold to the forest would have been safer for the group, but would have only hurt the horse-captain all the more; he needed to be carried on a level path that would not jostle him about and cause more bleeding. So we found the road and traveled down it, taking comfort in the strength of our numbers.

It was in the wee hours of the morning when we arrived back at the inn. We woke the innkeeper, who would not allow us back inside until one of the Baptines promised on his mother's honour that the damage to the outer wall would be paid for in silver.

"No paper money, I will accept specie only!" demanded the innkeeper.

Reluctantly, the innkeeper led us down a stairway to a large cellar room that was dusty but spacious, and had its own fireplace to drive out the night chill.

Rag-dan soon had the fireplace crackling with a flame that warmed our bones.

The Baptines had produced up-front the silver for the room, but when the innkeeper saw me pull some gold coins from my pocket, its mystic glint persuaded to bring us all some food from the kitchen, a portion of which the horsemen used to make a pot of broth for the captain that we helped them warm in the hearth-fire.

My gold also purchased a large kettle of fresh water and cloth for washing our wounds, as well as ointment to treat them.

As the man drift in and out of consciousness, his lieutenants looked after their captain with great care, washing and wrapping his stump, changing the blood-caked dressing, and packing his body in moist clothe to keep his fever at bay.

One had to admire such a band of brotherhood, even though there was little other cause for affection between us. As for the Dreadlock, we each looked after our own wounds as well, as none had emerged unscathed from the fight in the clearing.

Though the Baptines kept mostly to a corner of the room and to themselves, as we ate I noticed one of their lieutenants eyeing my scythe curiously. He looked to be the youngest of the bunch.

I had already washed the gore from it, so I took the weapon from where it rested by the hearthwall and walked over to him.

He wanted to ask me a question but was reluctant, I could tell, to converse with anyone his captain would disapprove of. But I already knew what was on his mind.

"Allow me to guess: you are wondering why I use the scythe in battle, rather than a more traditional weapon?"

My words seemed to break the iciness in his glare and he felt comfortable enough to reply.

"All of your men use swords, as do we. Your choice of the reaping device seems odd to me. How did you come to use a farmer's tool for demon hunting?"

"Indeed, on a farm the scythe is a superb utensil for cutting and harvesting stalks of grain. It was on the farm as a boy that I learned to use it as a tool as well as a weapon. I will tell you the story, if you will hear it."

He nodded that he would.

"I was but a lad of ten summers working one afternoon in the tall corn my father had grown near our barn. The corn was taller than I was at that age. Three men on horses rode up to where my father was working some cattle in the corral. I heard angry shouts and knew that the men had been sent from the local Lord to demand a tithe of my father's income as tribute. But a late frost had claimed nearly half the crop and father offered only half of what was expected. These publicans were not willing to accept the amount, and had dismounted their horses in order to teach father a lesson. As I round the corner of the barn, scythe still in my hands, I saw father smash the face of one of the men, but the other two got the jump on him and had pulled clubs to bash him with. But they did not account for me, and I came up from behind them."

"Did you go right for a kill?"

"Not at first. I only knew how to use the scythe as a farm tool, sweeping it low to the ground like I was cutting the stalks. That's what I first tried with these tax-collectors, sweeping the blade across the backs of their legs and ankles. My father had already been clubbed cold, but my first sweep clipped one of the men's Achilles' at the base of his heel, severing it.

"That man fell hard, clutching at the pain, and could not get up. But the other one turned on me with his club. I had gashed him across his calf muscle as well, but in a hurry I had not cut deeply enough, and my slash only served to enrage him. With my father it had only been business, but now that a boy had tried to lame him with a reaper's blade, he meant to do me serious harm, charging at me while swinging the club for my head.

"His first swing caught my nose with the tip of the club, breaking the bone. I tried to sweep the blade at the charging man's shin-bones, but all I got for my trouble was another goose egg under my scalp. I quickly realized that I could not keep the man off of me with ground-level sweeps of the blade, so I slid my grip down the handle closer to the blade for leverage, and on his next swing, which would have stove in my brain, I brought the blade up to meet his wrist.

"The man fell backwards clutching his wound. By that time his partner had regained just enough consciousness to collect their wounded trio and get them back to their horses. I stood over my father, scythe in hand, until the men rode off. My father recovered from the clubbing he had taken, and when he was able to stand up I made a present of the tax-collector's club, a severed hand still gripping it cold. Father looked me over strangely when I presented the object to him."

"What did you say to your father?" asked the Baptine lieutenant.

"I told him that if he still wanted to offer tribute, he should just leave the money in the severed hand, and perhaps the man would return for it in a few days."

"You did that, as a ten year old?"

"Yes, and my hands have never been far from a scythe since. Indeed, it was that occasion which branded me with the name of this harvest tool I now use as a weapon. The neighbors, upon hearing of the incident, would call me nothing but 'Scythe' from that day on. I tried to use a sword once, but found it too light. You see, the scythe is a tool designed for the human frame--it is in tune with the body. It takes the participation of the entire body to wield the scythe effectively; not just the arms, but the back, shoulders, hips, thighs, feet and even the toes. Every part must tense and flex and balance with and against the weight and shape of the scythe. It is a kind of dance."

"If it's a dance," replied the Baptine lieutenant, "it must be a dance of death. I noticed how handy you were with it during both fights I witnessed today."

About that time, his captain roused in semi-consciousness, calling out incoherent orders born of a mind overcome with fever.

The young lieutenant rushed to the older man's bedside, as did the other, but there was little they could do but keep the man comfortable and offer prayers for his recovery.

It was a few hours after daybreak before any of us rose from slumber. This late hour of rising could not be helped, yet I disliked it. I always felt a nagging guilt if the sun caught my feet in bed, but on this occasion it was unavoidable.

In fact, after each of us filled our bellies again with our leftover meat and bread, we all went back to sleep, so utterly exhausted were we. By turns, one man stayed awake and on guard. It was early the next morning, just before dawn, that we were all awakened by a pounding on the cellar door.

It was no enemy this time, but the innkeeper, and he carried a steaming hot pot of coffee along with a huge platter of fried eggs, topped off with fat strips of crispy bacon and a large loaf of buttered yeast bread.

Though bearing such a welcome feast, the innkeeper still seamed in a foul mood. He left us to eat our hearty breakfast, and just as we were finishing it off, as if on queue, we heard men approaching the door again.

SCYTHE

Chapter Nine
A Council Called

Double footfalls told us that there were two men who approached the cellar door this time. We heard the key turning in the lock. The first to appear was the innkeeper.

Ever protective of his domain, he was there to make a brief and irritated introduction of a guest whom he did not trust to find the cellar on his own. Having stepped aside long enough for the other man to enter the room, the innkeeper left straight away, shutting the heavy door with a thud.

Left standing there before us was a man heavily hooded, cloaked over broad shoulders, and of a fair height. He was young I could tell from the cut of his tight, clean shaven jaw, which was the only part of his face yet visible.

As he folded the hood back, a long mane of flowing golden hair was revealed, and I reckoned his age to be little more than a score. His cloak was of fine heavy wool, the folds of which he now opened for all to see. It was lined in red silk, a crimson red, the deepest blood-red I had ever seen, and clearly inscribed with the crest of the Archangel.

Kae-san looked at the inscription, looked at me, and then looked back to the young visitor. The crest of the Archangel was familiar to all Hunters of the Order, but rarely seen in public. As a symbol, it represented Jonasius the Whiteheart, the immediate body-servant of the Archangel.

Jonasius, whom I had met only twice before and whom some of my men had yet to meet, was said to be a direct communicant with the Archangel. I had never heard him make that claim, but he didn't have to. The commanding nature of his presence bore witness that he had been often in the company of the supernatural.

Some had rumored that Jonasius *is* the Archangel, disguised in the flesh and garb of a mere man. This I doubted, figuring it for the rantings of some youthful hunter with more zeal than knowledge, or else simply the ravings of some loon, with which the world seemed ever more supplied.

Nevertheless, we now knew that we were in the presence of a close comrade of Jonasius, for none but a fool ever dare take that crest upon their vestments that were less, and whatever he was, we could tell that this man was no fool.

It was proper and natural to stand in reverence to the crest when it was presented formally, and presented as authentication of a message to be delivered. Yet we all had been bloodied to one extent or another in the recent Ogdognal campaign. And this messenger was young and a little haughty looking, with no grey in his hair to suggest a tempering wisdom.

Although the two Baptines rose, none of the Dreadlock followed suit, though each one bowed his head respectfully. In order to avoid needless offense, I began to rise as representative of my team, but the messenger held forth a gloved hand as if to say that I could keep my seat without offending protocol. From the condition we were in, I was certain that the young messenger could sense our fatigue, and I suspected he knew more about us than we of him, a suspicion his own words soon confirmed.

"I am called Lukas Markus, messenger of Jonasius the Whiteheart, High Counselor to the Order of the Archangel." His voice was firm and manly, yet with a kindly edge that softened my own reply.

"Forgive our rudeness in not standing, Lukas. We respect your Master as our own, and you as a brother-at-arms. But we are heavily grated from battle, for we have just-"

"Yes, we know, Scythe," the young man interrupted, "Your victory over Crokow and his fellow hell-dogs is already known and recorded within the walls of Lionloff. I come from Lionloff, with congratulations from my Master, and with a message. Jonasius the Whiteheart sends his compliments to you all, and calls you--all of you, to a Council." He spoke his words crisply and without hesitation, waving his hand across the room to indicate that both Dreadlock and Baptine were included in the invitation. It went without saying that an invitation from Jonasius is one not lightly rejected.

No one spoke for a moment. How could anyone as far away as Lionloff possibly have heard the news of our victory already, a victory on which the blood was hardly dry? Lionloff is more than a full week's journey from the inn where we then lodged, and that with hard riding. The messenger, young as he was, sensed our astonishment and I think was somewhat amused by it.

"The next Council is not for two years hence, if I mistake not," replied I. "We are ready to fly to Jonasius' side whenever he calls, but why does he call this Council now, giving us so little time to order affairs?" I was surprised at my own protest, yet I had my men to think of, and they badly needed time to rest and heal, as did our mounts.

"I am come, not to give explanations, but merely to summon you, all of you, be ye Dreadlock or Baptine. Other than this, all I can say is that something is amiss amongst our kind which requires a called Council to repair," and then added gravely, "if it *can* be repaired."

With that remark, this messenger walked to the corner of the cellar where the Baptine Captain was bedded down behind a curtain partition. I watched as he dipped behind the curtain to kneel at the bedside, bowing his head close to the injured man, whispers passing between them.

I must have been too tired and irritable to be easily satisfied, for as the messenger emerged from behind the curtain I pressed him further for information.

"Has there been a major defeat for our side? Is there conflict among the hunters? What more can you tell us of the wedge that calls for this meeting," I asked. Then Kae-san added a question of his own.

"Does it involve the Dreadlock in some way? We would know, sir."

The messenger heard our questions and the intense curiosity in our voices, yet our questions were all in vain. Lukas remained silent as to the nature of a problem weighty enough to require a called Council.

"It is, brother Kae-san, what it is," he replied with finality. "The Council is set for the evening of the ninth day from this one. I can say no more than that, and that much must suffice." With those words he swept his cloak back around his body tightly, and pulled his hood back over his head, turning towards the door he had entered.

"Will you not rest a moment and take a share of food and drink," I offered. But the young messenger seemed all business and made no reply to my offer. He opened the door to leave, but turned at the last moment and said,

"I trust Captain Theologous will recover and serve long. Jonasius has prayed for him without ceasing since we received news of Crokow's attack. Bring him with you to Lionloff if possible, for his voice is much valued there." And with that the young man hurried out, pulling the door closed behind him.

So, the Council would within a few days convene within the Great Hall of Lionloff.

I allowed my mind to drift to scenes of that legendary place, a place I have entered only twice before. This Hall, though subterranean, was more grand as to its inner workings than anything I've ever seen above ground. It was situated somewhere underneath a hundred-thousand acre forest of ancient, towering oak. The canopy formed by this labyrinth of solid trees was so intense that no undergrowth bothered to compete for sunlight, and the forest floor remained clean.

Even if a traveler made it into that forest, scarce was there a way to determine one's direction. No road had ever been cut into the oak, there was no well worn path leading to the Great Hall, no road signs saying turn here or there. In other words, the address of the place was anonymous, you did not get there if not invited, if the Master did not desire you to find your way.

It is easy to get lost in such an unmarked, un-traveled forest. And if one were to stray even farther, one would find that this oak forest itself fringed the wilderness known as the Gawkellens, the vastness of which by comparison made even that forest seem local indeed. It was deep in the wilds of these Gawkellens that a young Rag-dan had been raised by his father, and almost eaten by the Ferocious.

After the messenger departed, I spoke to all in the room, asking if all would agree that we would allow for another day and night to rest, check our gear, gather supplies and to clean and sharpen weapons before mounting and striking out for the Council. Each Dreadknaught agreed to the worthiness of the plan, though the Baptines held their peace. I knew not what decision the horsemen would make, especially in light of the condition of their leader.

As far as I was concerned, they could do what they liked, for though we had fought with them and shared this cellar with them, each group still acted independently and there were no ties that bound us. At least the horsemen could put off until the morrow a decision about their captain's ability to travel.

For my part, I had my doubts about the saddle-worthy condition of a man so freshly stumped, but I would not argue the point with them, nor intrude upon their affairs in any way. That decision, and the burden of bearing their leader along the hard way, would belong to them alone, and to the captain himself if he regain enough mind to be worthy of an opinion on the matter. And so we looked to our gargoyles and our gear, and prepared to travel.

The next morning found the Dreadlock awake early, alert and ready. We took our breakfast in the regular dining room of the inn, having had enough of the cozy but stuffy cellar. The food was good, but we filled our stomachs only half full that we might ride light.

SCYTHE

Rag-dan had been up before any, harnessing and preparing our mounts, and we were now ready to ride. But before we departed, I made my way back to the cellar and spoke departing words to the Baptines.

"We are ready to ride now. If you wish to ride to the Council with us, we will help you rig a gurney for your captain to ride on, unless you think the trip would kill him. In that case, you had better leave him here and hire one of the locals to nurse him: Or if one of you wishes to stay, the other is welcome to ride with us so you can represent your captain at the Council."

Before the lieutenant could respond, I heard the weakened yet still gruff voice of the Baptine captain belch an order. His lieutenant rushed across the room to where his captain had rested on a pallet behind the curtain partition.

The lieutenant emerged from behind the curtain with the log arm of his captain draped around his neck. The captain was conscious and able to speak, though still very much weakened from the trauma of the past few days. His face was gaunt, boney-sunken, with as much color as an apparition, except for his eyeballs which were shot blood-red and surrounded by blackened circles, giving him an almost ghoulish look.

A wooden peg, roughly hewn I suppose sometime in the night, emerged from the leg of a fresh pair of riding trousers, standing in for the missing leg.

It was obvious that he should not have been out of bed, but an unbending pride seemed to support him and drive this man forward.

"Hurry now," he said with his head held as high as his strength would allow, "hurry to Lionloff, beast rider, for it would be to your eternal shame if a one legged man were to beat you there." His voice was low, but was laced with enough bitterness to make me clinch my own jaw.

"That leg you lost must have contained your brain, stern Baptine, for you have no business out of bed, much less in the saddle."

"See to yourselves and your hellish mounts, Dreadknaught. Your usefulness back in that clearing does not atone for the fact that you allowed, perhaps by design, that demon to follow you to this inn and drag me through the wall! And nothing you can say will ever regenerate my missing leg! You should not fancy me bonded to you in any way. We work on our own, and we ride on our own."

SCYTHE

My anger grew within me as the man spoke. It was clear that there was no befriending one so hubris-blind. I turned to leave but stopped short of the door and, turning to face the hollow-faced captain still leaning on his lieutenant, I produced from under my cape the object we had pulled from my gargoyle's neck after the battle.

"Oh yes," I said to him, holding his leg-bone high in front of me, "I almost forgot to return this to you. Even though it nearly killed my mount when he took it in the neck, I had him lick it clean with his forked tongue." I tossed the femur at his feet. If his face had looked gaunt before, I believe it now took on the very pale of death as he realized that the object skipping across the stone-cold floor of the cellar had recently been a beloved part of his own frame. I turned and walked away.

Rag-dan, with his usual proficiency, had our mounts ready and waiting, and so we were off without further delay. My thoughts, as we were leaving, were that this would surely be the last time I saw the Baptine captain alive. He seemed hell-bent on riding immediately for the Council, a hard and a long journey that I was certain would kill him if he attempted it without at least a month of rest. And if the journey did prove fatal to him, I was not sure I would mourn his passing. Was that because of his belligerence and insolence, or was it because we learned from Jonasius' messenger that this captain was held in high regard at Lionloff? Was my own jealousy getting the better of me? I felt a pang of guilt at the thought of it.

As we mounted our gargoyles and moved out, these questions and convictions made me uneasy, robbing my mind of its wanted peace.

SCYTHE

Chapter Ten
The Ferocious

The Dreadlock rode hard for five days with scant rest along the way before we reached the narrow mountain passes that would slow our pace considerably.

We were not going into the Gawkellens, but our journey would take us close to those lands, and as we drew closer to our destination our mounts seemed to sense the change. We edged ever closer to the lands which bore and raised them. They seemed to feel a connection to it, for their attitudes were never more lively than then, even though our pace was slowed by the terrain.

The men noticed the change in our mounts and, reminded of their history, the men put in to hear Rag-dan tell his story once again, the story of how he came to befriend the gargoyles that presently bore us along.

All of us had heard the story enough times that any one could recite it by heart, yet not one of us ever tired of the re-telling of it, as much as for the *way* Rag-dan described it as for the facts of the story themselves.

Finally surrendering to the pleading and cajoling of the others, he agreed to share again his earliest and most sacred memories. For my part, I was glad for the distraction from the turmoil that continued to plague my mind concerning the meaning of this called Council, and of our part in it.

And so, Rag-dan blessed us with his tale once more.

"I was but a lad of four or five when Mama died. My memories of her are as faint as the hazy clouds which now drift above our heads. Even so, I can still feel the warmth of her hand's touch upon my skin. The touch of her hand on my cheek was a thousand times better than a warm kiss from the morning's new sun. Her face, I think, was sharply yet gently featured, though the look of it has mixed in my mind with the look of many other women I have known, and I don't believe I could draw a picture of her even if Jonasius himself asked me to. Yet to this day she is still the best definition of 'love' that I have known. I think this is true of most every mother, for her son.

"My father took over my raising when she died, and I soon learned that the gentle part of my youth was over. I was with him in the fields and forests by day, every day, and at night he taught me my letters by candlelight. I know he loved me as well, though I never remember him being able to say the words. Or perhaps he could have, but wanted his love to have a harder edge. His affection was shown by teaching me those thing important to him; the lay of the land and the arts of his life, those being of field and stream and woods craft, and above all, the art of the hunt.

"He was a hunter and woodsman, and no farmer, though he enjoyed trading pelts for grain when perchance he happened to meet one. I heard him say once that farmers make the best kinds of men, being tied to the land as they are. But my father was also tied to the land, and the forest, to the glade and gorge, as much as if he had sprung from the ground himself, like one of the chestnut trees that surrounded our home in the wilderness. He was never truly at peace but when surrounded by the trees and rocks and creeks.

"His veins seemed to flow with river water--it was all part of him, and he of it. He never said any of this, for talk was not his game, but I believe he wanted me to know it. He wanted me to know that he loved the *wildness* in nature and of the land, and if the wilderness were to take his life, I should not grieve the loss. He thrived in the wildness of it, and if it brought him death, he was only being reclaimed by that which had sustained him in life.

"So when that cold winter day came when he did not return from one of his long lonely hunt-walks across the mountain, I never held it against the land. I never found his body but I am certain I know what killed him, and how his mortal flesh was disposed of. It was the mother of the beasts that we now ride that took him down, the Mother Ferocious.

"Father was the best tracker I have ever known, and I have known many of them and judge without partiality. He had tracked every beast known to man. When he was still young, even before he had met my mother, he would go down to the coast to be picked up by one of the passing ships who needed an extra hand. He would travel with these strangers to foreign lands, and there hunt every beast native to those climes.

"But before he disappeared, he told me that on his last few treks through our Gawkellens, something had stalked *him*, had followed *him*. He only caught a glimpse of it, he said, and it was no man, nor bear, nor any other animal known to his widely traveled mind. He described it best he could, and I could tell that he knew it was a beast of such size, quickness and strength that neither his axe nor his long-knife would be of much use against it should it attack him. Yet I knew father would go out and face it, if for no other reason than to draw it away from our cabin.

" When the day came, he forbade me accompany him, and made me swear an oath not to follow or even to come looking for him. If he was afraid he did not show it, but I was afraid enough for the both of us. Yet he would not allow me to let my own fear overwhelm me. I think that is how he forced me to become a man.

"When he left the cabin that last time, he looked me in the face with the most intense gaze I could imagine, steely yet full of love and grace. The grace of his eyes were green, green like the forest when the leaves are so darkly evergreen as to seem almost black. The story does not end well because what I feared the most came true and father did not return. The thing that killed him must have liked the taste of man-blood, for it was but three weeks after father disappeared that she found the cabin.

"It was the day after my fifteenth birthday, which I had celebrated alone in a cabin now my own, by baking a fresh skillet of cornbread. That day I had come to three conclusions. One was to accept that my father was gone and that I would never see him again. And it is not easy for a youngster with no other known kin to orphan himself in his own mind. Nonetheless, it was to do. The second conclusion was that my cabin was being watched and that I was now being stalked by whatever thing had taken my father from me. I had seen shadows, glimpses, grunts in the night that were new and horrible, and I knew it had come for me. Father had failed to draw it away. The third conclusion was easy and followed the first two neatly in my young heart: I was going to kill that thing if it meant that I must die in the trying.

"In truth, I had little hope of success, for that thing had disposed of my father and he was a big and capable man greatly skilled in the use of bladed weapons, yet none of that had kept him alive. I was just turning fifteen, and though already big and strong, my muscle and sinew had yet to be tempered as only the harshness of years can do. Yet the decision was made, and so I ate my cornbread. Besides, what choice had I?

"As night came on, I kept a good hearth-fire burning against the chill of the winter snow falling heavily from the sky to cover my world, and I prepared my own weapons. Hour after hour I pulled the blades of my long-knives and sword across the sharpening rock. Hour after hour the ring of steel-on-stone filled the little cabin, and it sounded like a harbinger of death, likely my own.

"And, though I should have been beaten for it, I found an old wineskin of my father's and began to drink. I had never tasted wine before, and it tasted rankly sour to me, but I kept drinking and quickly acquired the taste for it. I began to feel crazy, to feel wild, to dream that I could kill the beast, could kill anything. Steel continued to sing in harmony with the stone, and I felt like singing too. I sang a chant of the natives, a song of wild youth, a hymn of the old people, a song of battle and of dying young. I sang songs that spoke of loving girls, though I had scarce known any, much less kissed one. But I felt courage to sing, and when the blades all bore a razor's edge, I rubbed them down with oily sheep pelts so that the hearth-flame gleamed off them, and I sheathed them for battle.

"Late in the night I chanced a quick foray into the forest near the cabin to cut fresh wood for new arrows, all the while feeling great eyes upon me. Over the red-hot coals of the hearth-fire I melted down the head of father's battle axe, using the smoking ore to fashion new tips for my arrows. I chose to sacrifice the axe to the fire because I was not yet strong enough to wield its heft with confidence in a fight, and felt my chances of inflicting harm on the beast were best if I used the bow I had hunted with for years, along with my lighter blades.

"For hours I worked on the arrow tips, first shaping and sharpening the edges, then attaching them to the ends of the arrow shafts. After I had made twenty such arrows, I was ready to fill my quiver with them. Days before, I had run to a nearby creek which had not fully frozen over where I snatched up a sack-full of black winter serpents from the water's edge. These cold-blooded serpents are native only to the Gawkellens, serpents so deadly that a strike from one was known to grant even a large man only three paces before the venom cramped and killed him, dropping him in his tracks.

"Then, back at the cabin, I carefully milked the potent venom from their fangs, dipping the tips of my arrows into the thick black liquid-death before placing them in the quiver. Then I beheaded the snakes, skinned and cooked the meat over the fire to eat them. My father had taught me, as the natives had taught him, never to waste a good animal, or a bad one for that matter. And when you used an animal for food instead of discarding it, a portion of that animal's strength and cunning would pass to you.

SCYTHE

"I had just enough iron left from the axe head to fashion into a ring. Onto the ring I scratched the names of both my mother and father. I placed the ring on my finger, gathered my weapons close by, and lay down on a bed of thick bearskins to await the dawn. I did not have long to wait.

"With the first hint of the sun, I rose to what I was sure would be the last day of my life on earth. I would leave the cabin now, not by the door, but through a tunnel my father and I had dug years before. Father said we would need another way to escape the cabin if some enemy ever surrounded it. I did not know from what vantage point the beast was watching my cabin, but I thought the tunnel might give me at least somewhat of an edge as I carried out my plan.

"And I did have a plan. Father had said that you should never fight an enemy on ground of their choosing, on ground that would give your foe any advantage either of footing or of height. I knew that I had little chance in the coming struggle, but just to keep things interesting I had to even the odds a bit by finding some ground, some place or terrain that might nullify a bit of the strength and agility that this mysterious creature surely possessed. I could think of but one, that being a cave just over the nearest mountain, one I had discovered when but a lad.

"As a child, Father had forbidden me go there, but when he was away on a hunt I would go there to play anyway. Though it had been years since I had been there, I remembered that just inside the mouth of the cave, where the sun's light was enveloped by a perfect darkness, the floor of the cave dropped off suddenly. By torch-light one could see that the drop was some thirty or forty feet straight down to where the floor leveled off again.

When I had first discovered the cave, I could find no rope with which to climb down into the hole, so I borrowed my father's wood-axe and felled a tall thick pine that grew near the cave's mouth. It had taken me a week of hacking, but finally the tree fell across the mouth, the rocks of which were heavily iced, for it was then, as it was when the Ferocious came for me, the winter season. I cut the tree down to the length I needed to reach the cave floor, leveraged it over icy rock until one end went down into the cave, gravity pulling it head-long over the drop-off, the end slamming and wedging there on the lower level.

"I had left just enough of the tree's limbs attached so that they formed a kind of rough ladder for me to climb down. The cave had a clear, natural stream running through it. It emerged from crevices in the rock walls to flow through the heart of the cave, and in the summer months I would spend hours a day swimming that cool, pure water. I would even catch fish that had somehow come to live there. What a playground that cave had been for me as a boy, one I thought was my very own secret until one day when I had gone farther down into the cave than ever before. There, chalked on the cave wall I found, in Father's own handwriting,

RAG-DAN YOU ARE A VERY MISCHIEVOUS BOY

"Of course, my father had known all along of my forays into the cave, though neither of us ever mentioned his cave-note to the other. Perhaps, if things had gone differently, when I had grown older and had a son of my own, Father would have taken me and his grandson back to that cave and we would have explored it again, together. But that was a future that would never happen, and I knew I must destroy the creature that had taken those things from me when it had killed him.

"My plan was simple: I would sneak from the cabin via the tunnel, make my way to the mouth of the cave, lure the beast and find a way to kill it there in my childhood playground that I hoped would seem as an alien and confined landscape to the beast. I did not know exactly how I would kill it, but I could only hope that something would occur to me when the time came, when I was faced with a kill-or-be-killed proposition. I had heard that men often rise above themselves in such a pressure situation, and so I hoped it would be with me in the cave, though I knew in my heart that it was but to hope against all reason. Perhaps the best I should have dared hope for was to die *with* the beast--to get close enough to it to stick a blade deep enough to kill, which would be plenty close enough for it to embrace me to my death.

"There in the cabin, I loosened the floor planks to reveal the narrow entrance to the tunnel. I stopped a brief moment to pray, for Father always liked prayer, as long as it was short. Then I flung a fresh bundle of oil-soaked straw onto the fire. I hoped that whatever thing watched the cabin would have the sense to guess that heavy smoke from the cabin's chimney meant I was still there with no plans to leave. This might give me just enough advantage, just enough time to make the run to the mouth of the cave, which was just less than a mile from the cabin.

"And so, by light of a torch I made my way through the secret tunnel for some thirty yards, until I came to the end where the shaft turned upward towards the surface. This upward shaft was only half the width of the main shaft and it was all I could do, encumbered with weaponry, to shift and squeeze up the shaft a few feet to the surface. The tunnel exit was covered over with wooden planks and a few rough stones that Father had hewn from the face of a nearby cliff. He had planted a bank of ferns around the exit hole as camouflage, and the roots of these plants had attached themselves to both soil and stone, as well as to the planks that helped cover the hole. This formed a tough barrier that I had to break through in order to free myself from the tunnel. I had such a noisy struggle with the fern roots that I was sure I had alerted the creature as to my plan and that I had probably lost the battle before it had even started. Sand fell down into my eyes as I fought to break through.

"As I emerged from the hole in the ground, I squatted dead still with sword in hand. I listened to the sound of the early morning forest and strained my eyes in the darkness to find a creature waiting to pounce, but nothing was there. I moved a few yards to one side and waited again. Still, nothing happened. Had I gone unnoticed, or was the creature just toying with me before the meal? I could not know, so I assumed my escape had not been discovered, and I moved cautiously in the direction of the cave.

"It took me nearly a half-hour to cover the distance to the mouth of the cave, for I several times stopped to listen for anything that crept about me. Once I thought I heard a heavy crunch in the snow behind me, though I could not be certain. Now at the mouth of the cave, I retrieved from my pack some rags I had soaked in oil and quickly wrapped them around the end of one of my long knives and set it ablaze with a flint spark. I was not as careful now about being quiet. It was my plan to lure the beast to me and I knew it would take some noise to do that, along with the fire.

"With torch now lit, I searched the immediate area for dry fuel. I dug underneath a low snow drift until I found a few handfuls of dry pine needles. These I gathered together with what was left of my oily rags and started a small fire on a flat rock next to the cave's mouth which was little more than a jagged opening in the rocky ground. When the fire was well enough established, I took off one of my animal furs and tossed it on the fire. The fur was well oiled so as to give protection from rain and snow, and it was only a moment until it was ablaze as well, giving off bright red firelight, its smoke bearing a pungent odor into the silent snowy forest all around.

"Then I began to sing again, but this time I sang a mournful song, a dirge unto the memory of my father, and to my own memory. I felt my death was imminent, but what death is not? I sang at the top of my voice, the voice of a man-child still carrying the squeaky trace of a boyhood I was quickly leaving behind. Verse after verse, chorus after chorus, I belted them through the trees and freezing air in defiance of whatever beast was coming to drink my lifeblood.

"As I sang, a strange joy lifted my heart, and it was as if the wine were in my brain again, making me crazy. I swear to you that I began to dance, a death-dance in the snow around the fire. I danced and sang, sang to my father, to my mother, to my own death and to the death of the one I now dared to come and take me. Five songs I sang, then six, then a seventh time, and then on the eighth a tree heavy laden with ice fell not twenty feet from where I stood. I took that as a sign that I was no longer alone, and tossing my torch into the mouth of the cave, I dove headlong down into it. My target was the shaft of the old pine I had felled into the cave as a child, and the still un-rotted heart of it held firm as it caught my weight. I shimmied and slid down the shank of the tree all the way to the where it rest on the cave floor.

"Regaining my feet, I pulled my blades and crouched silently, trying to listen over my own nervous and heavy breath. My ears picked up the sound of the trickling stream that ran through the cave, the same stream that seemed a river to the tiny eyes of my childhood. I moved cautiously away from the tree, feeling for cave-wall behind me. My gloved hand found the cave's icy cold wall and working quickly in the dark, I sheathed the blades and pulled two arrows from my quiver and lay them before me. Then I again pulled both long knives and wedged them into crevices in the cave floor, just tight enough so that they stood on end, the handles within easy grasp. All this was done within a few feet of the cave wall, against which I now pressed my back firmly. My torch had bounced its way over the tree shaft when I tossed it down and lay now on the cave floor still aflame and giving light.

"I now had the position I wanted, with back to the wall, razor sharp long knives within quick reach, and a clear view of the mouth of the cave above me, which illumined more with every passing moment as the morning came on. Feeling for my bow, I pulled an arrow from the quiver and knocked it, looking above for any sign of movement. From my position I would be able to see the creature as it entered the mouth of the cave, maybe even catch its exposed underbelly as it came down to kill me. If I could stick the creature with an arrow or two, I might be able to cause it to fall the forty feet onto the cave floor, maybe breaking some bones in the fall. I needed to strike first, to let loose pain to do his work, to make blind with rage and panic. Then, if I could get near it I could do close-in work with my long-knives.

"Yes, I thought, a plan is finally coming together in my mind, but still I was afraid. I felt my body shivering, and not just from the cold damp of the winter cave. Fear of what I was about to go through, of my last moments of life on earth, and of crossing over the mystery of death. These fears threatened to overwhelm me and lock up my muscles. I could not let that happen--I must not allow Father's death to go un-avenged.

"To steady my breathing, which had grown erratic, I drew a deep breath--and almost doubled over gagging! I had not noticed till that moment, but the air of the cave was close, and thick with a wreaking stench. 'Bat Guano' was my first thought, but this smelt like no bat droppings I had encountered in my boyhood forays into this same cave. Had so much time passed that my nostrils had forgotten the smell of a bat infested, subterranean atmosphere? I tried to ignore the stench and concentrate on the mouth of the cave that loomed so high above me. I began to wonder if the creature had even followed me, or if it had heard the death-chants in my songs, or smelt my oily fire.

"Would I have to climb back up the felled tree and call out to the creature, displaying myself as so much bait on a hook? If that became necessary, any element of surprise that I thought I now enjoyed at the bottom of the cave would be lost. I waited another half-hour, trying to be patient, because Father said that a great hunter must be patient even if not brave. I wanted to be both, but the morning light hurried on now to bring the world above to fresh life.

"I felt myself losing intensity, the intensity of spirit which I must keep in order to contend with the beast. I could wait no longer, for I wanted a verdict on the day's struggle one way or another. I decided to climb back up the felled tree and try once more to attract the beast.

I sheathed my long knives, quivered my arrows and made a move towards the pine shaft.

"But as I made my way across the cave to the felled tree, my ears caught a sound that jelled my bowels in an instant--a deep, guttural growl from *within* the cave.

My legs locked in mid-stride. My heart seemed to drop into my stomach. I turned slowly to see what had made the sound, and there, locked onto me from the deep darkness of a corner of the cave were two huge red eyes.

"She had been there in the cave with me the whole time. It was the stench of her body waste that filled the cave's close air with the odor so strong it burned my eyes. Pale now with fear, I was also angry at myself. Instead of maintaining the element of surprise, I had stupidly let the beast turn that advantage on me and catch me totally off guard. For it is the victim of surprise that is most susceptible to panic. Only a childlike foolishness could have let me walk into such a trap, and now I could expect to pay for it with my life, no doubt after an excruciating death in the fanged mouth and crushing jaws of this monster.

"Why had she not yet attacked? Something had preoccupied her, had given her pause for a moment, but what? That thought vanished as she paused no longer. Now the red eyes grew larger and more fierce as she began to stalk slowly towards me. She came on steadily, closer, and her guttural grunt became a blood curdling grow as she steadied her bulk, preparing for a death-lunge. My mind was dizzy now with horror and fear and anger, and all I could do was to stumble backwards, tripping over the base of the tree and falling. As I hit the cave floor I knew my life could now be measured in seconds, yet I was faintly aware that my hand was on fire. When I tripped I had reached out my hand to break the fall and my palm had landed on the burning end of the makeshift blade-torch. The fire had burned me through the holes in my gloves.

"Instinctively I rolled over, taking the torch in hand. I began to beat the air between the creature and me with violent swings. And it was just in time because she had made her lunge and the first thing to meet her fanged mouth was the flame and blade of the torch. The fire and steel bit into her forked tongue and she recoiled as if surprised by my cunning. For my part I was still too afraid to do much of anything, although I was somewhat heartened by the effectiveness of the torch.

SCYTHE

"I regained enough presence of mind to pull another oily rag from my pack and wrap it around the torch. The light flared brighter now and in its glare I could make out the shape and fangs and red eyes of a nightmarish creature I had read of only in fairy tales. My brain recalled the word 'Gargoyle,' and somehow I realized that the thing now stalking me in the cave must be one of those. The huge waves of muscle wrapped around her massive frame cast an eerie silhouette against the cave wall behind her, mocking my own frame, a mere trifle in comparison. I had never beheld anything remotely like unto it. A waking nightmare was where I found myself, a surreal world in which my only worldly friend was the fire I held in my scorched hand.

"She continued to circle me patiently, forked tongue flicking bloody from her mouth. She was preparing to make another lunge, and this time I doubted any torch would stop her. I made a mental effort to think of a plan, but the only weapon that I could imagine would be of effective use against such a creature was a bigger fire. I needed more fire, but what to use for fuel? Then it hit me: the tree! The tree was my only handy source of fire-fuel in the cave and I had little choice but to use it.

"Recalling the small bottle of oil I carried within my coat, I quickly retrieved it, smashed it against the tree and stuck my torch to it. A flash of fire lit up the cave as flame touched oil. The beast was startled by the flash, but decided to make a lunge at me anyway. I watched her massive shoulder and leg muscles tense for the effort and knew she was about the make her leap. I backed my way underneath and around the fallen tree, putting it between the beast and me. The lunge came at me with outstretched claws. Her fore-paw had five claws, each one four inches long, thick, and sharp. A connecting blow would probably have beheaded me, but the claw whiffed inches from my face, missing me but tearing a chunk from the burning tree-shaft. But this served only to expose more dry wood and the flame burned brighter and stronger now, and the gargoyle retreated a few steps because of it.

"My confidence grew ever so slightly. Still, I knew that I must surely die at the bottom of the cave, but if I could work myself into a position from which I could get to her with my long knives without over-exposing my own body, I might be able to do enough damage to the creature that I would die knowing I had died well, and that my spirit could meet that of my father with no shame. My bones might forever haunt the bottom of a dark cave, but I would do my family proud with my last earthly effort.

"Those were mere hopes, and what move to make now I could hardly figure. The fire was helping me, confusing the creature, prolonging the fight. But I had to think of my next move, because the fire wouldn't keep the beast at bay for long.

"What options did I have left? My bow, I thought, my arrows! When I had first observed the size and ferocity of the creature, I had dismissed my bow and arrows as of little use against a creature of such mass, with dense hide insulated by short, spiky hair. I spotted a few patches of hide not covered with hair, and on her thick neck I noticed a wound, one that I had not made, for already it had begun to scab over, though it still oozed a bit. Had my father made that gash as he died in this creature's fangs? I could not know for sure, but took it as a sign that perhaps this opening in her flesh had been left there for me by Father so that I might finish what he had started. But even her un-haired hide looked as thick and tough as an elephant's ear. Yet the bow was my only option for now. If the arrows could not penetrate, at least they might infuriate the creature and lead to a misstep. Animals, like men, can lose their heads in more ways than one.

"Dropping quickly to one knee I forsook the torch for the bow and in a flash I had an arrow knocked and drawn on a tight string. There was no time for precise aiming but little need for it because the Gargoyle's nose was no more than twenty feet from the tip of my arrow. I let fly in the direction of the creature's head, hoping to hit a soft spot.

"As soon as the arrow left my string I was reaching for another in the quiver strapped across my back, all the while moving my position back and forth behind the burning stock of tree in order to keep it between me and the beast. What with the glare from the fire and the blood rushing to my head I did not see if my first arrow found a good mark, though a sharp cry from this leviathan gave me hope that it had. I had already let go of my second arrow, and then a third one before I gained a vantage point allowing me to clearly see what work my arrows had done. Two of them lay shattered on the cave floor, having splintered as they smashed into her mass. But a third one had found the oozing wound, perhaps made by my father, and had penetrated deeply with only half of the arrow left exposed.

"Whether it was the arrow head itself or the serpent poison I had laced it with that stung the creature, I cannot say. But for a moment the beast forgot about me and concentrated on removing it from her flesh. She cocked her head downwards awkwardly and tried to grasp the shaft in her fanged mouth but could not seem to reach the arrow implanted so closely under her chin. I knew now, at least, that the creature could be hurt, and if hurt then it could be killed as well!

"Of course the arrow had merely stung this colossus and it would take much greater and deeper wounds to draw life-blood from her huge, dreadful frame. Yet it was a start. My father had always remarked that I have extremely quick hands, and they never served me better than at that moment, for as the creature sought to dislodge the arrow in her neck, I drained my quiver of ten more arrows and sent them flying at her in rapid succession. One of the arrows caught her in the eye, penetrating deeply into the socket.

"The beast let out a blood-curdling screech that nearly deafened me in the cave, and I knew this was my chance. Leaping as high up onto the burning shaft of tree as I could, I shimmied up towards the mouth of the cave as quickly as possible. I dare not look back to see what the beast was doing for that would only slow me down. My clothing was set on fire by the burning tree, but I had no time to worry about that now. I felt the heat of the flame searing the flesh on my arms and legs, but the pain only made me climb faster. Now three-quarters of the way up, my hopes of making it to the cave-mouth were growing brighter as I drew closer to the fresh daylight above.

"Then she came on. I felt the tree jolt and then collapse as her bulk crashed into it. She had leapt thirty feet across the cave and onto the tree shaft, and the old wood proved no match for such an impact, snapping in two about halfway up its length.

"The top half of the tree was wedged in rock near the cave-mouth above and now hung suspended as the bottom half collapsed to the floor below. We all fell earthward together; a burning mass composed of me, the splintered and broken tree-wood, and the roaring creature.

"I landed face down with a thump on the cave floor, only half-conscious and in pain, burning debris falling all around me. Rolling over on my back, I looked up to try to see through the smoke, ash and dust that filled the shaft of light that beam down on us from the mouth of the cave above. My arrows were still lodged in her eye socket and in her throat, but these wounds, though no doubt painful, were more annoyance to her than life threatening. She had managed to land upright and on all fours. It was only then that I noticed that her feet were hoofed. What kind of hell-spawn is this, I wondered, that had hoofs and extendable claws on the same feet? No wonder she possessed both agility and quickness, as she could manage any terrain with those feet!

"She was tensed for another death-lunge toward me when it hit her. The top half of the old tree had dangled above for a few seconds, but the rock-formed wedge above could not hold it, and the thick shaft of heart-pine plunged now straight downward, pulled by gravity's inexorable strength. The broken and jagged end of the pine shaft hit her squarely on top of the head, smashing her jaw-first onto the solid cave-floor below with the sound of a great dull thud.

"Such was the force of the blow to her head, caught as it was between treeshaft and stone floor, that my now-bloody arrow barley missed *me* as it was ejected from her eye socket and flew past my ear. Several of her teeth and part of her forked tongue popped out of her mouth also. It was as if a mighty giant had delivered a stunning right fisted blow to the top of her skull and knocked her senseless. The beast lay there on the cave floor bleeding from about her head, mouth and ears, her movements barely perceptible.

"But I was in no shape to rejoice, neither could I make my way over to finish her, for my own fall had been a bad one onto the rough and cold solid rock floor of the cave. There was a burning pain in my left shoulder. I didn't know it at the time, but the fall had broken my shoulder, shattered the clavicle, and badly bruised my upper rib cage on one side. My sternum was also cracked, causing me to cough up bloody mucus.

"I drifted in and out of consciousness, in and out of this new world where monsters lurk in caves. I'm not sure exactly how long we both lie there on the cave floor, the creature and I. The sudden stop at the end of the fall had nearly done me in, while the tree-shaft taken to the head had rocked her brain. We lie there together, not fifteen feet apart, drifting in and out of consciousness, hovering so near to an end. The first to regain their senses could finish the other, but which one would it be?

"When I finally was able to sit up and focus my watery eyes, the beast was nowhere within the circle of light cast by the still burning remnants of pine. Managing to crawl at first, and then to walk-stumble, I made my way to the edge of the icy stream and plunged my head under the water. My mind and body was flooded with a confused mixture of pain and relief. The water was so cold, just above freezing, that it burned the skin of my face. Yet it also served to revive me and helped me regain my bearings.

"After checking out my injuries and determining that I could walk, I gathered what weapons I could find and began to move back towards the light of the burning tree. The stench in the air once again invaded my nostrils as I breathed deeply to refill my lungs with oxygen. But I felt stronger with each step and pulled my long knives with the hope of finding that the beast had crawled off into a corner, waiting helplessly for a carving. Despite my injuries, my confidence was high and my fear gone, but all I found was a bloody spot on the cave floor, and no gargoyle.

"She was gone, but to where? Was she still in the cave? I looked up the steep wall of the cave to the sun-lit mouth above and wondered if she could have scaled it, injured as she was. Pieces of the tree lay about the area, much of it still burning. Should I try to gather the debris and build the fire higher? I decided that a more immediate concern was to find a way out of the cave so that I might make it back to my cabin to hole up there and recuperate from my injuries.

"Reality told me it would be impossible to climb the steep wall with a busted shoulder. I had to find another way out, so I searched around until I had found my make-shift torch, rewrapped it with oily clothe and skins, and began to once again explore the cave I had played in as a boy. Only this time I *had* to go much deeper into its vast darkness, deep enough to find a way out. For my life now truly depended on it.

"For hours I wandered through the cave's tunnels, around the bends and over the natural humps and depressions in the floor. After some time I noticed that the air was less close, fresher somehow, and the nauseous stench that had so sickened me before was almost undetectable. That gave me hope, and I pushed on.

"Finally, after hours more of wandering through what might as well have been a stone maze, my eyes caught a glimpse of a faint light high above me. Yet the cave floor seemed to slope more kindly towards it, much less steeply than at my original entry point. I worked my way towards the light, yet the going was still slow. Each time I would look up the light seemed less bright, and I knew that the sun must be sinking now in the outside sky as night came on. I hurried on as best the pain in my shoulder would allow.

SCYTHE

"After another half-hour of painful climbing I felt a breeze of fresh air on my face and suddenly I was looking out of an opening the size of a wash basin. After several failed attempts to squeeze through the hole, I pulled my other long knife and began to probe into the soft earth around this opening that represented my last hope of life on earth. With great relief I discovered that I could tear away the soil and its attendant root structure that grew into it from the plant life outside. After removing enough earth so as to enlarge the hole to man-size, I prepared to exit the cave into the light of a fast-sinking sun.

"Just as I began my exit, I heard to my rear what sounded like rock sliding across stone somewhere in the cave. I harbored little doubt as to what caused the noise, but I ventured a look-see anyway. And there she stood, not fifty feet away. One red eye blazed at me hatefully from the dark, and I heard her deep guttural moan and felt a fresh chill in my spine. I knew this time she would end it.

"She made her move, coming at me with a renewed ferocity. I made for the opening, ramming my head, arms and torso through and pulling myself up and out of the cave.

"I was outside! I rolled twice and was on my feet, turning to face now the hole I had just crawled out of. In my rush I had thrown down the torch before exiting the cave. I quickly found the other long-knife sheathed at my waist, and pulling it, I gripped its handle tightly in my right hand, awaiting the beast that would soon burst-forth and be upon me. I felt the ground shake as she hit the hole at a charge, but only her massive head made it through, poking outside where I could clearly see it.

"Her shoulders were unnaturally wide and they would not push through the hole so easily. As her momentum stopped I wasted no time, charging towards her, hacking at her head and snapping jaws with my long-knife. It was here that a sword would have served me better, but mine had been lost somewhere in the cave. Still I hacked on, her one eye blazing at me, the other socket empty except for oozing blood and stringy, sticky mucus. Suddenly her head disappeared back into the hole and as a fool I thought she might be giving up. But the Ferocious never gives up. I watched as the earth around the hole began to move and give-way as if being ruptured from underneath. She was digging her way out, with thick, long claws, widening the hole, just as I had done to get through.

SCYTHE

"I knew now that she would never quit until she had killed me. I turned to run, looking for better ground from which to make my stand. But I was stopped in my tracks. I found myself looking out over a deep gorge, and realized that the place upon which I stood was but a rocky cliff hanging on the side of a mountain. I looked to my right for an answer but all I found was the steep side of mountain that formed a wall extending to the cliff's edge. I looked left and saw a thicket of bramble so dense that it would take an hour just to hack a man sized hole in it. I was walled in with no place to run. I turned to face the beast as she was about to burst through the cave opening. I had no fiery torch to stop her charges, nothing now to fight her with but the earth on which I stood, the long knife in my right hand, and the fierce pain in the heart of an orphaned son.

"And that is when, I swear to you, I heard my father order me to charge. He didn't speak to me in an audible voice, but through a voice much louder than that inside my heart. I obeyed without hesitation. Her head and one fore-leg were out of the hole now and in seconds her entire body would burst forth from this cave womb to consume me. I charged hacking at her, aiming for a point, that being the one good eye she still possessed.

"Massive jaws snapped at me as I forced myself, against all reason, to close within range of her teeth that I might get a good blow at her one remaining orb. Moving side to side in front of her I continued to swing away with my long knife, though it seemed to do little more than fire her anger.

"Then she winced--I had lanced the eye! Changing tactics now, I jabbed at her head with the long-knife, holding the handle with both my hands, poking and prodding again and again, moving my feet to avoid her jaws, spending my last ounce of strength. I saw that both eye sockets now oozed. I hacked once more as the newly punctured eye began to gush bloody fluid, and the beast howled with pain and rage. I backed away then, having blinded the creature, as she withdrew back into the hole. I allowed myself a deep breath, but I knew that she was not done, that she was not this easily whipped, and I held my breath short again as the earth shook and her entire body exploded through the hole, scattering a spray of soil and rock all about.

"We stood there together, me on my two feet and her on her four clawed hoofs. She tried to look about for me but could not see me, for she was indeed bind now, yet very much alive and able to kill me if she could make contact.

"Though she was the blind one, I looked behind and around me again, reminded that it was I who was the trapped animal. A gargoyle is hard to kill, and men die much easier, so even with her handicap the fight was likely to go her way. The beast might die of starvation later when she could hunt only blind. Perhaps a colossus-pack of giant wolves, which in the Gawkellens could number over a thousand, might manage to surround and wear her down. But she could live a long time slowly digesting my flesh within the relative safety of the cave, and I'm certain her instincts told her that I must be her first blind kill.

"I backed away from her and she was troubled to find me. She stood up on hinds then and began to sniff the air. And I knew that she could not see me, but could still locate me--not with sight but by scent! I moved hard to my right but I moved into the wind and she sniffed the air in my direction. When she came back down on all fours she had found my scent and moved towards me, snapping the air between us as she came on. It must end soon, I knew, and thought again of Father and stood my ground.

"I let her come close and hacked at her massive head again with my long knife. She snapped at me with dangerous jaws and razor-edged teeth, but I kept moving. I danced back and forth, a dance of death for us both, the creature and I, but I let her get too close and a fang tore through my clothing and into my abdominal muscles, drawing blood as her roars filled my head with confusion.

"Then a strange thing happened. She paused when she tasted my blood, and I knew she paused in remembrance of a former kill, and I knew that she tasted my father in my blood. This knowledge only enraged me more and I cast all caution to the abyss and rushed her, hacking and cursing her now for taking him from me. I chanced a lunge with my blade and the point entered her nostril and cut her deeply there and she came on harder now in a rage of her own, forcing me backwards, and the cliff's edge waited for me just a few feet away. She had me, was on top of me now and I wanted her to follow me to my death, ending our pain. She bit into me again as we both tumbled over the edge of the cliff together.

"And instinct alone made me reach out, my hand finding a thick thorn-vine growing on the cliff-face. The thorns penetrated my hand, but I would not release the vine. The beast's fangs had pierced my flesh, and the vine tightened for a split second, but I felt her jaws release and unfang me when she felt no ground underneath her. I held the vine with a death-grip and feared it would tear free, but it had grown deep into the cleft of the rock and would not let go.

"I watched her body fall through the air, limbs flailing, and she moaned back at me as she fell, the mournful cry of one who leaves behind helpless young. Instantly, I knew. The realization came to me as to why she had killed my father and sought to kill me, and almost in that instant I would have reached out to save her if I could have. For I knew that when I worked my way back through the cave I would find a nest, and hours later I did and there they were, asleep in it. Her young, four of them, in a rounded nest some eight feet across, formed of twisted oak saplings and mounds of wiregrass. And when I awakened them they opened fanged mouths wide to be fed and I raised my long-knife to slay them, but could not. Instead I gathered them and one by one got them up and out of the cave and back to my cabin and they suckled there by my warm fire on the blood of wild hogs that I killed and drained for them.

"They grew rapidly, with voracious appetites. Many a wild boar lost its life to their bellies and I cared for them as if they were my own. And now they have grown nearly as strong as their mother had been when I killed her. Or should I more honestly say when I lured her to fall to her own death, for that beast that killed my father and fed his blood to her young was more than a match for me."

"How long," Invictus asked, "did it take for you to tame them?"

"I never tamed them, Invictus, for they are quite untamable. Some beasts were made to tame, others to befriend, still others to be killed. Let us say that we, the four of them and I, agreed to live in friendship together, and they agreed also to let me ride on their backs and put reigns about their heads. No man tames a gargoyle-beast, but I am glad to have the friendship and service of these we now ride. Always remember, my brothers, these beasts *allow us* to ride them, and not the other way around. We are not the masters of them, and never shall be. I helped them to live when they had no mother left to care for them. And they gave me a reason to live when I had no father. That is all, and that is enough."

And so Rag-dan's tale once again relieved our boredom and took our minds off the cares and troubles that presently weighed upon us as we passed through the narrow mountains. Soon enough we found ourselves in the open grassy fields where our beasts could match their muscles and thick tendons against wide open terra-firma, and on we sped, making excellent strides, marking excellent time.

SCYTHE

Chapter Eleven
Curtain of Iron

Arriving at the edge of the oak forest, the Dreadlock knew we must find near the geographic center of it a little four cornered building that might have been no more than a small and ill-placed inn.

This building was not the great hall, obviously, where the Council would convene. It was but a marker, yet the little building itself was marked on no map. Its location was untraceable, and direction was of little use, for once a man uninvited crossed the forest boundary, his sense of direction went array and his feet invariably lost their way. That forest was not evil, but it *was* dangerous, just as every good Hunter must be.

But even those who are called must depend on some supernatural help if they are not to be forever lost wandering about. Even they possess no map or direction finder that would work here; a higher source of direction was necessary.

So it was on a kind of blind faith that we penetrated the forest's edge, trusting that along with Jonasius' invitation would come guidance from above. And help we sorely needed for we had traveled not a hundred yards into the forest when we came upon a high, dense and massive wall of woven reed-thicket standing impenetrable against our progress.

As the Dreadlock drew up to face it, we looked at it and then at one another, appalled. Finally all the men looked to me, as if I could produce some ancient incantation that would part this sea of reeds, but it was new to me as well.

"How do we get through this, or can we go around it?" asked Invictus.

"I'm not sure how to penetrate such a barrier, and there's no telling how long it runs in either direction," I answered.

"How did you get through it on your previous trips?" Kae-san asked.

"It was not here before, Kae-san. This is new. I've never seen anything like this."

"How can that be, Scythe? This growth looks to be very old. Judging from the height and thickness of this wall, it must have been planted here an age ago," replied Kae-san as he took a closer look.

Then it began to move. Only slightly at first, a tremble from within its mass. Then, whole sections of the wall begin to sway slightly, first this way, then that way, and we could now see the movement clearly.

The cracking sounds of thick reeds moving against one another, bending one another, echoed from the interior workings of it. The gargoyles grew nervous and backed away, not sure what to make of it.

"It moves--even without a wind to sway it, it moves as if it were alive," said Invictus, his eyes wide with wonder.

"Maybe it's growing," added Kae-san, with a bit of sardonic wit, "maybe it grows up around men, and they are never heard from again."

I told the others that I wanted to scout around a bit, and warned them not to leave the spot or do anything rash, and to remember that we should count ourselves as guests on the lands of another. Guests do not take too many liberties, I reminded them.

But, it seems, warning a young man not to do a thing is tantamount to daring him not to do it, and after I departed each of the remaining three Hunters felt compelled to dismount and inspect the thicket wall, admiring its woven, twisted growth pattern that defied a man's arm to reach into it even to elbow depth. The weave of the living wall was made up of two-inch thick stalks that might as well have been iron bamboo, with each stalk extending some forty feet in the air. Each of these poles was tightly packed into the mass of others, as well as being ringed and wrapped to its neighboring pole by thick cords of wiry thorn-vine.

When I returned I asked the men to remount so that we might work our way around the wall if possible, though I had found no break in its exterior as I scouted about.

About the time I took note that only Invictus was missing from our quartet, we heard a sharp yelp that could only have come from him. Running towards the sound, we found him struggling at the wall in obvious pain, his gloved hand firmly stuck within the thicket.

"It closed on me, I tell you it wrapped itself around my hand as I reached into it," said the young man, his face now red with pain and fresh beads of sweat. Indeed, the thick reeds had pulled themselves tightly around Invictus' hand and wrist, and the thorny vine had quickly wrapped itself around both tightly, as if to bind him to the wall forever. Each of us grabbed hold to Invictus' arm and upper body and began to try to pull his hand loose. He shrieked and yelled, begging us to stop, but we knew his hand had to come out. We heaved with all our might, but the hand budged not a whit.

We gave up the struggle for the moment, much to Invictus' relief. I examined the situation again and saw that the thorns were now penetrating the skin causing trickles of blood to run down his bare arm. The reed thicket moved then, seeming to tighten its grip around Invitus' hand, and I could hear knuckles and bones beginning to crack as he growled angry now with pain, his grimaced face shading to a pure crimson.

Sprinting to my mount, I retrieved my scythe, calling on the others to retrieve their weapons as well. Returning to Invictus' side, I sought to wedge the long, broad scythe blade between the stalks that were binding the hand.

"Don't bother to hack at the wall. The shafts are as iron. His hand is wedged in, and we must wedge it out!" I shouted.

The others joined me with their swords and we jabbed our blades through the weave of the thicket as near Invictus' hand as we dared, and with all our might we pried the reeds apart and pulled until finally the hand came free.

Invictus fell writhing to the ground. He clutched the hand to his breast, holding it there with his uninjured hand as if it contained all of the world's torturous wealth. Finally the pain eased enough that he could extend it for us to examine.

Easing the gauntlet off of it, we stood staring, baffled. No swelling was visible. No bruising, no torn skin, no blood. Invictus began to flex the fingers, and then to make a fist. I knew I had heard the bones crack, but the hand was as good as new. A look at his smiling face told me there was no lasting damage or even pain.

As we attended him, a massive shudder vibrated through the length of the reed-wall as far as our eyes could see in either direction, though the air did not stir of wind. Talking it over for a moment, we reminded ourselves that this wall belonged to our Master, and decided to take the event as a discipline, a severe grace from His Hand, teaching a young servant not to over-reach.

After this, we mounted and made our way along the thicket wall, taking the trusting attitude that if we were meant to find our way, then we would. We followed it for some time but no way through the wall opened to us. The men were beginning to show signs of frustration, but I reminded them that no worthy trail is ever easily followed, and if we were indeed called, a way would open to us soon enough if we but persevere.

And so we continued to follow the way around the impenetrable wall until finally, after hours on our mounts and with no warning, we came upon a narrow opening in the thicket. It was a space no more than four feet across, barely wide enough for one mounted Dreadknaught to pass through at a time.

The Dreadlock gathered around it before entering. I looked at Kae-san, and watched him examine the ground around the opening.

"Scythe, look at the ground of the opening in the wall. It is newly disheveled--it looks as if something has just been torn from it, something that was deeply rooted there." We looked around, but there was no one there, and there were no tracks to prove anyone other than us had recently come this way.

I looked at Kae-san, his eyes already locked on me. We both looked back at the thicket wall, reaching the same conclusion. The wall had *opened itself*. No other explanation would lend itself to the facts before us. This conclusion was at once encouraging and frightening. A thicket that could will itself open could just as easily will itself closed. Going through this newly made entrance would be taking a serious risk, but I knew of no other choice to make.

I nudged my mount towards the opening, showing my men that I was willing to lead the way into either blessing or curse that waited somewhere on the other side. Those from whom I had learned years before taught me that a leader should never order men into a place that he himself was not willing to go.

My mount approached the doorway, his head down, sniffing loudly with huge nostrils, blowing around the freshly turned soil. Then it raised its nose to the wall to sniff it. It shook its massive head a few times, working its ears to and fro, as if to ease its own doubts, pawed the ground a few times, then jaunted heartily into and through the opening as the Dreadlock followed me through.

As we passed through, I looked at Rag-dan, who himself was shaking his head in disbelief at the walls' thickness.

"Impregnable," I head him say, and so this barrier was to any hostiles who led less than an army with machines of war that could batter its way through the natural bars, or else find a way over it, though its forty foot height ending in what looked from the ground like needle points would be a hellacious challenge for any number of determined foes. Even for an army of Ogdognals twice the size of Crokow.

One also had to consider that this barrier contained some innate ability to move and shift itself, making it formidable indeed.

We pressed on.

We did not pass other Hunters as we entered the forest. Whether that was due to the others having arrived early, or because we had been led to a more conspicuous route, it was impossible to say. Whatever the reason, the Dreadlock did not mind it, for we rather liked keeping to ourselves. That characteristic, a contentedness with being alone or at least only being forced to keep company with those most like one's self, was true of us to a man. It was born of our individual personal histories.

Rag-dan's life is well known, raised motherless by a quiet woodsman father who might speak no more than five or six words on any given day.

As for Invictus' life, one could understand how it might also have led to a loner mentality.

As a boy, Invictus had a father that was standoffish. Perhaps in reaction to that fact his mother had doted on the boy and spoiled him. But she went too far, as parents sometimes do, by deciding to plan his life for him.

Thinking the boy so full of love and kindness, she decided he must be destined for the ministry. Early on, his mother started putting back silver for Invictus' religious training and education, and when he turned sixteen she enrolled him in the finest religious school that she could afford.

But Invictus had a wilder side that his mother could not, or perhaps, would not see. While Invictus shared all of his mother's theological convictions, he was less inclined to practice the acceptable social habits that usually followed with them. In other words, while his fellow seminarians were gathered somewhere for religious discussions and debates, Invictus might be found in another place enjoying the company of the local examples of beautiful young womanhood, along with a lightly blushed wine and the dark tobacco of a gold-ringed, hand-rolled cigar.

So it came as a surprise to his faithful and gentle mother when Invictus was kicked out of the seminary after an incident in a local tavern.

SCYTHE

It seems that Invictus had been insulted by a fellow patron, and sought recourse through the breaking of a billiard stick across the face of his antagonist.

The seminary Head-Master was called to investigate, and Invictus was called before the school's Board of Discipline. Having heard the facts as presented by the Head-Master, but without Invictus' own testimony, the board demanded an apology from Invictus, to be followed by six months of probation, each day of which would require one act of penance.

Invictus, being all of seventeen years old, asked for and was given one hour to think over the board's requirements. When that hour was expired Invictus was called back before the board to give his decision, at which time he promptly demanded the right to address the board in his own defense.

The facts Invictus presented to the board, and that he felt justified his conduct in the tavern, were as follows: For one, the music in the tavern had been especially lively on the evening in question, probably due to the fact that a new piano player had just been hired.

Secondly, Invictus continued, the wine being served that evening was from the proprietor's own private stock and had both a delicate bouquet as well as a fairly strong kick, requiring Invictus to drink at least a pitcher full.

Thirdly, the power of the wine had mixed in Invictus' brain with the effects of a hand rolled cigar made from dark brown tobacco, also from the owner's private reserves. These together had carried Invictus' mind into climes previously un-encountered by the young man.

Finally, to top it all off, the tavern owner had just that very day hired as waitresses all three of the Johnson triplets, each of which were fairly bursting forth with girlish pride. Furthermore, Invictus informed the board, the triplets' mother is quite a seamstress and had made them all new dresses which were perfectly tailored to compliment their ample feminine forms.

Invictus' defense was simple. The aforementioned influences, none of which in and of themselves were sinful, had nevertheless combined to put Invictus in a situation in which a challenge to his manhood could not possibly have been met with tolerance on his part. And when a fellow tavern dweller supplied said insult, there was but one and only one possible outcome, that being the use of a billiard stick to answer the insult and correct the attitude of said fellow patron.

SCYTHE

In conclusion, Invictus stated, the incident could be said to have been, in practical theological terms, predestined.

That was Invictus' last day at seminary. And after six months of aimless wondering from tavern to tavern, in the last of which the Dreadlock rescued him from three angry men wielding daggers, Invictus joined our merry band
and found that he could serve his mother's cause by hunting along side of us, albeit in a way somewhat less gentle than his sweet mother had imagined.

On we pressed through the wide forest of old oak and spruce, ancient woods towering above us. We were hoping to come across a beaten path that would lead us to our mark. Still, we felt the need to rely on our unseen guide to bring us to Lionloff.

We rode for hours, heading to what we generally thought might be the central interior of the forest. Carried on as much by the instincts of our mounts as our own, finally we came to what we later were told was the very geographic center of the forest.

There before us sat a small four-cornered building, wood-framed, a building that might have been no more than a small, ill-placed inn.

SCYTHE

Chapter Twelve
The Great Hall Lionloff

Lionloff is one of the Three Grand Halls to which a Hunter might ever be called for the purpose of attending a Council, the location of each Hall a secret closely kept, the paths to them guarded with a holy jealousy. And of the three, it is said, only Lionloff is sub-earth, built entirely under the ground. It lay in fact underneath the small building, running a hundred times that little building's length and breadth, beneath the ground, in all directions.

Before we even dismounted, a crusty old man had made his way out the door and was limping towards our party as we emerged from the woods. As he looked up, I could see the man was startled at the sight of our mounts, and for a moment he moved not a hair. Yet, I liked him instantly. He had a countenance that seemed at the same time kindly but crankily suspicious as well, if that be possible. I sensed goodness in him.

Though I had not met him on my previous visits, I had heard of him, had heard that he was one of Jonasius' oldest and most trusted servants. As we approached him, he asked uneasily, as he eyed our beasts, if he might have a boy tend to our mounts. Rag-dan thanked him and said that our mounts only cared to be tended to by Rag-dan himself. The old man looked relieved at having been spared the task, duty alone having forced him to offer. We later learned that he had been forewarned that Hunters would come in, riding strange mounts, and it then occurred to me that even one expecting to see men riding gargoyles are nonetheless startled at the novelty of it, if not at the sight of such wild and vicious looking creatures performing that role.

After dismounting, we followed him into the little building where he introduced himself to each of us. Then we were led to a hallway, the floor of which was made not of individual planks, but of a piece, twelve inch solid hardwood, taken no doubt from the heart of a massive oak sacrificed from among those standing guard for acres all around.

After exchanging several signs, passwords and the like, the guest-master skillfully moved an unseen lever which caused the hallway floor to give way, dropping instantly a foot in depth and rolling quietly underneath the adjoining floor and out of the way. A stairway leading some thirty feet downward was revealed.

Wall-mounted torches below cast light upon the steps which led to a corridor that must have been fifteen to twenty feet wide. Its floor was formed of massive flat slate-stones, all polished to a brilliant, impeccable shine.

Each stone itself looked large enough to require a small army of men to move it, and was streaked with just enough of the colors of a peacock's feathers to break its monotony of grey.

The stairway within this small building was the only way in or out of Lionloff, according to all to whom I had spoken that claimed knowledge of the place. I could not help but to wonder if there were other places of entry or exit from the great underground Hall, and if the Archangel himself ever visited Jonasius here. But Lionloff is a place about which one does not ask too many questions when visiting, even as an invited guest.

Once inside the sub-earth Hall, a strange atmosphere surrounds a man. One could feel it in the very air one breathed, a change you could not explain but knew was as real as your own flesh. It was as if the walls of the place held their own power.

Hunters would come from every quarter to attend a Council, speaking in perhaps threescore different tongues and dialects. However, once they made their descent of the staircase down into the Great Hall, a startling change took place. Though every man still spoke his own language, each man heard the words spoken by others as if spoken in the hearers own native tongue. This was part of it, but there was even greater mystery and power still to be found in Lionloff, even so much, it was said, as to allow men of pure heart to read one another's thoughts without the aid of the spoken word.

In this place, hours of conversation were said to have occurred with lips never moving but with the clearest of understanding having been achieved, without the possibility of deceit.

I had never had such an encounter and did not expect one now, for my heart told me that the Dreadlock had been called to this Council for a contention, and contentiousness rarely lends itself to purity of heart.

Having descended the stairway, we followed our guide through the corridor which was brightly lit all along the way by glowing wall-mounted torches.

As we walked, I took notice of the old man again. I wondered what the past had held for him. Was it years of walking these rock floors that had taken their toll on his body? How long had he been at this post? Had he welcomed Hunters to Councils his whole life? Or, I thought, perhaps this Hall-duty, as honourable as any other though less dangerous, was a type of reward for many years of service in the field. Had he at one time been a Hunter like the rest of us?

I had heard stories, legends of those called The Holy Twelve, ancient ones and blood kin all, chosen by the Archangel himself as the first band of brothers to take up the Call of the Hunt. I looked our guide over again and he must have felt my eyes upon him, for he turned his face sharply in my direction, a harsh yet un-angry grimace on his face. He held my eyes for a few steps with a knowing look, then turned away as the corridor made a corner. I took stock of his height, and he looked to be a little shorter than me. But looking again I saw that it was the bend of his back and squat of his old legs that made him look shorter. Stretched out in youth, I surmised, he would have equaled my height at least.

Perhaps he *had* been a Hunter-- perhaps he had charged an Ogdognal in days gone by, thundering across an open field aboard a brilliant white steed, its ears pinned back against a fierce cold wind, and the dented steel of his sword had torn through claw, scale and bone.

Though I ventured not to ask him, for again this was not a place to ask uninvited questions, I decided for my own satisfaction that, yes, he had been a Demon-Hunter in years gone by. And it was at that very moment that my thoughts were interrupted as we made our last corner.

The light from a great hearth-fire suddenly enveloped us, leaping yellow and pale orange onto the peacock slate floor and solid grey walls of the corridor. At last, we had reached the gathering room of the Great Hall.

And I heard voices, thousands of voices, flooding to meet us as we neared the wide doorway opening into the gigantic room where Hunters gathered. Our old guide led us limping through the doorway and we saw hundreds of men, demon- Hunters each and every one, men feared in hell, seated row after row in chairs and pews of solid oak. Looking around I tried to take in the scene, and my heart, though anxious, swelled at the sight.

What a variety was there represented! I saw short, stumpy, hairy men, their large heads sitting almost neck-less atop thick shoulders and massive barrel chests. Their gourd-like heads were covered with thick hair on top and thick beards below, eyes and noses visible between, just. Their attire was heavy layered woolen clothes and short scarves, suggesting that they hailed from colder climes. These were known to be rock dwellers, mountain men, climbers as well as diggers, cave seekers, hewers of stone and fearlessly ferocious in battle. They are called the Gogwallers by some.

Each variety of Hunter had some specialty, some claim to special honour. For these Gogwallers it was that they were known to go into tight caves if necessary to dig a Wormwood demon out of its layer. Their squat size no doubt helped them to maneuver in such close areas, but still, a large helping of raw nerve was required to go sub-terrain to challenge in its own lair a demon of even the lowest form.

Another group of men stood out in the crowd as well. They were tall, each over seven feet in height, but slim up and down and narrow at both hip and shoulder. Called The Fierce, they lack a traditional manly build but were yet a fierce looking lot. Numbering about ten, each had fiery eyes and steel grey hair and matching beards that might as well have been formed of woven barbed wire. With skin dark leather tan, their long lapelled dusters added to their wiry appearance, giving them a dangerous look.

And between the squat and the long-lean were mixed every shape, size and appearance of men that would dare be called into such a profession as Demon Hunter, if profession it could be called.

All of them together in one place was enough to make one stand in awe, for each and all of them were ruthless fighters when they had to be, yet each and all were fiercely passionate and loyal to their cause. Men of conviction, of resourcefulness, and of duty-bound integrity salted with, at times, reckless courage.

Looking them over, I wondered for a moment if the world was worthy of such men before I remembered with shame and pride that it was for this very world that we fought. The Hoy Ground, the Master's Province.

Each man spoke to their friends among those gathered in the Hall as they ignored those they had little use for. There was some disregard felt by some Hunters for others in the Order. Not all of them liked all the others, for each lived according to his own fashion, which was bound to rub the next fellow wrong from time to time, be he comrade in arms or nay.

Just as we had had our own personal conflict with the Baptines, so did many of the Hunters have one with another. Yet the knowledge that we all served the same Master and worked towards the same goal had kept a general order and peace amongst our kind for as long as anyone could remember. It was important that this general tolerance continue to exist amongst the Hunters; we must never allow the enemy to divide and conquer us. And though each unit worked independently of the others, there might come a time when the entire order be called together to form a close knit army, perhaps under the direct command of Jonasius himself.

The Hunters presently gathered were not segregated by any space or grouping, but seated in close rows. Even so, a keen, remembering eye could still tell which were members of a single unit. By their matching clothes, or by matching weapons, or else by some other common trait one could identify the teams of five, the pairs of two, the groups of ten, the squads of eight or packs of a dozen.

This diversity of numbers among the groups was owed to the fact that Hunters were free to organize themselves and their membership according more to practical needs and situations as opposed to any strictly defined number pressed on them from above.

In other words, a hunt-pack might just as well consist of six men as of eight or four or eleven, numbers being adjusted up or down by either the attrition of battle death or the recruitment of new members.

Recruitment was an ongoing thing amongst us in as much as sudden bloody death was natural to our line of work. A hunting party could consist of twelve today and be cut to six tomorrow, half having been cut down in one battle. And that lost six might be replaced by as few as one or as many as six or more, all according to the availability of ready recruits.

Whenever our kind crossed paths out in the wild, one of the first questions asked was if any recent battles had been joined, and if so, was any life lost. And though no set-in-stone policy ruled us, a few general principles were followed.

The first principle was that, generally speaking, the members of each party could consist of as few as two, but should not climb much over a dozen, just to keep things manageable.

A second principle was that, when and if a member was lost in battle, a replacement should be added as soon as practical concerns allowed, but only if each and every member had no serious doubt as to the worthiness of the replacement. If a pair were cut down to one, then that sole survivor is free to either find a replacement to remake the pair, or else join himself to another hunt-party, but he cannot remain on his own as a maverick. His joining himself to an already established pack seldom occurred for the simple reason that each party operated with a strong sense of independence, strong enough even to prejudice them against a Hunter who had been a member of another hunt-pack. Whether this last fact was an admirable trait amongst our kind, I will not judge. But for good or ill, it remains a practice nonetheless.

Our guide did not hesitate at the door but plowed into the rows of men, and we quickly followed like obedient pups. We had no idea where he was leading us, but we followed blindly on until four empty oaks appeared out of the rows of man-flesh. The guide, neither pausing nor looking back, merely gestured towards our seating, a short flip of his right hand as he walked that could just as well have been meant to balance his teetering stride. The Dreadlock took its seat amongst the hundreds, few if any taking notice of us.

The mass of entangled voices grew louder by the moment and it seemed that every hunter in the room must have been trying to talk over each of the others.

As I listened I began to focus on faces and was drawn to the fact that not every mouth was moving. Yet I could swear that the voices of those men whose mouths were silent were yet filling the air with force equal to every other speaking man in the room.

Intrigued now, I began to lock eyes with some of them, and knew from their eyes that they were speaking, or should I say creating words and voices, as clearly as if their lips and cords vibrated to form the sounds I was now hearing as clearly as if a tongue had spoken to me.

Then my eye caught a familiar jaw. It was the young square profile of the messenger, Lukas Markus, who had visited us in the cellar of the village inn. He turned to look at me with lips unmoving, yet I heard him call out to me,

"Scythe," and his voice I heard above all others because we were seeing eye to eye. I waited on his next words, but they did not come, and the spell was broken by a sudden hush and every head turned face forward as Lukas Markus mounted a stone-fronted stage at one end of the Hall. The whole room sank into their seats without a word as the young man, recognized by most for who he was, prepared to address the meeting. He wasted no time, but got right to the point.

"Greetings to all. I am Lukas Markus, servant to Jonasius the Whiteheart, who is the High Counselor to the Order of the Archangel."

SCYTHE

The whole room had taken seats when Lukas Markus began, but now each and every Hunter rose to stand in honour as Jonasius the Whiteheart emerged from behind a wall of heavy crimson veil.

He looked to be nearly seven feet in height. His hair was long and straight and as white as the lightning that flashes across a dark stormy sky at midnight. His face was angular, with defined nose and cheek bones. He looked to be a man above middle age, but how could one tell his age when it was known he had been in the presence of those from that other world, which is said to keep a man's youth from running away.

A robe of pale gray, hemmed in crimson, draped itself over his muscular shoulders, the crest of the Archangel worked into the cloth where the garment covered his heart.

And he began to speak to us in toned words that only his silver throat could have produced--and the words held great volume and music, yet were not painfully loud to our hearing.

"Warriors of Honour! Soldiers of the Realm! It is with gratitude that I welcome you into the Great Hall of Lionloff! You, each one and all of you have ridden here in honour, and some of you have ridden fresh from battle with our ancient foe, having mixed your own blood with that of our enemies--and you are here but they are dead!"

This was a greeting we all needed to hear, especially my own men, and they joined every other man within the Hall in a hearty eruption of joyous cheering. Our hearts were at once melted with humility and filled with a robust pride that we were allowed to be called warriors in an Order so holy and sacred. Cheers, loud yet respectful, went up from every lung and tongue in the place, as if the very vibrations were drawn from our throats. Jonasius lifted a hand, and we quieted with an obedience so perfect that a dripping ball of candle wax could be heard striking the stone floor.

"In the name of the Archangel, in whose ranks and at whose pleasure you serve, I salute you as men of a Separate Courage, Men and Brothers-at-Arms!"

Again now loud and throaty 'hurrahs' went up, bounced off the marble ceiling, and ran away down vast corridors in thunderous speeding echoes.

"We have much to rejoice in, my friends and brothers. Battles have been joined, and many kills have been made, many of our own martyrs created--and another giant step taken in the long march towards a victory that has ever been unwaveringly certain, yet growing more certain every moment!"

The rejoicing reached now a fever pitch. Jonasius paused long enough to allow the cheers to subside, then paused longer still. And we were then reminded that certain-purpose and self-control never yet have been found without self-mortification. I looked at my men and them at me, and we were excited to be there, and thought back a few days to our own victory over Crokow. I could see the confidence of the Dreadlock swell in their faces, our apprehensions disappearing as wind-blown leaves off a pitched roof. But we had not yet heard it all.

"And now, my friends and brothers, I wish to thank you once again for coming with such speed and diligence to this called Council. You will see that the gravity of my concerns fully justify the sudden nature of this meeting.

"The purpose of this meeting is this: In the past few months, evidence has been presented to me, evidence of a plot to destroy our sacred Order, and I must find the truth of the matter. Of course, hell's fury comes against us daily, against you brave warriors in the fields and forests and even the cities of this world. But it is not these outward, expected attacks that concern me today, for the enemy could never conquer us from without." Here he paused just a moment to let that truth sink in, and I think, to foreshadow in our minds his next revelation.

"I have reason to believe that our sacred Order has been infiltrated by agents of the enemy. We have evidence that the enemy now seeks to destroy us, not only from without, but from within." Another pause here, allowing the hammer blow to sink into the crowd of now silent men.

My own heart had stumbled over a precipice and was falling fast. Joy turned to dread in an instant. His pause continued, allowing silent speculation.

The Great Hall was wrapped in a perfect veil of silence, not like the reverent silence of a moment before, but in a fearful and mysterious absence of belief at the words we just heard.

I looked around the hall to see the reaction of the Hunters. Many eyes were still fixed on Jonasius, and many jaws dropped at the devastating news delivered to us by our beloved leader. No one spoke a word, but I noticed that other Hunters were looking around them,

suspicious already of who amongst our number might be guilty of
treason and betrayal.

I saw one Hunter, seated one row behind ours and a few seats
down, look squarely at me. I looked away from his gaze, not knowing
if his look bore accusation, and not wanting to know. Jonasius
continued.

"I have not come to this conclusion alone, my friends, nor did I
arrive at such a serious place in haste. You need to know that I have
had the benefit of wise counsel, and feel the need to share with you
who these advisors are."

He looked then to his right, where there was a doorway that
opened to another room, and at his bidding a line of men emerged
from the doorway and walked over to stand on either side of Jonasius.
One by one they entered, and I counted them as they came...seven,
eight, nine.

I recognized none of them until the last one, the tenth, emerged.
His entry was presaged by the sound of solid and steady rapping of
oak on the solid slate floor, growing louder by the second as he
approached. If my heart was sinking before, when I saw this last man
hobble forth, my heart crashed to the ground and nearly shattered.

There he was, dressed in his long black overcoat, face still hollowed
and ghostly pale. Clearly in pain, his face would grimace each time
his oak peg struck the floor, yet he made his way with inhuman effort
across to stand near Jonasius. And when he took his place in line I'm
certain that of all the hundreds of men in that place, his piercing blue
eyes singled me out amidst the crowd.

I pride myself on fearing no man, but when his eyes met mine, a
bolt of dread ran through my soul as never before. It was not fear of
that Baptine captain, but rather fear that he had used his position
with Jonasius to undermine a man that he hated without cause, a
man called Scythe.

The stumped horseman had hobbled close enough to Jonasius now
to lean upon the arm that The Whiteheart extended to steady the
Baptine captain. A pure heart it was who did not at that moment
envy the horse captain, being in such a favored position next to
Jonasius. The two men clearly shared a confidence, one that took me
by total surprise. And Jonasius clearly wanted all the hunt-class to
know that this captain was among his closest advisors, and so he
spoke again.

"I have chosen to give any of my advisors who so desires an opportunity to address this gathering." There was a long pause again, punctuated by not a sound from anyone. Not a cough, sneeze, nor even an exhaled breath could be heard.

When the Baptine Captain shifted his weight about, the creaking sound from his wooden stump squeaked loudly through the still air hanging over the Hall. And I knew, as soon as I heard his movement, that he had chosen to speak.

Stepping forward as he released his hold on the arm of Jonasius, he again looked my way. Then his blue eyes, made all the more penetrating by the man's ghastly appearance, scanned across the whole gathering.

Any would have to admit that, at that moment, he cut quite a figure on that stage. A fresh sweat had broken out on his hollow, pale skin, and dark rings encircled his eye sockets. His clothing, so perfectly cut and neat at our first meeting, now hung limply on his gaunt frame. It all combined to give him the look of a specter in search of a healthy body in which to take up residence.

"Men at arms," he began with a voice so strong it surprised me, "I salute you as fellow warriors in our eternal struggle for good over evil. Most of you know me, for I am Theologous, Captain of the Baptine Hunters, Deacon of Demon Destroyers, and Horseman of the Realm of Light." Rag-dan leaned over and whispered in my ear,

"That seems a lot of titles for one man." I shushed him as the Baptine continued.

"I am the slayer of countless demons, and a loyal servant in the Order of the Archangel. For over thirty years I have fought the good fight of our Holy Cause, and I carry many a scar in what is left of my flesh as witness of my deeds." This last remark drew direct attention to his missing leg, in the place of which now stood an oak peg.

Nothing so ingratiates a fellow Hunter as the willingness to sacrifice one's life and limbs for the Cause, and I could feel the crowd moving under the sway of this man who hated me and my Dreadlock.

"I have witnessed things in recent days, things that have greatly distressed me--strange things, things never before seen. I have seen men who claim to be servants of our holy Order having contact with things from hell. (A gasp went up from the crowd.) I have seen hunters riding on the backs of fiendish, ghoulish beasts--hellhounds that are not of this worldly realm! (More gasps and groans.) I have seen demons come to the aide and rescue of men by slaying their fellow hell-kind, to deliver their favored ones--even some who sit here among us this very moment!"

At this the whole Hall erupted in a snarling, righteous anger at what they had heard, men beginning to rise from their seats. And those most enraged cast about them for a culprit, for a face to match with the accusation. My own heart seemed to ache within my very breast, as if it would tear itself out of its protective rib-cage. Out in the fields, I found the enmity of the Baptine captain little to worry about. But here in the Hall, with him standing as a confidant at the side of Jonasius The Whiteheart, his enmity had the power to cast me in a most unkind light, or even to bring formal charges against me and my Dreadlock.

Looking around, I saw men huddled together, some looking and nodding in my direction. I looked another way and saw a finger pointing towards me. Rag-dan, Kae-san and Invictus, I could tell, were growing nervous under the growing number of glares and stares cast our way. Many were moving about in their seats, and one man seated behind us, on purpose or by accident, bumped Invictus. Out of the corner of my eye I saw my young comrade flinch defensively and begin to rise from his seat to face the older, bigger man who had bumped him. Instinctively I darted over to Invictus, pushing him back down in his seat.

"Invictus, please sit down. This is no time to take offense. It will be over soon enough. This is a Council in the Great Hall, not a brawl in a tavern!"

Invictus looked hard at me, and then at the big man seated behind him. He seemed as angry at me for restraining him as he was at the man who offended him. As I stood over Invictus, the Baptine's voice boomed once again across the Hall.

"Look who stands as the dreadful news of betrayal is revealed. I have fingered no persons, but do the guilty not often reveal themselves? Why stand ye without recognition before Jonasius? Is it a swollen conscience that makes you rise, and does guilt cause you to pace about, beast rider?"

Suddenly I realized that the whole gathering was again seated, I alone standing on my feet among the thousands. The Hall grew deathly quiet and I felt all eyes upon me. The Baptine captain had spoken directly to me and thereby focused all attention on me. I was in a position now of having been singled out from the crowd with a half-accusation launched as a fireball from the stage. There was no choice but to turn boldly and answer manfully.

Turning to face my accuser, I summoned strength to my spine, spread my feet apart and stood bolt-upright to defend myself and the Dreadlock. And so I took my stand, and spoke.

"Guilt, sir? Guilt is a matter in which I must defer to you, Baptine captain, since you have for so long used it as a ready weapon to intimidate those around you."

This stinging rebuke made the captain cringe with anger. Men all around me were startled at my harsh response, but none more than me. He had the position of favor, and I was walking on dangerous ground by insulting him. But I could not--I *would not* allow myself or the Dreadlock to be so falsely painted by any man. My eyes were locked in a stare-down with his, which looked now even more sunken into his sweaty skull. Yet he had a ready tongue, fired by an unseen hate.

"Guilt belongs to the guilty, and how can one escape his guilt when helped by Hell itself? The devils know me as an enemy who comes to slay them. That is why they took my leg from me, (he pointed down to his stump). They wanted to kill me, but I've witnessed one kill a fellow demon to save your life, (he pointed his finger directly at me now). I am no friend of Hell, yet Hell befriends you. Tell us why, beast rider!"

Jeers, hoots and hollers rose accusingly around me and all through the Great Hall. And though the Dreadlock was there with me, I never remember feeling so alone as at that moment.

The hunt-life is all I have known, and I could feel it so suddenly and unjustly being taken from me. I wanted more than anything to be known among the Order as a faithful warrior above reproach. That desired reputation I also felt slipping from my grasp.

My eyes remained locked with those of the Baptine. I ventured a glimpse at Jonasius to gauge his reaction, but his face was stone and eyes marble, revealing every bit of nothing. If the floor had opened up and swallowed me whole I would not have complained. But the slate did not part, and I had to make an answer to him.

"Many times have I ridden to a death meeting with demons, to bleed them, or be bled by them. Not once have I ever made league with a Hellion, yet more than once within the last fortnight have I risked my own neck to save yours and that of your men, stern Baptine!"

SCYTHE

Oos and Ahs now rose from the crowd. Many Hunters were no doubt ready to believe the Horseman's accusations against me. Yet, not a few were ready to hear my part as well. But the captain had one last barb.

"Oh what a savior you are, beast rider, judging from my torn flesh. You carry the weapon of a reaper and ride creatures of the darkness. You could have saved my leg, but you were late to battle!"

Late to battle. What a slap in the face that was for a Hunter of our Order! It's almost as bad as talking about one's mother. It was a jab that found its mark in my own pride, and I winced at the blow, yet all looked to me now to see how I would hold up.

"I am called Scythe, and my name rings like 'Knife' and well so, because my blade has cut down many a Fallen One, dispatching their shriveled souls back to the pits of hell. I am here today because I was summoned here, just as you all were, and in obedience to our great leader Jonasius I came.

"Some of you I have met in the fields of this present world, and you know I charge into battle on the backs of the Ferocious, borne upon the shoulders of beasts we call gargoyle, a creature which looks every bit as menacing as it proves to be in close combat. Along with my three fellow warriors we form the battle team known as the Dreadlock, and the Dreadlock rides here with fresh Ogdognal blood on our blades."

I had said all this to the crowd around me, for in any confrontation like this one it is important to win the crowd. But I had something to say to my accuser, so I turned to face the cripple on stage and pointed at him.

"And though I fight with an unorthodox weapon, and though we ride to battle aboard strange war-beasts, I swear to all this day that the hearts of the Dreadlock are just as pure, if not as puritan, as yours, stern Baptine. We serve with an honour equal to any in this Great Hall, and I will not be accused by a man I saw snatched through a wall, a man I found nearly dead and strapped to a tree, helpless as a babe and ready to be made a meal of by hungry demons that were cut down by our blades."

"You are alive and stand before us today because of my efforts, by my hand and weapon, and by those of my gargoyle riding Dreadknaughts!"

At that point I ventured a glance about me, and I could see the once hard, suspicious expressions on the faces of the hunters softening with my words. They were listening, at least, to my self defense. I looked the Baptine in the eyes as I drove home my final point.

"And yes, there in that clearing in the deep forest, where your life hung by a thread, an unknown devil did charge in and strike one of its own kind. And though I can find no reason for the action and offer no explanation at this time, let me remind this Council and all under the sound of my voice that when that hellion cut down one of its own, it saved not only my life, but that of my accuser as well. And though I was hard pressed at the time, it was not I who was lashed, stumped and bleeding, to a tree trunk."

I had finished in a flurry of defiant words, and I could hear mumbling voices throughout the Hall, and even a few hoots and shouts of support.

Jonasius waited a moment for the Baptine captain to respond, but the man uttered not another word aloud, but turned finally to whisper something in the ear of The Whiteheart. Then Jonasius stepped forward.

The crowd had grown louder with talk as the Hunters discussed what they had just heard, but Jonasius raised his hand. With that slight movement the entire Hall almost instantly came to a perfect silence. Jonasius had taken control of the Great Hall and would make a final address.

"Despite what you have heard, no formal charges have been presented before me." At this point Jonasius gave a quick glance in the direction of the Baptine Captain. Did I see a trace of disapproval in Jonasius' eyes, was it a chastening look he cast at Theologous? Or was it just my hopeful imagination grasping for any straw it could find? Whatever the intent, the horseman remained unmoved, his chin granite, his head unbowed and un-shamed.

"There are two hunt-teams who did not answer the call the Council. They will be found, and we will know the reason for their absence. If they are the traitors, they will be exposed for what they are. As to what we have heard here this day, as far as I am concerned, all Hunters leave here on equal footing, under no public suspicions." Jonasius paused now to step forward, even to the very front edge of the dias, and though he already had our full attention, everyone's ears perked up for his final, emphatic statement.

"But as you return to your duties, return to the fields of blood and sword, know this: those who betray The Whiteheart Order, those who let fly in the face of the very Master in whose service they enlisted and to whose glory they are solemnly sworn, those Hunters will become the ones I hunt. They shall become my prey. They shall be driven from us, for they are not truly of us. I will personally ride them down and mix their blood with that of hell's rebels, and together banish them to the chains of darkness!"

All was silence as Jonasius' final words hung like like a sword over the Hall. With his entourage of advisors, Jonasius The Whiteheart strode off the stage, thus ending the Council.

Each hunt-group waited to be escorted back down the long corridor and up the staircase. When our turn came, it was the same old man whom we met upon our arrival that led us back out the same way we had come in. As our group moved through the still crowded hall, a few reached up to give an encouraging slap on our shoulders, though we also received many a grim look from fellow hunters. Yet all of my men, including Invictus, kept cool heads as we made our way out. I tried to remember that these our fellows were good men, and that they had been rattled by what had just taken place in the Great Hall, and that it is only human nature to look for someone to blame when all does not go well. If suspicion were cast upon all, then most will look for a scapegoat to vicariously remove suspicion from them. That is simply the world we live in.

Though the air inside the underground Hall had not been unpleasant, I needed to get to fresh air as soon as I could. I needed to pull in a great breath of nature in order to clear my head. It never failed to refresh me, and I needed that so I could think through what had just taken place.

But my plan for a quick exit would be delayed, though not by my choosing.

As we progressed down the hallway leaving the Council chamber with its voices and echoes at our backs, our guide without hesitation made a sharp left turn. I had not noticed a doorway there before and at firs appearance it looked like no more than a shadow cast on the wall, but as my silent guide ducked below the stone header of the doorway I quietly followed without question, as if bidden by fate itself.

The flickering lights of the torch-lined hallway were quickly left behind as we worked our way through the twisting and turning tunnels which remained unlit save the warm beacon of the old man's hand-held torch.

SCYTHE

After what seemed like half an hour of fast paced travel through the dark corridor we stopped abruptly at a thick oaken door upon which the guide began to rap with the scar-knarred knuckles of his free hand. It was the first time that I noticed that his hands were unnaturally large for one his stature.

A voice from behind the door uttered a word I could not discern but which apparently allowed entrance for the guide turned the knob and pushed against the oak as the old door hinges creaked as if in protest of this intrusion upon their rusty sleep.

As if to spite the hinges, the inviting breath-light of a hearth fire beckoned me enter and I stepped through. Sensing a stillness at my back, it was only then that I turned to see that I had at some point been separated from my Dreadlock. I cast a questioning eye over the guide but he gave me a knowing look and wink that said 'All is well.' He backed out of the doorway into the hallway and closed the door behind him.

I found myself in a room not over-large, but large enough to hold a stone hearth which was the only source of heat and light in the room. The room appeared to be a living quarter for it was furnished sparingly with a bed and a table strewn with parchment, and an armchair covered in forest furs.

It was then that I noticed a fairly tall and sturdy silhouette against the light of the fire. It was a man wearing a heavy coat or cloak and had on heavy leather riding boots. His head was uncovered and his hair grew down past his shoulders.

I wanted to be cooperative but was uncomfortable being separated from my men. Along with the accusations that had been pointed toward the Dreadlock, the circumstances of the present moment were making me tense. The silhouette still had his back to me when he spoke.

"The magic of this place still amazes me though I have tread her halls for many a year."

He turned to face me then and he looked familiar to me but I could not be sure with his face now leeward of the fire. My mind, under the shadow of this new uncertainty, raced to assess the tone of his unknown voice. Much had been said in the Council and though Lionloff boasted a high level of security I was far from certain that even this great hide could not be infiltrated by some form of devilry. I noticed that he wore a sheathed blade, and as his sword hand moved toward the hilt I readied to defend myself. To my relief his hand stopped on his belt buckle where he unfastened it and laid both belt and blade over the arm chair, his sword resting neatly against the fur covered backrest. Not little relieved, I could not see that he noticed either my tension or the release of it. He was clearly at ease in the present situation.

I needed to see his face clearly and he noticed me looking at the oil-lamp on the table. He nodded towards it and I struck a match to the wick and held the lamp towards him for a closer look. Then I knew; he was one of the Ten of Jonasius' inner circle that had sat with The Whiteheart during the Council. He was of middle age with streaks of grey in his hair and beard, and wore a dark green tunic underneath his cloak, along with a black vest and breeks. They were fine clothes though well-worn. He removed the dark leather gloves he had worn in the Council, the act revealing a sword hand minus the tips of two fingers. The left hand had all its fingers though, with its twisted skin and scars, it looked as if it had left some of its meat on the fangs of some hell-thing.

Moving back to the fire, he cast more wood into it, stoking it so that the flames grew to cast our shadows larger about the roomwalls.

"You come to this place beneath a grim shadow, Beast-rider. There are men here who would not mourn you should ye fall by the hand of a hellion or be found a traitor and dispatched forthwith by The Whiteheart himself." He paused a moment as if to let that sink in. "But I would wish neither the former nor the later end for you John. I would rather hope to call you a friend and an ally."

"Forgive me sir, you seem to know who I am, which puts me at a disadvantage since I am unfamiliar with you, save that you are one of the ten confidants of Jonasius."

"I am called Aol-bren."

"The Noble Blade?" I asked. He snickered at that.

"So some translate it. As to the Order, I am an Elder-Hunter. As to the World, I am a Lord of Lands. As to this Hall, I am its Keeper."

I looked about the room again, wondering if it could be that of the Keeper. He read my thoughts.

"What? You imagined the Keeper of such a Hall would have a grander private chamber? I see, but remember, simplicity is the key to humility."

"My real question, Lord Aol-bren, concerns why I have been brought to your chambers without my men. In light of recent events, sharing a private meeting with the 'beast-rider' might cast doubt on your loyalties." He considered my words a moment, then paced back across to where I stood.

"Amongst the Baptines, perhaps, and those that would be quick to join the Horse-Captain's harsh and unproven accusations, even against a man that may have saved his life. But you will find me one of the few who can call Jonasius an old friend and as long as my stance is right in his eyes I care not what devisive tongues would speak against me. Or against you, Scythe. I am no friend of Theologous, though at present I have no personal quarrel with him as he seems to have with you."

"If that man were," I replied, "a whit more cold and stiff, I believe he would shatter like ice."

"And if he were an ounce more stubborn he might bray like a mule rather than speak as a man," said Aol-bren.

We were both smiling now and I relaxed another measure at his humor, my comfort level growing more easily now.

"Still, of all the Hunters you could have chosen to cross, the Baptine Captain was not the most tactical of choices. He is both an elder-Hunter and a favorite of Jonasius—a powerful and influential position. And though I hold no fondness of the man, we must both admit that he commands a presence, all the more with that stumped leg still bloody. The hearts of men are often swayed by such sacrifice."

"True enough," I admitted. "I never wanted to be his enemy, but I must say that however peculiar our circumstances in the wood that night, I hardly think it should warrant suspicion of my allegiance." Aol-bren nodded in agreement and crossed the room to a cupboard from which he produced two small wooden dups and a corked bottle. He poured the shimmering liquid and handed me a cup.

"This, Scythe, is the very matter for which I had you brought here. As you may recall from Jonasius' speech, there is great suspicion of a traitor amongst the order. And though you may have not yet realized it, this goes beyond the Baptine and that night with Crockow in the wood. I know you have not forgotten what Jonasius said just a few moments ago about the Hunters who did not respond to the summons to this Council." I nodded that I did indeed recall. "This is just the latest of the troubling events that have plagued us recently."

He paused and I took the moment to sip the drink. I did not recognize the taste but it was not unpleasant, thicker than I had expected, like unto a broth, and it warmed me almost instantly as it went down. I noted then in his face a baleful stare that reflected the troubles we were discussing. It was the first look of worry I had seen in the man.

"The enemy is moving Scythe. We have yet to divine their larger strategy, but we are sure that a major offensive is in the offing." As he spoke it seemed that the room began to blacken. The shadows advanced from the far corners of the chamber where they had been held at bay by the hearth light, threatening now to overcome it. Though I knew not if it was the fire that was dying, the strange magic of the place, or the dark uncertainty of his tone, yet I sensed the very physical presence of some great menace, a whisper of fear echoing within the inner reaches of my mind. "There is a stirring in the dark amongst devils and men. There are words being spoken in secret places that heaven and earth have not heard in half a millennia. And I fear that if we do not discover what new evil hell is birthing, and react swiftly, it might be that we are the ones hunted across the Holy Ground of this earth.

His words hung in the room like an unwelcome guest, a stagnant and foul apparition, and I realized that my breathe had gone shallow and I could feel the strong steady pump of my own heart. Aol-bren had turned back to the fire.

"Alo-bren, you know as well as I that Scythe is no large reputation in this Order, even less so after today. Why then, I ask, would you confide all of this to me?"

He stood a moment as if lost in thought, but then turned sharply to face me.

"Because your name is known in hell. Feared even. From the information we have from Jonasius' well-placed spies, 'Scythe' is not a name there cheered but one that brings a devil-hiss from their wretched lips. Some even, it is said, look to see if this 'Scythe' lurks in the shadows of empty spaces with death's reaping-blade ready to return them to the pit! A reputation amongst your enemy is more valued to me than one amongst friends. Friends want to admire but the enemy is forced into fear. You and your men will soon be needed, Scythe, and if you would answer the oath that you swore then I will put a word in the ear of The Whiteheart that you are his man, indeed. I suspect that these recent events are being coordinated to draw the attention of the Council toward your Dreadlock. Though it would not be wise at this point to push the matter in open debate, I will continue to investigate what is truly happening amongst our ranks, and try to get to the bottom of this skullduggery."

I stiffened my spine to reply.

"I made my oath to our master's Cause as a Dreadnaught many moons ago, with a blade in my hand. And it is with a blade I have since dedicated every breathe granted me to bleed hell dry. My Scythe belongs to The Whiteheart and the Order of the Archangel, as do the blades of my men. The resolve of the Dreadlock is absolute, and the man who questions it does to his own peril. I thank you for your trust Aol-bren, please know that it will not be betrayed."

He waited a moment, measuring my words, then smiled and replied,

"I trust that it shall not be."

Downing the last of my drink, we clasped forearms and with that goodbye I left him there. The old guide had been waiting and as I stepped through the doorway he began to shuffle back the way we had come without a word as I followed through the maze of cornered corridors. In a moment I found myself back in the wide, well-lit hallway that we had used to exit the Council earlier. Hearing voices behind me I turned to see my men, the three of them, following behind. They were still discussing the events of the Council, and gave no sign that I had been anywhere else but walking with them the whole time.

Soon enough we were outdoors again, and the darkness of night covered all. We made our way back to the edge of the woods where we had tied off our mounts. The old guest-master accompanied us as far as the trees. Before he turned to go, though unbidden, he spoke to the four of us.

"Sometimes I have found myself in a lonesome place. Sometimes in an unknowable place, without direction. I have found, at times like those, that it is good to return to where one started, to where it all began. Farewell." And without giving us a chance to reply or question him, he turned and was gone.

His words still haunting me, I mounted my beast and led the men away, backtracking the way that we had come in as best we could discern.

Coming at last to the wall of reeds, we found that the portion that had opened to allow us entry had closed itself off again, the inter-twine and thickness of the reeds giving no hint it had ever been parted. All we could do was to try to keep up our faith and move along the length of the wall, hoping to be granted another point of exit. A bright moon had risen high in the sky and gave much light for our travel. After nearly an hour's ride along the wall we came to a place where once again the upturned soil showed signs that the reeds had uprooted themselves and retreated to clear a path for us.

Riding through, we thought of camping just on the other side, if that we might be privileged to see the wall of living, moving reeds move back together to close the breach up again. But I decided that we had no time for that. Though we had no place to rush to, I felt like we needed to put some distance between us and that place. I needed room to think, and so we rode on.

SCYTHE

SCYTHE

Chapter Thirteen
River of Rest

Silent was I, and distracted, as the Dreadlock made its way along the road away from the Council. My friends must have recognized my disposition, for they left me alone to my thoughts, talking in hushed tones among themselves when they did speak. I had much on my mind, and as the leader of the Dreadlock, I had decisions to make, decisions that might take me and my men in a different and even more dangerous direction than ever before.

Like any man who enjoys life and self-preservation, I had concerns for my own future. But those concerns were small compared with the concerns I had for the young men under my charge. Even though I am but a few years their senior, I was feeling the weight of responsibility for their lives more every day. I had always been taught that a good leader is one who cares deeply for those under his care. Now, more than ever, I was feeling the true iron of those words.

As for the men, they would not want me to worry about them, for though they were young, they were men grown and each had been blooded in battle many times.

Furthermore, they saw themselves more as independent fighters gathered in a loose confederacy as opposed to being strictly under my care and command. Still, in any band of brothers there will always be one upon whom falls the privileges and responsibilities of leadership. In the Dreadlock, it clearly fell to me. And no matter how much the others protested their own ideals of the unbound and carefree Knight Errant, I have always felt a great duty to see that each lived to see the next summer of their young lives. One fact did serve to ease my mind a bit, this being that none of them had yet married or started families. And so if one died in battle alongside me, he would leave no grieving wife and child behind. Come to think of it, the Dreadlock itself was really the closest thing to a family that any of us had. And so we had made our sacred pact: to live, fight and even die together in pursuit of mankind's worst enemies.

We rode through the night and into a grey, somber morning without stopping, a slow pace that covered little ground. I could think better at a slower pace, and the men could sense my burden. No one pushed ahead too quickly. Late in the evening the sound of moving water and a grove of stocky elm bid us to make camp there in the midst of trees, and so we did. The grove stood on a grassy hillock that overlooked a slow moving stream of blackish-green water. The locals called this stream a river, even though it was no wider than thirty feet across at any point we could see. Drifting smoke told us a village was nearby.

With our mounts tied off as perimeter sentries, the men gathered dry driftwood for a fire. I sat alone with my thoughts on the river bank, allowing the trickle of the swirling water to stream through my mind. The worries inside my head were little boats, dinghies getting caught in the flow of the stream noise, and I closed my eyes as I rest on the grass of the hillside, and the little boats bore my cares away for a brief moment.

But when I opened my eyes again, the dinghies had floated to the sea and across all the world's oceans, then sailed straight back to the forefront of my mind.

I could not stop asking questions. Why had the Dreadlock been singled out? Was this whole thing just a contest of wills between the Baptine captain and myself, or was something deeper and more sinister going on, an unseen reality behind the outward appearances? How persuasive were the accusations that had obviously reached the ears of the highest leadership in the order, perhaps to the Archangel himself? And if so, what could be done about it? What were we to do next? We could not simply return to the hunt. Things were no longer that simple.

But why, I asked myself in frustration, couldn't life be simple, with one side all-good opposed by the other side all-evil? Why must there be in-fighting on the side of the good? With this in-fighting, all the simplicity of the hunt life vanished as into the very surrounding air, and the peace of my mind with it. Before, I had thought it all clear cut, them verses us, good verses evil, heaven's friends locked in total, desperate war with hell's spawn. But now we find ourselves a part of a struggle *within* the side of the good, a very in-fight among warriors of light. To say the least, this was a distraction from the wider war that my Dreadlock had sworn to wage against the demons.

With camp made, we lingered beside the river.

I was tired. We all were tired. But for me, the fatigue ran deeper than just tired muscles. It was an exhaustion of the spirit as well as of the mind and body. Even so, I felt restless, like I needed to get back on the road to take action that would fix everything. My anxiety was all too real, and I must have been wearing the worry like an old garment, for my friend Kae-san walked out to me as I sit by the riverbank one evening.

"Scythe, I thought I might find you here," said Kae-san as he walked up.

"Yes Kae-san, the sound and sight of a moving river helps me to relax and to ponder. A river is one of the earth's great marvels, in my mind. Did you know that a man can never sit by the same river twice?"

"So I've heard, Scythe, because yesterday's river has traveled far down-land by now, perhaps even to the sea."

"Exactly so, Kae-san, for the river rolling past us now, though called by the same name, rolled down new and fresh from some mountainous land this morning."

"And what a beautiful day it has been," he replied.

"Beautiful indeed. I only wish my mind were untangled enough to enjoy it."

"Scythe," Kae-san said kindly, "I know that it is a heavy burden you bear. I can see it in your face. So can the others," he continued as he took rest beside me. "You have many concerns, many worries, but you should remember that whatever problems you face, none are so great that we cannot overcome them together, as the Dreadlock. You must also remember what we have been through during the past few weeks. A desperate hunt for Crokow and his fellow devils, then our meeting with the Baptines, the two battles and to top it all off we had to ride hard for over a week just to make it on time for the Council. And the Council itself was not without its own conflicts. Any other group of hunters would take months of rest after such an ordeal. We must also take rest, and try to relax so that our bodies and minds can renew themselves. I have seen you do things in the past few days very few men could do, but even you have your limits."

"You are right Kae-san, but there is a claw in my brain, and until the clouds of disloyalty and dishonour no longer overshadow me, I will enjoy no peace."

"Those who ride and fight beside you know that your honour is clean. What others think matters very little in the long run," Kae-san said. He hesitated before he continued, as if being careful with his words. "Perhaps Scythe, it is your reputation that concerns you more than your honour." I bristled at Kae-san's insinuation, yet deep in my heart I knew he was right. My own father had warned me that the human heart is but a wrestling ring where pride and love battle for supremacy, one desiring the applause of man, the other desiring to serve mankind. And before he died a few years ago, my father had confided in me that though he was proud that his son had done deeds worthy of a reputation, yet he was even more thankful that those deeds were done for a cause greater than my own self.

"Kae-san, once again you are right. Once again you prove that the wounds of a friend are faithful and meant for good. I'll admit that I enjoy walking through a village when the crowd parts to make way for me. I hear them whisper 'there is the one who fights with the scythe, see how the blade gleams above his heard.'

"Did you expect a similar treatment at the Council?"

"Well Kae-san, if I did I was sorely disappointed. Rather than being celebrated, I was more or less denounced publicly as a traitor. Can you tell me that the Great Hall was not growing warm as that Baptine Captain spoke against us?"

"Warm indeed, Scythe. Still, we are denounced by a man who had no right to make that denouncement, and no grounds for his claims. He didn't have a leg to stand on," Kae-san blurted out before he caught himself.

"Wrong Kae-san, he still had at least one leg to stand on." We both enjoyed a chuckle at the play on words.

"Nonetheless, Scythe, the key thing to remember is that this captain, whether well connected or not, is not your judge. A greater One waits to judge us all, and His judgment is as unerring as it is gracious."

"Kae-san, you are a good friend as well as an encourager," I said, rising with him to shake his hand. "From now on I will think better thoughts. I will try to have faith and remember the things you have said. Now tell me, Kae-san, after we take our needed rest here, what plan of action do you advise?"

"Well, what does your heart tell you?"

"My heart tells me that the advice of that old Hall Guest-Master was offered in good faith. Some may wear their gray hair as a fool's cap, but his, I think, is a crown of wisdom."

"And what was the advice he offered?"

"He said to go back to the beginning, to the original things, to where I started from."

"My guess is, that for you, that would mean a return to your Hunt-Master."

"Yes, Kae-san, I think so. But the prospect of it troubles me. My Hunt-Master and I did not part on the best of terms."

"Ah yes," replied Kae-san, "his daughter....what was her name?" I looked away from Kae-san, out across the rolling river and into the green forest beyond.

"Pristine."

"Pristine," he repeated.

SCYTHE

SCYTHE

Chapter Fourteen
Memories of The Bower Green

We camped there by that flowing water for another few weeks, taking much needed rest. The river was healthy with fishlife and we found bait in the high grass.

The men had met some folk who came up from the nearby village to visit. I sat by the river and watched, from a distance, as they laughed and talked with the villagers, who offered generous samples of the local cuisine.

Encouraged as I was that the men had found new fellowship, I knew it would not last, that we could not stay there for long. I was reminded of what a lonely life a Hunter must so often lead. No more-stark reminder of that fact could I have had than my thoughts of Pristine. Of all the sacrifices I have made for The Cause, she was by far the greatest.

Sitting there by the trickling waters, I looked up into the sky, searching for hope. But the sky was a plowed field, row after row of grey cloud, tightly packed against an eternal expanse of blue. I closed my eyes, forlorn, and allowed my mind to drift to memories of The Bower Green.

When I first came under his care, her father, my trainer and Hunt-Master, had warned me to count the cost of the path I had chosen, and to be sure that I could walk away from what I loved most. But that had been in the beginning, before I had fallen in love with his daughter.

All of sixteen years old, I had been so sure of my commitment to the Cause. But that was before Pristine, before our long afternoon walks under acres of dogwoods and cherry trees, the blossoms falling around us like bliss itself. On two of those walks we had held hands, and pledged our love to one another forever. Those were the last two walks we had taken together. By then I had been under her father's authority and training for most of two years. He had made sure that those were the hardest years I had ever known.

His name was Ell-ory, and months before, on my first day in his house, he had hardly spoken to me. Then, before sunup on my second morning with him, he shook me harshly awake. My training had begun, in earnest. It was still well-dark when he led me deep into the forest.

The trek alone, burdened with heavy pack, had been enough to blister me to-blood on both my shoulders and heels. But as soon as we had made camp, with no thought of food or rest, he came to me with a hemp rope in his hands.

First he tied the end of the rope around my waist, then ordered me to follow him down yet another path that was familiar to him if not to me. He told me to keep the free end of the rope coiled around my arm. I noticed, of course, that he carried two huge war axes with him, one in each hand.

I followed him down the path until it split into two smaller paths, which were no more than pig trails. Neither turning to look at me nor uttering a word, Ell-ory threw one of the axes a few feet down the right trail and pointed to it as he himself veered to take the left trail. I took that to mean I should take the right trail. That I did, picking up the war-axe as I went. The weight of the axe was appalling; the thickness of the oak handle, the massive iron of the double-blades.

On and on I walked down my trail as the way grew harder and the brush thicker, my clothing already drenched in sweat.

The sweat covered my face as well, dust and debris caking around my lips and stinging my eyes. I had no idea where my trainer was, but as I had sworn complete subservience to him as my Hunt-Master, I had no choice but to carry on down the trail.

I walked on alone through the day until darkness again overshadow the land. My body wanted to stop for rest, but my mind was determined not to fail my first assignment. My arms and shoulders ached and cramped from holding the heavy war-axe. I tied the loose end of the rope around the shoulder of the axe, where the handle connected to the iron axe-head, and slung it over my back to take the weight off my arms, though it only made my back hurt worse.

Going on as far as I could physically go, just before I dropped in exhaustion, I took one last step. But there was nothing solid to catch my booted foot as it came down. It felt as if I had steeped into a pot of thick soup, though the pot had no bottom because my foot continued to sink, finding no ground. I tried to pull my weight back from whatever I had stepped into but the weight of the axe pushed me forward.

Just as my face went under the surface of the quicksand, I tried snatching the rope to fling the axe forward in hopes that it would catch on something and become an anchor I could hold to. But my arms had no strength left in them and the axe never made it off my back. Instead of an anchor to hold me, the axe was as an anvil strapped to my back, pushing me down into an abyss of liquid rot. How strange and disappointing, I thought as I plunged deeper in the mire, that I was dying on my very first day of training. When I fell into the muck-pit, my mouth must have been agape in fear, for I swallowed a mouthful of the filth, which my stomach rejected back out through my nose and mouth. It was as if I were breathing this very gook I was submerged in, and I knew death was nearby. The light faded, the darkness beckoned.

Strong hands took hold of me, meat hooks of steel, unforgiving iron fingers. How they reached me or from what direction, I never knew, for I was nearly unconscious when my Hunt-Master pulled me back into the world of the living. Choking, spitting, coughing up what looked to be parts of myself, I regained a semblance of consciousness lying at his feet. He was not laughing, that much I remember, not because I didn't make a funny site but because I didn't need to be made fun of at that particular moment.

You see, everything my Hunt-Master did to me had a purpose, was meant to harden some part of me, either physically or mentally, for the demon-hunt. He knew that the prey I would be pursuing is as physically overwhelming as it is remorseless. In the Hunt-Master's mind, there is no place for weakness in the life of one by him trained. Every student of his takes his sign, seared into the skin of the right shoulder, a hollow X. And wearing his brand is akin to taking his name--he doesn't give it out lightly. He claimed the sign was an ancient emblem of defiance of evil, though I had never seen its like.

The first year that I was under his training was the most intense year of my life. If you came to a Hunt-Master with heroic ideals of glorious, easy battles and of hearing your name celebrated in songs of the renowned, Ell-ory would give you, in a day, such an introduction to reality that would quickly rob you of your false romanticism. And *he* would enjoy it, if you did not.

Nothing has ever been harder, before or since, not even my worst battles with the Damned. He called it the 'high-water mark of pain' and offered me daily, in those first few months, opportunity to reconsider, to walk away with no dishonour. My body wanted to go, but my mind made me stick it out. The mind taking control from the body was indeed his goal for me.

SCYTHE

After hundreds of days of being cold, tired, hungry, bloody and having several near-death experiences, he announced that my first year of training was over. He knew that my jaded mind had lost count of the days, and that's why he had to remind me of the date.

That year of physical torture hardened me. My skin, my muscle, even parts of my soul became rough and calloused. The second year of training would still be physically trying, but it would be more for the refinement of the skills of the hunt: learning about the enemy, how to recognize it and how to kill it. Learning to track. Learning to use bladed weapons. Learning woods craft. Six days a week we trained, fourteen hours a day without exception. And for the first six months of that second year I saw my Hunt-Master grow happy with my progress. He trained me with the sword first, but so pleased was he with my progress in the use of that legendary blade, he allowed me to work with a scythe as well, knowing how much I wanted to use it as a weapon.

But in the second half of that year, things changed. They changed because two things happened. First, the daughter of my Hunt-Master, Pristine, returned from an extended visit with her cousins. Second, a new trainee joined us, for Ell-ory, though he preferred one student at a time, would sometimes take on a second. So it was that Pristine and Ar-ric entered my life in the same week. I watched her for three days, trying to catch her eye. Then Ar-ric came, and we both tried to catch her eye. Even so, most of it was still innocent at that point, no one was serious or in love yet, therefore no one was jealous. Yet.

Meanwhile, Ar-ric and I became fast friends, trained together, and decided that when we left the Hunt-Master's care we would form our own hunt-team. Ar-ric even thought up a name for it: The Dreadlock.

But then it happened. Ar-ric and I were out in the woods one morning learning how to set up an ambush. Pristine happened to choose a nearby path for her morning walk, and her path led straight to us. Ar-ric and I saw her at precisely the same time, but something was different in all of us that day. Indeed, for whatever twist of fortune, none of us were ever the same again. Fateful day indeed.

Ar-ric and I both put away our weapons and went, without speaking or even looking at one another, to her in the pathway. She saw us both, saw that we both craved her attention, having forgotten our training. But she moved towards me and we together walked away from Ar-ric, who was left there standing alone. I did not mean to hurt Ar-ric, I think, for I was thinking only of Pristine.

SCYTHE

Yet I must admit that at that moment, when she first looked into my eyes, holding her gaze there, I would not have cared what our decision meant to Ar-ric or anyone else. It was the kind of moment one waits for all their lives, a moment when all the world around you dissolves into a blur about the edges of the nature-framed picture of the beloved. Idolatry, no doubt, but I was as guilty as I could be and helpless in it.

She and I walked and laughed together that day, and her smile became the very joy of my existence. I had not known the world could even contain such beauty. It was a smile that could warm the coldest heart. My heart did not merely warm, it melted. From that day on I thought only of her.

We spent every available moment together, always out of her father's sight. But if my Hunt-Master did not see my love for his daughter, he certainly noticed that my skills had suffered. I had lost the focus and intensity of my earlier training. He complained that my mind seemed to be somewhere else. Nothing could get my attention, even when he roughed me up in our blade work, leaving me bloody though not deeply cut.

And all the while Ar-ric watched, brooding. He kept trying to talk with Pristine, to get her to notice him. But it was no use, her eyes could see me only. And that's when Ar-ric began to change. I remember the stages of his conversion. Irritable at first, moody, glum. Then the moodiness turned to outright bitterness, then to red anger. Anger gave rise to hostility. I tried to explain things to him, but he would not hear it. Our sparing matches, which had always been intense, became bloody affairs. More than once I ducked the hard sweep of his sword that could have cut me deeply, even have killed me perhaps.

When Pristine and I would walk together, Ar-ric would sometimes follow us at a distance, spying from behind a tree or shrub. His spirit grew colder, meaner every day.

One day I heard angry voices near the woodshed, and I rushed out to see what was going on. I found Ar-ric with Pristine, holding her forcefully by the arm. He was demanding that she walk with him, but she refused. As I rounded the corner I saw that he was yelling loudly, his angry face close to her tear-stained cheeks. She looked frightened. That, along with jealousy, enraged me, and I came on strong, plowing into Ar-ric shoulder first, pounding him to the ground.

SCYTHE

It was a hard blow, but Ar-ric was tough and strong and no sissy, and he was powerful enough to throw me off him. We both rose to our feet, measured one another briefly, then attacked. We kicked and beat one another bloody for a full twenty minutes before our Hunt-Master heard the ruckus and found us. That picture told him all he needed to know. After ordering us to stay put, he took Pristine into the main house to question her for the whole story.

She told her father all that she felt, and because it was me and not Ar-ric that Pristine confessed love for, it was me who bore the brunt of his wrath. When he came out of the house, he came straight to me. He walked right up to me and punched me square on the chin, knocking me nearly out of my boots. When I regained enough mind to listen, he gave me an ultimatum: I could finish out my final two months of training if I swore never to so much as look at Pristine again. Then I could leave a Hunter, but only if I further swore never to return, and never to see her again. It took me nearly three seconds to form my answer. I told him that I respected him, but that he was crazy if he thought I could ever forget Pristine.

"Then you will leave this place," he replied, and drawing a dagger from his belt he said, "but first I will cut my mark from your flesh. You will not carry my mark from here without my blessings." He had branded me with the mark only a week before, and having earned it, I decided to keep it.

Backing away from him, I moved through an open door of a storage barn. When I emerged, my scythe was in my hands, hands that were like stone from my training. Ar-ric stood close by, enjoying my humiliation. He said between malicious laughter,

"Look? The boy who defies his own Master with a--a farmer's tool! Mighty Scythe has come out to fight!" I ignored him for the moment, speaking to my Hunt-Master.

"No one will cut my flesh from me this day, not even you Hunt-Master, unless you want to lose an arm, or worse."

"Then collect your things and go. You are no longer welcome in my presence, or in that of my daughter. I will let you keep the mark if you leave, never to return. But if I see you again, you will die--now get out!" I looked around for Pristine, but she was locked away inside the house. It looked as if I was short on options.

"Then I will go and never return. Your mark will not suffer embarrassment due to me, I assure you. But as I go, know this. My respect for you remains strong and I am grateful for the training I have received at your hand. But you cannot keep your daughter from Love. If you try to, you will ruin her. I have come to love her more than I have words to express, yet I go from here alone. If you will not let her love me, remember that she must love someone, sometime, Hunt-Master!" I collected my few belongings and walked away, the only sound in my ears came through an open window, the pitiful desperate sobbing of Pristine.

Ar-ric stayed on and continued his training. He hoped Pristine's love for me would cool, and that she might learn to love him. But when she continued to reject him, Ar-ric's heart turned to something truly evil. The kernels that remained of his faith and hope dissolved into a pool of hate. After he had learned all he could from the Hunt-Master, he walked into the night, enveloped in evil.

The next time Ar-ric was seen, he was riding with demons, taking the heads of Hunters as trophies. He had made a pact with the enemy. Having lost all faith in the Light and in Love, Ar-ric cut a deal with The Dark. He made his choice, and would take his chances with Hell rather than simply living without Pristine.

Pristine. Even now, to speak her name brings pain, the pain of loving something you know you can never have. Now I would have to return to that place where I had met and had fallen in love with her, that place I had been banished from because I could not, would not stop loving her. Going back there, I was certain, would be almost the hardest thing I had ever done, second only to leaving her the first time.

SCYTHE

Chapter Fifteen
Chasing Shadows

The men eventually grew restless at our camp by the river. I could tell that they also had questions, the kind of questions that Hunters always come to wrestle with. Do our lives as demon slayers really count for anything? Does anyone really appreciate all that we do or the sacrifices we make? What would my life be like if I had chosen a different path?

I knew what they were feeling, having asked these same questions of myself many times over the past few years. When doubt seeps into the mind, doubt of even an underpinning you thought long settled and not open to doubt, it can be a very confusing thing. Having been there myself, I knew that there was no one on earth that could answer these questions for the men but the men themselves. Yet each man deals, to an extent, with such things in his own way, after his own fashion.

Invictus, as young as he was, still mostly celebrated the moment, the delightful joys of youth, and was therefore less contemplative than the others.

Kae-san had the mind of a tracker and was most at peace in the wooded glens and forests. Whenever he sought solace and solitude amongst the trees I knew that there was something that burdened his mind.

Rag-dan usually spent his spare time working with the Ferocious, which he sometimes called his 'untamed children.' And so I found it a bit odd one day when I noticed him leaving the camp, taking a narrow path, alone, off the eastern side of our encampment. It was only later that we would learn what happened to Rag-dan on his long, lonely walk.

This shepherd to our unique mounts had walked alone over a mile from our camp that day. The sun was still bright when he entered the woods, and he would later tell us of a shadow that swept over the trees above his head, rustling the leaves of the tree canopy from above, startling him. The tree canopy was just sparse enough to allow a shadow to slip through to Rag-dan, but just dense enough to keep him from getting a clear view of what cast it.

From what he could see, it looked to him to have the shape of some great wing. He hardly believed his eyes though, for no bird could be large enough to cast such a shadow.

Captivated then, Rag-dan began to chase on foot after the figure that was sweeping the tree tops, wanting a better look at the thing that skirted just beyond the edges of his vision. But it was moving so fast that, for the trees and the speed of the thing, he was able to catch only the slightest glimpse of it. Yet there was something about the thing, some familiarity, that so pricked Rag-dan's curiosity that he would not give up that easily.

On he ran after the sweeping, circling shadow, but the thing refused to pass over an opening in the tree tops and show itself. Rag-dan realized he had to somehow get above the leafy roof to identify whatever the thing was. If it be some agent of Hell this close to our camp, we had to know about it.

Looking ahead, he saw a possible opportunity. A giant pine tree had been bent over, obviously since its youth, by a nearby tree that had fallen against it. The deformed pine had not died, but continued to grow at a forced angle. The pine was now so long that, even leaning, its upper end ran nearly to the ceiling of the leaf canopy.

Without breaking stride, Rag-dan jumped onto the leaning pine and began to run up its angled length. There was no telling how old the pine was, but its thick crusty bark held tight under his boots, making for excellent traction. Upwards he charged, building speed, running up the tilted pine even as its girth grew more and more narrow.

As he ran, Rag-dan could see that the shadow was coming back, making another pass over the forest. Suddenly he was at the end of the pine, but so close was he to the top of the forest that Rag-dan leapt and grabbed the high limb of a nearby maple, pulling himself upright on that limb, a limb barely stout enough to hold a man's weight.

With the agility and balance of a circus star Rag-dan stood to his feet on the limb, poking his head right up and through the treetops into the bright sky above. But the sunlight was immediately blotted out as some huge thing swept down upon him as if to knock him back through the roof of the forest. Rag-dan was blinded as a storm of leaves, twigs and limbs enveloped him, debris which was cast about by what seemed to be massive, beating wings slamming into the canopy.

SCYTHE

Rag-dan, his eyes clogged now with grit, could see nothing and felt only warm, leathery skin brush across his face as he lost his footing on the maple limb. A pungent, choking odor filled Rag-dan's nostrils and lungs, and he was barely aware of the limbs slapping his body as he fell towards the forest floor, though the limbs did serve to slow his fall considerably. Into a thick bed of musty-old, decaying leaves he plunged, and by the time he swam his way out of the damp pile and cleared his vision, the flying shadow was long gone.

It was a shaken, limb-scratched Rag-dan that wondered back into camp that evening. He would say little as to what had happened to him in the forest, for though he did not get a solid sighting of whatever it was that flew over him, he could not shake one unbelievable conclusion from his mind. Nor could he answer the question of how the scent that filled his head and lungs could possibly be. For that smell was unique to only one beast of the earth, the unmistakable musk of a gargoyle.

We would stay at that encampment by the river weeks longer, for Rag-dan was about to take a chance that would, one way or another, change the fate of the Dreadlock forever.

SCYTHE

Chapter Sixteen
Wings

"What is the matter with Rag-dan?" asked Invictus, "He's been acting strange all day."

"I have noticed," said Kae-san. "Usually he's a good natured lad, but the last few days have found him solemn and withdrawn, having little to do with any of us. Do you know what his problem is, Scythe?"

In truth I did not know. I too had watched Rag-dan's strange behavior. For days he had stayed with his personal gargoyle mount out in the woods, away from the rest of us. A couple of times I had gone out to see him, once to find him sitting beside the beast, staring at it as if it contained one of the great mysteries of life.

Another time I found him lying on the ground *under* the standing creature, with his hands pressed firmly into its belly. I did not disturb his work, though I found it quite strange. I passed it off, concluding that the creature must have shown sign of illness, and Rag-dan was attempting to examine the beast. After all, it's not like there are many gargoyle physicians in the area that make house-calls. But if the beast was ill, ill enough to alter the effectiveness of the Dreadlock, why would faithful Rag-dan not have shared that with me?

"I don't know what the problem is exactly," I replied, "but there's definitely something bothering Rag-dan. I asked him yesterday evening if something was wrong, or something that he needed to talk about, but he just walked away shaking his head 'no' and mumbling under his breath. It could be an issue with one of the mounts. But the truth is, Rag-dan hasn't been himself since he returned scratched and bewildered from the forest that day a few weeks ago."

Whatever he encountered in the forest that day had rocked his mind.

"He was gone from camp for three days last week," replied Kae-san. "Does anyone know where he was? And what did he bring the rope for? I saw his mount laden with the thickest ropes I have ever seen!"

Young Invictus must have caught a tone in Kae-san's voice, for he took offense on Rag-dan's behalf, as the young-brash ones often will. Invictus snapped back defensively at Kae-san.

"What business is it of yours, Kae-san, where he goes or when he goes. He's as free as any man to come and go by his own leave. You don't play the part of his father, and it is none of your concern!" This uncalled-for, sharp tempered response was met with a quick and stern reaction from Kae-san, who wheeled to face Invictus, his hand finding a quick grip on the handle of his sword.

"Do not venture to accuse me, boy. I have ridden and bled alongside Rag-dan for years before you ever came along! You are the one who broached the subject!" Invictus' face turned red with anger as his hand also fell to his sword.

I decided to step between the two men. In the past I have let the men work out their differences physically, even coming to blows, as long as no one drew a blade. They would batter one another for a few moments, grow tired of the melee, shake hands and go about their business as if nothing had happened. Those were more sporting matches than actual fights.

But our times had grown hard, and it looked like these two would now skip the blows and go right to swords. So I filled the space between the two, preaching hard to their shame.

"Dreadnaughts! Is this your brotherhood on display? Is this your self-control in action? Harsh words and blows are hard enough to get over, but I see both of you reaching for swords. I remind you that we never draw blades unless we fully intend to blood them. I believe your hands fell to swords more from habit than from any desire to harm your brother, but if you draw them over nothing more than a slight insult, you can be sure that my scythe will not remain in its cradle, but will flash to further try the skill of which ever of the two of you is unbloody at the end!"

Both men allowed their hands to drop from sword handles, though neither took a step back, not wanting to be the first to retreat. The moment was tense, because even if they unstrapped sheaths and chose to settle it with fists, we already had plenty of enemies to fight without fighting amongst ourselves. But the tension of the moment was suddenly broken by the very subject of the dispute, as Rag-dan emerged from the edge of the woods surrounding the clearing we had camped in. Apparently he had overheard the argument, and I was glad to hear him speak his first cogent words in days.

"Gentlemen! I trust I haven't become the source of a brawl amongst men as honourable as I know you both to be? If its excitement that you crave, perhaps you would like to see what has been troubling me for the last few days. Follow me."

"Now, there's that," I said with relief and pushed past the two to follow Rag-dan into the woods. Boys will be boys, and the other two quickly forgot their squabble and followed as well, their curiosity easily overcoming their belligerence.

Rag-dan led us some four hundred yards into the woods until we came upon a strange sight indeed. There, in the midst of another clearing, lay Rag-dan's gargoyle mount, on its back! The feet and legs of the beast were spread apart, held by the massive ropes, exposing the thick dark skin of the underbelly.

Each limb was solidly wrapped about with the heavy rope that Kae-san had asked about earlier, and each rope was stretched taut and tied off to trunks of stout trees which surrounded the clearing. The gargoyle seemed confused, humiliated even. Its face bore what must have been a mournful frown, and sadly pathetic groans vibrated up from deep within the creature's massive throat. It turned its head, looking back and forth at us, as if for explanation of its plight, and the fact that its face was upside down, jowls sagging, only added to the dolefulness of its countenance. One couldn't help but to be touched by the scene.

Rag-dan's well known fondness of these creatures was all that kept us from drawing weapons to slice the rope and set the beast free. We knew that Rag-dan was the only man alive who could have convinced one of these wild creatures to allow itself to be so rolled, tied and bound. I would have asked what the purpose of binding the creature was, but Rag-dan lifted a gauntleted hand to hush any questions, and with the other hand unsheathed his dagger, its double razor edges dazzling in the sunlight. Facing now one of those he had raised from the nest, one he had fed from its very infancy as a mother would feed her young, he spoke to it as if apologizing for what he was about to do, which made me even more apprehensive.

"I am sorry for this, old friend, but I think there is more to you than meets the eye. You have been earthbound long enough. Without pain there can be no gain. You must be released and be free!" And with that Rag-dan rushed upon the creature, lifting the short-sword high above his head and plunging the blade deeply into its belly just below its chest-bone.

Downward he pulled the blade toward the hind end, slicing the beast open as he cut! Such a cry went forth from the beast that our hearts melted within us as it began to struggle mightily, fighting with all its strength against the ropes. But Rag-dan had knotted the beast perfectly, and without any upright leverage, even the enormity of its strength would not break its bonds. We would have rushed upon

Rag-dan to stop the madness, but to a man we were stunned into complete and utter paralysis. Why would Rag-dan do such a thing? Our minds could simply not digest it.

Rag-dan's blade had carved a ghastly wound some two feet long in the gargoyle's belly. Blood and mucus poured freely from the wound, and the blood seemed to drive Rag-dan to a knew height of madness as he tossed the blood-drenched blade to the grass and shoved his hands *into* the gapping wound, as if to pull the beast's very entrails out!

This could be no attempt to help the animal, I thought, and my anger at Rag-dan's betrayal of the animal's trust shocked me to my senses.

I rushed from my place at the edge of the clearing, headlong into Rag-dan, tackling him hard from behind. We both fell over and onto the bloodied creature as I yelled for Rag-dan to cease this madness. Rag-dan turned to throw me off, angry at my interference.

Then I felt it underneath us, as if something was erupting from the animal's belly. Something hard and unforgiving had emerged from the fresh wound, and thrust upward and into my shoulder, hard as if a war-hammer had hit me, jolting me upward. This was followed by a short pause as the object withdrew back into the wound.

Confused and covered now with gargoyle blood, I caught a glimpse of something again emerging from the long gash Rag-dan had so cruelly made in the belly of the beast. But my mind had no time to understand what was happening because that emerging object exploded upward now into both me and Rag-dan, violently punching us up and into the air.

We were thrown, sprawling, near the wood's edge. Lying on my face, I looked up at the creature that had carried Rag-dan into so many battles. As the beast struggled against the ropes, two long, pointy and mucus-dripping spears of what looked to be black, jointed bone were protruding from the belly wound.

Each spear looked to be eight to ten inches thick, tapering to pointed ends, and each had two joints and were bent at those joints. Upward the jointed spears continued to thrust until they were stiff and the tips were pointing straight up. Each must have been some fifteen feet in length when stretched straight out.

The other men were all aghast at the scene as well. All, that is, save Rag-dan. I looked at his face and saw that he had a frightening and wide-eyed smile across his blood spotted face. He bore the look of a man who might have just discovered the cure for all disease, or a pirate's buried goldchest, and yet, at the same time, dreaming of all the more that could be.

I felt something warm and runny slap the skin of my face. The spears emerging from its belly were flexing now, at the joints up and down, throwing blood and mucus all about. Then they began to spread apart, one to the right and one to the left of the gargoyle, which still lie on its back, still moaning and struggling against the thick ropes. As the spears flapped in the air, something began to expand from them.

Faster they flapped and ripped through the air--and we saw that smaller spears of black bone were separating from the main shaft, but still connected by flaps of translucent skin. As the flapping and spreading continued we could identify dark veins running through and across the flaps.

And with more flapping and spreading, the more we could tell that it was blood that was filling and rushing through the veins, carrying the life-giving substance to every part of what we finally realized were two wide, powerful and massive wings protruding from the rip in the beast's belly!

Rag-dan knew, of course, from the first eruption of the black bone-spears that he had guessed right. He yelled out above the noise of the groaning beast and its flapping wings,

"Cut the ropes! Set it free! Set it free! It must be allowed to fly to force the blood all the way to the wing tips." And with that Rag-dan led the way, rushing back into the clearing to grab his dagger and cut the ropes. But just as he reached the gargoyle, one of the massive wings swept powerfully against his body, the under-part of the wing catching him full and tossing him back into the air. He landed unharmed in a bed of ferns, the only damage done to his pride.

At that point the gargoyle's throaty cries took on a deeper, and for it a more normal sound, and the wings began to flap and fly at an enormous pace, slapping the ground now with solid thuds and spraying dirt and debris all around.

Our worry now was that the beast would harm itself trying to get free of the ropes. We wanted to rush in and cut it free but the wingspan was now a ripsaw of blinding and blurred movement that no one dared creep near.

We soon saw that our worries were unfounded, because we noticed that the massive taut ropes were beginning to fray.

SCYTHE

The shaft of either wing was made of large black bone, and the leading edge of the bone was compressed to a almost-edge. The Gargoyle had discovered this new tool and was whipping the sharp edge of wing bone into the ropes like a knife, cutting deeper into the rope with each beat of the wing.

Suddenly two of the ropes sprang apart with a popping noise as they were cut in two almost simultaneously. These were the ropes that had held the beast's front legs. Its front legs free now, it used its wings to throw itself over and back on its feet, held now only by the ropes on the hind legs.

Upright and proud, and dreadful the gargoyle stood, its chest swelled with the strength it clearly felt in its new wingspan. Its eyes seemed to glow.

Though emerging from the underbelly, the wings curved from there upward around the ribcage, flattening at the withers to extend perpendicularly outward.

The beast swiveled its head from side to side, looking at each of us, and for a moment we were deathly afraid of what revenge it might take on us. Yes, it was the same gargoyle, but clearly it had been reborn, remade now with new wings, the birth canal of which had been opened by Rag-dan's blade.

It extended its wings fully and from tip to tip they spread all the way across the thirty foot clearing. It began to flap both wings up and down, slowly at first, with controlled lifts and falls. It was feeling the strength emerge, growing into the newness of it. As the blood continued to flow through the wings the skin flaps lost their transparency, turning a rugged black before our eyes. The creature looked down at the two remaining ropes, following their length to the trees where they were tied. The ropes seemed to anger it and it beat its wings faster against the air now. The belly-wound had already gathered itself, like a drawstring gathers the top of a sack, about the base of the wings.

Hiding at the edge of the clearing, we could feel the whipping wind coming off the new wings as the beast worked them harder and harder with a mixture of rage and beast-joy.

Then, the gargoyle dropped its chin and bent its front legs, squatting its chest low to the ground. With tremendous force the beast sprang upwards, its head reaching high, its open mouth reaching skyward as if to swallow the clouds, wings whipping and beating with more force than ever. Its feet left the ground as we watched, and the upward force created by the wings was too much for even the thickness of Rag-dan's ropes.

The ropes began to twist and stretch and then to fray, small strands splitting and popping, surrendering to the wings' power. We watched the sight, awestruck, from the clearing's edge. Finally the fraying ropes could take no more and they snapped in two.

Free now, with more freedom than it had ever have known, the gargoyle rose into the air and above the trees. Hurrying into the center of the clearing, we gazed upward into the sky as the great land-beast hovered there above us on beating wings. Looking down on us a brief moment, it let go a terrible roar, a roar of freedom and found purpose. It then flew away from us, far up and away on new wings, wings that it might never have known of save for Rag-dan's inexorable curiosity.

SCYTHE

Chapter Seventeen
Balance of Power

Two weeks passed as we waited for the newly liberated gargoyle to return, but we saw not so much as a hair of it. During the day we stayed busy by tending to and mending our weapons and gear as well as the three remaining mounts, keeping one man always on sky-watch with instructions to call out to the rest of us if our prodigal returned.

Late in the night as we slept, a flying shadow would pass over the moon and a great and distant roaring echo would bounce about the heavens, serving only to haunt our dreams. We longed for the return of that which was lost, but it had been set free.

For us, and especially for Rag-dan, it was one of those moments when you doubt that a thing was ever really yours because, having tasted freedom, it chose not to return. And if it did not return, no one could claim the beast as their own, not even Rag-dan. Another week passed without a sign, and I called the men together for a council of our own.

"Rag-dan," I began, "it has been three weeks since the gargoyle left us. We all want it back but we can't stay here forever. An open camp gives us scant protection against attack, and we don't know how active the enemy is in this area. We must prepare our next move, and make it."

"Yes, I know," he replied. "I thought it would have returned, as a friend wounded, in a day or two after, after I cut it. I must admit that my hopes have been fading for its return now that it has been gone this long. The cries that woke us in the night gave me some fresh hope, but hope quickly turned to gall when the beast did not appear. Who knows but if those night cries, even if made by the gargoyle, are nothing more than the mockery of one who is glad to be free of my ropes?"

Invictus then voiced the question that all of us had been asking ourselves since the cutting of the beast.

"What about the other three mounts? Do we know for sure they too have bound-up wings inside? And are we going to cut them open to find out?" All of us had watched the past weeks as Rag-dan examined the three as he had done their now absent comrade, and Invictus, though quick to speak, had not asked a poor question.

"And if we butcher the three Invictus," replied Kae-san, "and no magical wings pop out, but their life-blood does, what then? We will have killed our only means of transport, not to mention the loss of their abilities as scent tracers and war mounts. They do things horses cannot do for us! Their sense of smell surpasses even that of a bear."

Kae-san made a valid point, but so did young Invictus. The men looked to me for an answer, and I was not afraid to make the decision that could end the Dreadlock as it was known...a four soldiered machine of war riding into battle on the backs of raw, untamed vengeance. But first I would know the mind of the one who had found and raised and trained the creatures. I owed him that much.

"Rag-dan, I am ready to make the guess, for that is all it will be, but I want you to educate my guess first. I have watched you examine the other three gargoyles for the past weeks, everyday. None of us have interfered with your examinations, for no one knows the beasts like you. It seems to me that you want to believe that they too have secret wings inside, but unless I read you wrong, you are not at all sure, are you?"

Rag-dan bowed his head. When he looked up, his eyes were glassy, though no tear fell. He knew a decision about the remaining three was necessary but he feared the wrong one might be made.

"As usual, Scythe, you read me rightly, for I am not at all certain. The other three may contain wings--or they may not. There is no guarantee that the flight-trait is common among the siblings. Their mother had no wings, or if she did she never discovered them. That is certainly the only reason I am still alive, for when she fell over that cliff she could simply have swept back around and through the air, taking my life there on the mountainside."

Rag-dan said these words with a gloomy, mournful voice, almost as if he remembered his victory over the mother–beast with regret. I have always found Rag-dan's way of looking upon the creatures and their mother interesting, and puzzling. One would almost think he would have little regret now if she had taken him in that cave, and his blood had suckled her young. Whether this was due to a contented trust in providence, or a blind trust in fate I cannot judge.

Perhaps it was just that he had come to see his own life so inexorably tied to that of the gargoyles. Whatever the case, this was one of the toughest decisions I have ever been forced to make.

"Well," I began, explaining the decision I had come to, "as things stand, we four are down to three mounts. That makes our task as hunters much more difficult, yet still doable. We *could* cut our losses, live with things as they are, taking turns riding double. And when battle *is* joined we will adjust our tactics accordingly. We might proceed with this strategy, never taking a chance by cutting the beasts. This would be the safest course to take.

"Another course would be to risk it all, open the guts of all three with the reckless hope of transforming the Dreadlock into a force indeed to be reckoned with, one that could attack from the ground or from on high, or to split up and attack from both at the same time."

"Assuming the other three would not also fly away from us," added Rag-dan.

"Assuming so," I continued, "assuming that we find ways and means to keep the creatures from being overwhelmed by their new powers of flight, to help them grow gradually into their wings, if indeed they have them. But, if we risk it all and lose the gamble, we will have killed three creatures unique on this earth, and ones who have been good and faithful companions to us. Not to mention that we will have put ourselves afoot as well. After we have charged to battle mounted on aback the gargoyles for so long, are any of us really ready to become horsemen again? I doubt it, gentlemen. I think that if all our mounts be lost, then the Dreadlock itself will dissolve."

Grim faces looked back at me from the small circle of men, the weight of my words sinking in deeply. I let the words sit a moment before I gave a third option.

"I choose a third option, one more risky than the first but less than the second. We will separate one beast, tie it off, and roll the dice by opening its belly. If we find no wings and it bleeds out, then we are down to two mounts, and the Dreadlock, though changed, will survive. But if we discover wings in that one, we will open another, taking our chances with it as well. If that one also has the secret, we open the fourth as well. This is my plan. Agreed?"

Three reluctant but grimly determined replies echoed agreement back to me. Truth be known, we were all afraid of the change that was upon us, coming as it had with little warning. But what man lives very long without change? There exists a certain comfort in regimen and consistency, but the hard realities of life quite often break up our regularity, long before we are ready.

And so we set immediately to our task, recovering the thick rope we needed. We allowed Rag-dan to choose which of the three would be cut first, and he chose Invictus' mount, much to the chagrin of that young rider. Invictus didn't like it, but helped us fashion the knots that would hold a creature of such enormous strength.

SCYTHE

As an extra precaution we worked some smaller rope into netting that we fixed and tied off at tree top level over the clearing where the 'procedure' would take place. This would serve as a catch net that we hoped would keep the beast from flying away as the first one did. Besides the thick ropes wrapping each gargoyle limb, smaller ropes were attached about its neck and body to be used to pull the creature back to earth before it went truly, irreversibly airborne.

The plan was ready, the beast tied down on its back, all preparations made. We said a short prayer for success, and then Rag-dan repeated the same cutting maneuver he had made to the belly of the first gargoyle. Just like the first one, this beast reacted with an awful shriek of pained betrayal and began to resist its bindings.

Our hearts sank when, suddenly, the beast froze in time, its whole body going rigid, as some deep inner pain overtook it. But our fears were short-lived, and great relief swept across our sweaty faces as two boney black spears emerged from the belly gash. We watched, still amazed, as the wings emerged and stretched and strengthened, in much the same way as those of the first beast.

The ropes and netting helped us to keep this one from flying away. We did allow it enough room to flap and feel the strength of its new wings, exercising the blood throughout their span. More sure of ourselves now, we repeated the procedure with both the other gargoyles. Finally, there before us stood the three of them, winged and ready to fly.

When Rag-dan thought the time right, we allowed them one by one to lift themselves off the ground to just above the tree tops, the four of us manning ropes still attached to them. I imagine that either beast could have easily flown away with us dangling at the ropes' ends, but we wrapped the ropes around three trunks as pulleys for leverage, and held tight. This gave us the leverage we needed to control the amount of slack in the ropes. The gargoyles learned in this manner that they could fly and stretch their wings without leaving the Dreadlock behind.

Each day of flight training found us giving them more and more slack in the ropes until the beasts were flying some five tree lengths above us with only one rope attached to its body at the neck. It was essentially flying at the end of a three hundred foot leash.

The day soon came when we decided to allow the beasts to fly high on the leash, and then release the leash so the animal was truly free.

SCYTHE

We hoped it would return to us, but had no way of knowing, since the first one had not retuned at all.

It was on a Friday morning when we released the three. As the first one had done, each seemed to enjoy the new found freedom to fly unhindered and in a moment had flown out of sight. We did not see them for two anxious days, but on Sunday morning we heard their cries filling the air above us.

Rushing out of our tents, we saw not three but four mighty winged gargoyles, our war mounts, sweeping towards us in even formation on outstretched wings. The three had found the prodigal, and now all were retuning to the Dreadlock. They could not know how lost we felt without them, or how relieved we were to see them return.

I looked at Rag-dan as the beasts made landfall around us. We were both thinking the same thing--that a shift in the balance of power between demon and Dreadlock had just occurred, and for us it was a shift sorely needed. With these new weapons, these flying mounts, we now had invaluable tools to pursue the task before us, to clear our names and recover our honour among the Order. And we desired nothing above that.

Our gargoyles had learned the art of flight. Now, the Dreadlock had to learn to fly them, to fly them back into the pain of my past, back to Pristine.

SCYTHE

SCYTHE

Chapter Eighteen
Return to Pristine

The home of a Hunt-Master is not easily found. It is not supposed to be, even by those who have visited it before. If it were readily known where to find those who train the Hunters, surely the enemy would concentrate dark forces there to assassinate these the masters of our holy, deadly craft.

The Hunt-Masters are the linchpin that holds together the line that runs from raw recruits to field-ready Warriors of Light. Hunters emerge from their training 'schools' as newly born, bruised and battered but also hardened in the violent birth canal of instruction. Always the student emerges with the utmost respect for, if not always love for, these hard men, the Hunt-Masters, who have sharpened them as a blade, to cut evil deeply.

It had been so long, and so much had passed since that day I walked away from the Bower Green. As a sixteen year old volunteer, I had been blindfolded and placed in the back of a wagon when I had first been taken on the long journey to my Hunt-Master's home. And at the end, when Ell-ory had sent me away in anger, it is true that I had to walk afoot on my own. My Master had merely pointed an angry finger towards the surrounding forest, and I was not sure but assumed he meant that was the direction I should leave in.

For days I had walked through wooded lands, descending hollows, and then *down* the steep side of a mountain range. I found this to be strange and confusing because, even in a wagon and blindfolded on the way to my Hunt-Master's place, I had not sensed that I was being taken *up* a mountain.

Like a refugee I wandered about in a vast, wild land that I had neither knowledge nor remembrance of. I kept walking for days until my strength was nearly spent and only a few stale morsels of bread bounced about the bottom of my leather pouch.

That is when I stumbled upon Kae-san, literally.

I had come to a strong flowing river whose waters had exposed rock and boulder all around. One huge outcropping of rock blocked my way, so I began to climb over it. Topping the last of the rock, I slid down the other side.

But I had not been careful to check what was on the other side, and I landed right on top of another Hunter. At first we were both naturally shocked and untrusting, both drawing blades.

That anger soon passed as we explained one to the other how we had come to be at the same time and place. After talking with one another for a while, we soon counted one another friends, realizing that we could be of great help to the other.

Kae-san explained that he was a Hunter-in-training as well, under the Hunt-Master Skyn-gilliad, a man with a reputation for training that was as solid as that of Ell-ory.

At that moment Kae-san was in his final month of training. He had been put out in that wilderness to track a thousand-pound boar-hog. His Master had given that one final task, and its completion would mean a successful conclusion to Kae-san's training.

Though the beast outweighed him by some eight hundred pounds and was armed with a pair of razor-sharp tusks at least two feet long, Kae-san was charged with killing it single handedly. And though he was armed only with weapons suited to close-in work, those being a sword and two long-knives, I found Kae-san anxious and ready to make meat out of the half-ton beast he was tracking. And that's when I knew I would ask the young man to join me as I began to form the Dreadlock.

Making fast friends, I asked to tag along with him in his pursuit of the wild boar. Closing in on the beast, I told Kae-san that we could supply half the known world with bacon off this one, and he laughed so hard we almost spooked our prey into the thick brush where we would never have found him. But the beast did not take to the brush, and I helped Kae-san maneuver it into a mud-bog where its immense strength could be worked down.

We cut oak saplings into long spears and moved in on the creature, prodding and goading it through the thick muck of the bog until it spent most of its will to resist. The beast charged us both several times, and we both took shallow cuts from the tusks. But the muck was thick and the thing began to tire. Kae-san insisted on making the kill by himself since that was his assignment and he wanted to be able to report honestly to his Master. I was impressed when he tossed the spear aside. It takes more courage to kill closely, Kae-san explained, and if he did not make the kill with the sword, working close-in, it would mean little and less. He did so with several deep thrusts of the blade, the wild swings of the animal's tusks grazing his skin once again in the process. Kae-san used a long-knife to carve the tusks from the carcass, the proof of his success he would offer his Hunt-Master.

We made it out of the bog but became hopelessly lost after that. But Skyn-gilliad knew right where to find us it seemed, and retrieved us after a few weeks. After presenting the tusks to his Master, Kae-san was discharged in good favor by Skyn-gilliad, taking his brand. The Dreadlock was officially born.

Presently, I required Kae-san's help to feel our way back to the area where my old Hunt Master's encampment was located. Yet even with Kae-san's skill and knowledge of the land, it would have been next to impossible to find Ell-ory's place, tucked away as it was from the world. Ell-ory had chosen his place well, actually a valley within a mountain, so concealed that one could walk all around it without ever knowing it existed.

But walking around is entirely different from flying over. From the backs of our air-borne gargoyles we searched the land for the encampment until we spotted a green bower below us that would otherwise have gone unnoticed. We circled in the air for a moment, and when we spotted no movement below we brought out beasts down in a clearing not far from the main settlement, walking in afoot.

The place was deserted. An eerie pall hung over the place, once so full of life when Pristine's gentle steps had graced this ground. Even the grass, I remembered, seemed brighter and full of spring-life when she tread there.

We examined the entire area, walking the outer ring, and looked through the buildings. Very little had been left behind. Clearly, Ell-ory and Pristine had left on their own and in no rush. They were not hurried, it seemed, and that gave me a rush of relief, for my mind, so distraught at the prospect of seeing her again, now had to wrestle with what could have happened to her.

Why they were gone was not evident, though I could not help but think it had something to do with the two former trainees Ell-ory did not want to be found by. Though for different reasons, Ar-ric and I were both banished from the lives of Pristine and her father.

The irony of all that made me chuckle, then growl. I had chosen loyalty to my sworn cause, while Ar-ric had converted to the darkness, yet both of these very different choices yielded the same result in regards to Pristine. We were both banished from her presence as long as Ell-ory drew breath. Would I change my choices if I could go back,

I wondered? I was not sure, but that hardly mattered now. What is done is done, I told myself. And I still needed to speak with my Hunt-Master. I called the Dreadlock to gather about me.

"Kae-san, what do you make of these leavings?"

"Well," the tracker replied, "no personal goods were left, no pots or pans. This means that they had been planning the move for a while." I looked at Rag-dan for his take on things.

"I agree with Kae-san," added Rag-dan, "but I did find these in one of the out-buildings." He held up some blankets and a couple of iron files. "Why would your Hunt-Master leave behind good wool blankets and good iron files?"

"May be that he had no more room on his wagon," offered Invictus.

"May be," said I, "and that would mean that these were the least needed. He always taught me to leave behind only that which you don't need or that which can be easily replaced."

"Where does one go where one wouldn't need blankets and iron files?" asked Invictus.

"One goes," answered Kae-san, "where it's too warm for much need of heavy blankets and where there is plenty of iron-ore for making new files."

"And where might that be?" asked Invictus, looking to me.

"Many places, Invictus, but the closest one would be the Isles of Eeglass. There the weather is mild even in the heart of winter, and one hardly has to dig for iron ore. The volcano that forms the island did the work years ago, regurgitating the metal up from earthly deeps, scattering it all around. The tide washes up a new crop every morning for those who will walk the beeches in search of it, or so I have heard." Rag-dan stepped forward, placing a hand on my shoulder.

"Then that is where we should look next, and perhaps you will find what you seek there. Perhaps she will be there, walking the beaches, searching for whatever the deep places of the earth will surrender." I looked at Rag-dan, and he had the trace of a mischievous grin on his face. I smiled at my arm-brother's teasing of my heart. A good friend knows when you need to smile.

"Then it is to these Isles we go, my friends," I replied, moving towards the clearing, "and I'll wager a whole boar hog that my mount can get there ahead of those winged sheep you fellows are riding!"

And we rose, a strong wind at our backs, warriors in search of answers.

SCYTHE

The winds were kind to us, pushing us onward, towards destiny. Still, it took days to make the journey, following the coast till it jutted out towards the open sea, pointing the way to the Islands of Eeglass. On we flew over open ocean for another three hours.

Then we saw them. Appearing out of the sea-mist, the Isles were sparkling jewels with hearts of jade, thinly outlined in white thread. White-capped waves broke on jagged rock that surrounded each island, defending the beaches against unwanted visitors who might approach by ship. Tactically sound, I was thinking as I surveyed the Isles, difficult to reach and well chosen by my Hunt-Master, Ell-ory. No surprise, that.

There were three of the islands, one far larger than the other two, separated by channels of clear, shallow water, and more jutting rock.

I gave hand signals to the Dreadlock, indicating which island each should search. They knew instinctively not to make contact with anyone they spotted until they had first found me. Ell-ory would not recognize them, and I wanted to avoid a confrontation, if that be possible.

Invictus I sent to the smaller island to the north, Rag-dan to the one west. Kae-san and I would go south, searching the largest of the three islands by separating and circling it in opposite directions, first the beaches, then the hinterland.

We headed out, moving in separate directions. The sun was bright and the day clear. From the back of my beast I could see miles of coastline as I flew, the salt-wind whipping my hair. My winged friend had carried me nearly a quarter of the way around the Isle when I saw a figure on the beach, a mere black dot against the sugar-white sands. The dot was moving slowly in my direction as I flew towards it.

Soon I was close enough to make out that it was a person, and a moment later the outline of a girl emerged. I realized that if I was close enough to see that she was a young lady, she was close enough to see that I was no bird on the wing. I did not want to frighten her with the sight of a gargoyle hovering over her head. So I kicked my mount to hurry and fly past her, though I had no plan of what I would do next.

But just as my mount increased its speed, she spotted us. I saw her mouth fall open, her hands coming up to cover it, as her mind tried to conceive what terrible thing flew above her. A bag she was holding plopped on the wet sand, the gentle rolling sea-foam rushing up to encircle it.

She turned and began to run away, back through her own tracks in the sand. I urged my beast on until we had passed beyond her running figure. Then I pulled the gargoyle around and had it to drop itself quick and hard onto the beach some hundred yards ahead of her, the beast's muscled legs absorbing the shock of its own weight coming down hard into the wet sand.

Pristine saw us land and pulled to a halt with a sharp scream. She turned to run away again before I could dismount. I slid out of the bone-saddle onto a wing, and from there jumped to the sand below. I had yet to get a good look at her face. Still, there was no mistaking that form so perfectly emblazoned in my mind. I wanted to run her down, to show her who I was and that there was no need to fear, but my legs were bloodless and stiff from the long mounted flight. I was trying to move but I was losing the footrace, so I called out to her with all my breath and heart.

"Pristine!" I yelled, "I am John...John from the Bower Green."

She stopped to look back, and she was afraid, I could tell, but not of me. She seemed to be looking around me to see where my beast was at. I had to reassure her that she was safe.

"Pristine! That creature is with me and is harmless to my friends. I am your old friend, John. Do you remember me?" Her face now seemed more angry than afraid, and she turned and ran away from me again.

She had every right to be angry, I admitted to myself. What man in his right mind leaves a girl he is in love with only to return, years later, dropping from the sky on such a creature?

"Pristine!" I yelled out again, and saw her slow. "Pristine," I called out with less throat. The female form stopped, but did not look back to me, not at first anyway. I wondered at that moment what she was thinking. *What voice is that, strange yet familiar? How can it be, after so long? How could he have come to this place?* She did not move.

I kept walking towards her, saying nothing, allowing the questions to run their course through her heart and mind. If she was afraid, I was more so. How could I know her reaction? How could I know if she would even care to see me? My whole life turned on her decision. I was close enough then to speak her name, gently.

"Pristine."

SCYTHE

I stopped as she turned slowly, head slightly bowed. Her dark hair flowed in the sea breeze, wispy about her face. As she lifted her brow to face me fully I realized that she seemed not to have aged at all. We looked into one another's eyes for the first time in years. Our eyes spoke volumes, though tongues uttered no words for a long moment.

Then, slowly, I began to ease towards her, and I felt my knees weaken and I was so afraid she would turn away, but she refused to.

Close enough to touch her, I dared not, for I knew not if she belonged now to another, though I saw no rings on her fingers.

And even if she was still free, after the way we had parted, with neither words nor messages passing between us these years, I knew not whether her heart was as tender as flesh or cold as flint towards me.

Neither of us, I think, wanted to be the first to speak. I saw a heavy tear drop from her eye just before she bowed her head again. As the one who had come seeking, I knew the duty fell to me to speak first, but I was not at all sure of myself.

"Pristine...it has been so long...I...I..." She looked back into my face, both eyes filled now with tears. She did not stumble over her words as I had.

"Why did you leave me? Why did you never return for me? I wanted you to come back," she said, her voice trailing off in sobs that broke me inside.

I have been cut by many blades and dug into by many claws, pierced even by fangs, but none ever bore so deeply into me as did her wet green eyes, two gleaming gems, at that moment.

She had been there that day when her father banished me, so she knew the cold facts, but for a girl's heart, cold facts are nearly never enough. She needed to hear me explain it. She had needed to hear it from me, I realized now, for all these years, and I was ashamed that I kept my promise to her father and had not found her and spoken with her before that day on the beach. It was the first time I have ever been ashamed of doing what I thought was my duty. But sometimes, I suppose, promises made to a daughter should override those made to her father.

"Pristine, he was my Hunt-Master, and I was a young fool--what else could I have done at the time?" She hung her head again. "I'm sorry for whatever I have put you through. You owe me nothing, but if it means anything, I have thought of you constantly. Over the years, you have never been far from my mind."

SCYTHE

The sounds of the eternal sea, the waves and gulls, waft around us, but she stayed silent. Her head was still bowed, the wind playing with the curls of her hair. It seemed to me that she was deciding the matter in her mind.

Did this mean that she was still free, at least free enough to consider my request for forgiveness? And if free and forgiving, did it mean she wanted something more? I had dared not hope that she would even remember me, or remembering, forgive me. Much less had I ventured a hope for a future with Pristine. I had not even allowed my mind to entertain the idea, not because I did not want it, but because I dare not take my soul to such heights of expectation only to fall, smashed upon the cold rocks of her just rejection.

But the moment we locked eyes on that beach all discipline had forsaken me, all resistance faded away, and I knew that I belonged to her if she would have me. She had but to ask. As she pondered I knew my future hung in the balance of her decision.

When Pristine looked up, her eyes were still moist with tears, making them all the more beautiful to me. She said nothing, not with words at least, she only reached out a hand to me, which I took with both of mine and pressing it to my lips, kneeling there in the sand and tide. She let me kneel before her for a moment, then tugged at me to rise. Still silent, she held my hand and we walked towards a trail that led off the beach.

I said not a word, but motioned with my free hand for my gargoyle to fetch the bag she had dropped on the sand and to follow us, although not too closely. The beast gave me a curious look, but scooped up the cloth sack in its fanged mouth and muddled along behind us at a safe distance.

Silently we walked hand in hand down a well beaten path, inland through palm forests.

Soon we began to pass signs of domestication. There were sheep grazing upon a grassy knoll. I looked back to see my gargoyle looking longingly at the sheep, its slick forked tongue sliding out of its mouth. He received a hard look from me that said 'no'. The beast shook its massive head about, and I heard its several stomachs growl. But it pulled its long tongue back behind its fangs and followed us, leaving the sheep unmolested.

It was not long before I spotted some buildings up the path. I wanted to stop before we entered the settlement. We needed to talk about her father. But Pristine was leading and seemed to have made up her mind. She would not stop but led me into the clearing between what looked to be the main house of the settlement and some out-buildings.

I was nervous, armed only with my hand sickles. If her father, my former Hunt-Master, desired to do damage to me for breaking my vow never to return, I suppose I would just have to let him do it. I had decided instantly on that beach that his daughter was worth the risk, and that was the easiest decision I had ever made.

The sounds of a hammer banging on iron were coming from inside one of the work buildings, and Pristine turned to face its open door before calling out to her father.

"Father! Father, can you take a moment's rest and come outside?" The noise of the work stopped. He came walking out of the door, a pleasant look for his daughter was on his round, sweaty face.

A big hammer was in his hand, its head the size of two man-fists stacked together. I noticed immediately that, like his daughter, he seemed barely to have aged. He was a bit stouter than I remembered, but not by much.

Patches of grey flaked his hair about the edges, but his arms and shoulders still bulged with muscle. I almost bowed to him out of reverence. I owed him much, and knew it. He had put me through hell as a boy that I might battle Hell as a man, and I would always respect him for that, no matter what he did now.

He seemed not to notice me for a second, so focused was he on his daughter. Then his eye caught me and the smile left him, his gaze freezing over in an instant. I was the last thing he expected to see.

"You!" He spit the word at me. "You!" and held the hammer towards me as if to point me out to the world, though only he and Pristine were there to see. He held the heavy hammer out towards me with powerful ease, his fist grasping the end of a three foot long hickory handle, a feat of strength itself that made the muscles of his forearm roll and ripple.

"Yes, Hunt-Master, it is I, and I have returned-"

"He has returned to us unharmed, Father, and I am happy to see John again." She had cut me off mid-sentence as she moved between us men, shielding me of his harsh gaze as she began to make the apology for my return. I suppose she thought it would be better coming from her lips rather than mine.

"John, was it?" he said, cocking his head a little as if to get a better angle of sight at me. "I remember a John--I remember a boy who brought trouble into my family, and shame onto my training ground!"

I tried to control my temper, to keep my answer soft, but his words were needles in my pride. I stepped past her now and towards her father, letting go of her hand. I did not want him to think I was hiding behind his daughter. I loved her but I would not use her as protection from my former mentor.

"I am that John whom you once trained with honour, to whom you imparted skill and craft, and though our parting was not as I would have liked, I am that John who has ever held you in reverence and esteem, both in my own heart as well as among the hunt-class."

"Aye--a man of honour are you? Well, do you honour your own vows, or are they so easily cast aside?"

I knew he spoke of my promise to never return to his presence. He had to bring it up, I knew. And I had to give my reasons, though I was not at all sure he would accept them. He could easily reject them and thereby shame me for having tossed aside a solemn vow, condemning me as an oath breaker. I was ready with an answer, but Pristine spoke before I could, taking my hand in hers again as she spoke.

"John comes to us as a friend, Father. He comes in peace, and I have welcomed him with all my heart. I ask you to do the same."

"Comes in peace, does he? I'll wager he comes in need, looking for a handout, or maybe a hideout." He stepped closer to me now, close enough that I could smell the sweat he had worked up in the smithy. He pressed the head of the hammer firmly against the center of my chest as if to drive home his point.

"This Isle is no hideout for slackers, or those who run from battle. And holding my daughter's hand will not keep you from losing yours."

Those words coming from any other man would have seen blood spilt, mine or his, but I felt Pristine take my hand again and squeeze it. I relented, taking a deep breath, trying once more to salve the old wounds.

"Sir Ell-ory, I indeed come to your home in need, but not for a handout, not for a place to hide. I have found no need to hide from my enemies since I entered the field of service. Remember, you taught me that I should always be on the attack if at all possible. I have not forgotten my lessons. Your tactics have served me well in battle. Though the name 'John' may not be known among my enemies, I dare say the name 'Scythe' is."

SCYTHE

With that statement, I slowly but firmly moved the hammer-head away from me, having felt its cold iron long enough. At the mention of the name 'Scythe' I noticed the ends of his lips curl just a bit, and I knew that he was not ignorant of my life since I left his care.

A Hunt-Master as well known as Ell-ory would not be without knowledge of the happenings of the war we were engaged in. And even a man as hard as Ell-ory would enjoy the thought of his battle-doctrine being used in the field to dispatch demons with ruthless efficiency. No man wants to think his work has been wasted. But he was wondering about my mount.

"And what of the stories that come to me about a group of hunters who ride strange beasts into battle? What am I to think of that?"

"Decide for yourself," I said as I put two fingers to my mouth and blew a sharp whistle. Out of the brush emerged my gargoyle, trotting lightly on its feet as if in a playful mood. It stopped in the clearing, jerking its head to toss Pristine's cloth bag of iron-ore towards us. The beast then yawned widely, revealing a mouth full of fangs and a long forked tongue. It then extended its wings, stretching them widely and shaking its body before re-gathering them. It pawed at the ground a few times and lay down to rest. I looked at Ell-ory, who looked at the gargoyle with an expression half appalled, half intrigued.

Ell-ory then looked at me intensely, then over to his daughter, then at the gargoyle again, and then at me again. He was trying to make sense of it all.

"In the house," he said finally, irritably, with a jerk of his head towards the dwelling. Then he turned to re-enter the work shed. I heard the sound of a hammer being set aside as Pristine pulled me towards the nearby house, and I knew I had at least gained the opportunity to explain why I had returned. I counted it a grace-gift, for clearly this man felt he owed me nothing.

The inner workings of the house were simple. The home had one central room that served both as a kitchen and living area, with a couple of sleeping rooms off of a small hallway. In the center of the room an iron stove served as both a source of heat and for cooking meals.

A solid hickory table sat nearby, surrounded by wooden chairs. Pristine directed me to one of the chairs. On the table sat a loaf of wheat bread, a small bowl of honey, and a dish with butter and goat cheese. Pristine offered me a share of the food but I was too nervous to eat. Her father entered behind us, walked over to the table and sat down opposite me.

"Well, if you're not going to eat, start talking." Right to the point, just as I remembered him to be. With Pristine holding my hand firmly the whole time, I recounted to them the basic happenings of my life since I left them. The Dreadlock, the gargoyles, the battles--I told them all of it, though in brief form so as to not wear out my welcome. Soon enough I came to the reason for my return.

"Sir Ell-ory, I vowed never to return to your presence. I had every intention of keeping that vow, no matter how much it hurt," I added, looking over at Pristine, who brushed away a tear with her free hand. "My love for your daughter has never cooled, not for a moment. I assumed she would have met another by now, but now I see that this is not the case. And for that I am more glad than you could ever know. With your permission I will return to this island to pursue a future with Pristine. But first I have a mission to accomplish, a mission to clear the name of the Dreadlock from accusations made against me and my men at the recent Council. Has news of this council reached your island?"

"I have heard bits and pieces," replied Ell-ory, coldly. "Go on."

"At the Council recently held at the great Hall of Lionloff, my hunt-team was publicly accused of being traitors, though not formally charged. The accuser was one Theologous, a Baptine captain. We had encountered these Baptines in the field, even helped to save this captain's life in battle with Ogdognals. One Ogdognal leader called Crokow targeted this captain, ripping the horseman's leg off before we could join battle. There is no doubt he would have died in the forest if the Dreadlock had not intervened, yet for our trouble he accuses us of treachery."

Ell-ory had listened closely to the tale. He stood up and moved over to the wood stove in which a cook-fire crackled. Turning, he began to speak, and his words were both shocking and powerful to my ears.

"I know this 'Theologous'. He is about my age. We trained together when young. After training we hunted together for a time. He was a good Hunter, excellent with both horse and sword. He could be counted on to do his part in the fighting, yet his devotion took such a rigid form that it seemed to rob him of the very joy of life. After a few months with him I could tolerate life in his doleful presence no longer. I told him we must part ways. Theologous was

offended that I no longer wanted to hunt at his side. He even
suggested that I didn't have the stomach for the fight. When our
disagreement came to a head, Jonasius himself intervened. We were
sent our separate ways. I would hunt for twenty years more before
entering the Hunt-Mastery.

"Theologous joined himself to a sub-order within the Hunters
known as the Baptines, and quickly became a leader within that group.
As my training ground began, in time, to turn out young Hunters,
word came back to me that Theologous, when encountering one of
them in the field, would often disparage them, looking to find fault in
my trainees. It is said that he will cast aspersions on any that do
things differently or use tactics other than the ones he finds suitable.
But none of my students ever gave any real cause of embarrassment
until that day you and your fellow trainee, Ar-ric, declared war on one
another in my yard."

I felt a pang of guilt at those words. I had never thought that war
had been declared between Ar-ric and me, but Ell-ory's words were
giving me a new perspective on things. Yet I wanted to clear the air.

"I did not fight Ar-ric to give you embarrassment, sir Ell-ory. I
fought him because I felt he had threatened your daughter. If I have
caused my Hunt-Master embarrassment, it is with great regret."

His face was stone, showing neither acceptance nor rejection of my
apology.

"And in threatening my daughter he offended your pride, John,
since you had come to think of Pristine as your own."

"Perhaps," I answered, dropping my gaze as if to study the bread
and cheese.

"Perhaps," he repeated, "but you John, though troublesome, were
not the real cause of embarrassment. You did not let your
disappointment turn to hatred, as Ar-ric did. In embracing the
darkness, Ar-ric disowned the Light, denying its power to save us
from our selfishness. And this Baptine captain has used Ar-ric's
desertion to disparage my training ground. I suppose that is his way
of repaying an old debt."

"Well," I said, "now he is disparaging me and my men, and that
before a very Council. Because of the status he has attained among
our kind, I will be looked upon with suspicion from now on because of
his accusation. And that is why I broke my vow, that is why I have
returned, Ell-ory. I need your advice as to how I clear my name. I did
not know of the history you share with the Baptine captain, but I

count that as an added blessing, and think it will only enhance your wisdom as to what direction I should now take."

Ell-ory hesitated for moments. He drifted over to a window, looking out at my gargoyle resting in his yard. Still looking out the window, he spoke.

"Take Ar-ric."

He let the words hang in the air a moment, as a tight swarm of bees ready to sting.

He walked back over to stand by the table, his hands folded behind him.

"You must take Ar-ric. You must find him and bring him to the justice of the Council. But I doubt you can take him alive. Ar-ric has vowed a gehena-vow not to be taken alive by Jonasius, and he has been given strong protection."

"Ell-ory," I said, letting go of the girl's hand as I rose, "I need to know all you can tell me about Ar-ric. I have heard stories, but who knows how much of it is true?"

Ell-ory looked at his daughter sadly, as already in mourning for her coming loss.

"Pristine, would you leave us alone?" But the girl showed her sand, refusing to go.

"I will never leave John's side again, unless he bid me to." Her words thrilled my heart, but her father was unmoved.

"I must speak of things now that should not pass a girl's ears," he said to her, but she had inherited a portion of his stubborn will and would not leave. He gave in reluctantly, looking back to me.

"Ar-ric has become a personal favorite of the Dark One. He has been given a platoon of Blue Wings as a private guard. What know you of the Blue Wings?"

The Blue Wings. No wonder my old Hunt-Master's face was shrouded in pall.

I had never laid eyes on a Blue Wing Demon. Few if any Hunters ever have and lived to tell it. Bits and pieces of description are taken from ancient stories, passed around from Hunter to Hunter. Massive in size, roughly in the shape of some grotesque bird-like thing, they are said to fly through the air on long wings.

Having no discernable head, in its place is a razor sharp beak that always drips with black blood. Underneath are talons long and vicious enough to pierce a man clean through. And their favorite way to kill a Hunter--wrapping the talons around his head and ripping it off at the neck. Worst of all, it is impossible for them to forget a Hunter once encountered, and they will never stop hunting him until he is dead.

Old warriors, having survived an encounter, have been said to go mad with worry, running into the wilderness after hearing the flush of wings in the night, lost to all until one day their bodies are found headless. These Blue Wings have no place on the class-scale of demons. Bred for personal service to the Dark One, you might say they are in a class by themselves.

I stood stunned by the news, lost in dark thoughts until Pristine's hand touched me, bringing me back into the room.

"This platoon of Blue Wings, how many do they number?" I asked.

"No one knows--perhaps less than ten." I swallowed hard at the number.

"So my four man team will be outnumbered?"

"John, you still don't understand, do you? If there was but one Blue Wing to face, your four would be outnumbered still!" Ell-ory's point could not be ignored. Whether he liked me or not, this old Hunt-Master could call battle odds as well as any man in the Hunt craft.

"And what more do we know of Ar-ric?"

"After leaving our side, Ar-ric hunted our kind for a few years, growing in skill and power. He took many lives in that time, even some of those I had trained."

Ell-ory winced at his own admission, clearly pained for those he had lost, but kept going. "But Ar-ric made a mistake. In his arrogance he over-reached. He so desired to make his name truly infamous that he planned a master stroke against our side--he wanted to bring the head of Jonasius himself back to the Dark One. At that time he had only two Blue Wings and a few Ogdognals to help him. He secretly trailed some Hunter to where he thought Jonasius could be trapped. Instead, three teams of Hunters ambushed him, wounding but not killing him. Most of those Hunters were killed in the battle, and of the couple that did survive, one was last seen screaming and running off a white cliff by the sea, though they said his body never hit the water. The other one went into hiding and no one knows his whereabouts to this day.

"After that, Ar-ric knew he was also a hunted man. Jonasius, like the Blue Wings, remembers. More Blue Wings came to Ar-ric and they flew him, it is said, to the peak of a far mountain, though Jonasius has not yet found which one."

Pristine's father looked at me then, and I caught a suggestive glimmer in his eye, ever slight, though his face was stone still.

"Jonasius," I said, "does not know which mountain, but perhaps someone else has guessed it. And perhaps only *that* one has guessed it because only *that* one trained Ar-ric."

Ell-ory stood motionless for a moment, contemplating. Again, it was one of those moments in my life, I realized, where someone else was deciding my future.

"Over here," he said, jerking his head towards an old trunk sitting against the wall. I followed him over to the trunk and he bent down to unlock it, lifting up the heavy lid. His knotty scarred fingers rummaged the contents of the trunk for a moment until he pulled out a dusty piece of parchment. He closed the lid and unfolded the parchment on top of the trunk.

"Here," he said, pointing to the edge of the map, "look here."

"I don't recognize the land, but this map is very well drawn with precise lines and symbols, though it is torn at that edge," I observed.

"That is right, John. Torn there at that edge. But it was not torn before Ar-ric deserted our side. I had looked at this map just the night before he disappeared into the forest. After we realized he had gone, I noticed someone had been in my private desk where this map was kept. Pristine would never do that, so I knew it must have been Ar-ric. See how cleanly the paper was torn? He creased it so that it would leave no jagged edges, thinking it would go unnoticed. But he was not as careful as he should have been."

"What was on the stolen part of the map?" I asked. Pristine now tried to interrupt our conversation, pulling me back towards the table. She sensed another heartache in the making, that another broken dream was in her near future.

"We can talk these things over some other time. Come, let's eat this bread before it goes stale." I heard the trace of worry in her voice, and knew what she was trying to do. I hurt for Pristine, but I had to do what I had to do.

"Stop, Pristine," I said firmly, "I will hear the rest of this. I *must* hear it." Ell-ory looked coldly at both of us, realizing what was to come.

SCYTHE

"Don't leave it there, sir. I would hear it all," I said to him. He looked again at his daughter, who wept now. Then he looked back down to the map. His finger ran along the map as he spoke.

"This is the forest known as Saul's Liver. It is beyond the Gawkellens."

"I know of the Gawkellens. One of the Dreadknaughts was raised in them, and that is where he dicovered our mounts." Ell-ory just grunted a 'humph' at that bit of information, seeming unimpressed, but continued.

"The forest of Saul's Liver is bordered by yet another great forest. Within that forest there is a mountain. It is not a range of mountains--it is one mountain, one tall, shear-sided shock of smooth stone jutting out of the ground where no mountain should be. It is a surprise to the very earth. By the few who have seen it, it is called the Rock of the Ages—it is also called the Unclimbable Mountain."

"Do you think that is where the Blue Wings took Ar-ric?"

"I do not know--all I know is that that part of my map is missing."

"I'll take that as a yes--I have no other choice." Ell-ory seemed to ignore my words, walking over to his daughter.

"Pristine, I will speak to John alone now. I am not asking this time." Pristine looked at me with tearful eyes, now angry--or was it disappointment I saw there? She rushed from the room. Her father turned to me.

"You can go to this mountain if you wish, but you will not return from it. It is an act of self-murder to even attempt it. I don't know what you think of your men--these ones you call Dreadknaughts, but if you care for them at all you will not lead them there. Even if any of them survive, their lives will be haunted until death, likely not a nice death either."

"My men hunt at their own will. They are not forced."

"And my daughter? What will it be like for her? Listen John, and listen closely. If you attempt this madness, Ar-ric and all the Blue Wings must be killed. It is an impossible thought that you could even prevail over them, but perchance you did, then your victory must be complete. None must survive to remember you. If even one does, then you will never be allowed near my daughter. I will not have winged things coming for her in the night. I promise you here and now, by all that is holy, I will take your life myself before I let that happen." I knew he meant it.

- 153 -

"If that is how you see it, why did you choose to show me the map at all?"

"I thought it might make you leave."

"It will, but what makes you think I will not return?" I realized the stupidity of the question as soon as it left my mouth. Ell-ory smiled anyway.

"Something ancient, evil and darkly blue."

"Why is it called the Unclimable Mountain?"

"As I said, the sides of this mountain are tall, smooth and have little angle. Hard to get a grip on. Ar-ric, if still there, surely lives at the top of it, at the very peak, and never does he leave it."

"Perhaps I can reach him there, without climbing."

Ell-ory looked at me, grinning now. He walked back to the window, the map held in hands again folded behind him. He looked out the window at my gargoyle.

"Interesting beast" he commented, "a winged beast--what can it do?" I walked over to the window and looked with him out at my gargoyle.

"It has talent. And it has three siblings, one for each of the Dreadknaughts." He paused for a moment, then, without looking at me, he held out the map.

"Go."

Chapter Nineteen
A Good Day to Die:
The Rock of The Ages

The Dreadlock approached the Rock of the Ages, Ar-ric's alleged mountain fortress, by a trail through thick forest that led east towards the base of the mountain. Little more than a game trail used by deer and rabbits, it served merely to give us a general direction to follow through the woods.

Our beasts and our blades beat back the brush, vine and briarwood that choked our way. Though we saw no spies in the forest, if Ar-ric had posted sentries in these woods they certainly would hear us coming. As our mounts forced their way through the brush, Invictus asked me a question.

"Scythe, how are we going to do this--when we get to the mountain, how will we assault it? If we simply fly up to the top, Ar-ric may escape us as soon as he takes sight of us. Even if we find his quarters inside the mountain, there could be a score of cave tunnels, with twice that many exit points from which he can escape us."

"You are right Invictus. We cannot simply fly to the top. Even if we left one man at the base of the mountain to guard an escape attempt, leaving us with only three to make the assault, there is no way that one only could patrol the entire base of the mountain. We must take a different tact. We will, you and I that is, Invictus, attack directly at the base of the mountain. We will get a grip on it and begin to climb this unclimbable Rock."

About this time we came to a clearing in the tree canopy telling us we were near the point where the forest ran up almost to the mountain's base. A cloud moved to uncover the glorious golden ball of sun displayed against a brightly blue sky. The sun's rays knifed through a hole in the forest, chasing the frost off of our faces in the cool of the morning. Invictus looked especially spry in the morning light, full of life and that special itch for battle as only the youngest of Hunters can feel.

"I hope they are here!" said the young man with enthusiasm. "I hope they are waiting for us at the mountain!" We all looked at him, admiring his boldness yet acutely aware that the eagerness of youth could easily rob him of the caution a worthy foe was due. And if ever an enemy bore a close watching, it was the Blue Wings.

"Easy young brother" cautioned Kae-san, "the Blue Wings are not to be taken lightly."

"What's wrong Kae-san? It is a good day to be alive--a good day for fighting!" intoned the younger Dreadknaught.

"Yes," Kae-san answered as he reached over to give a good natured slap on Invictus back, "A good day to live, and for a demon hunter, a good day to die." Invictus looked back at Kae-san, the young man's face showing a bit more soberness at the thought of dieing so young. I took the opportunity to encourage the men.

"Let us not die today for our cause, gentlemen. Let's make our enemies die for theirs."

Invictus was peering upward at the Rock, and he asked while trying to let no fear crack his voice,

"Scythe, do you expect immediate resistance?"

"No," I answered, "Why should they defend the base of a mountain that neither man nor beast could possibly climb?" Invictus looked at me, curiously. I continued,

"Let us hope they indeed do see us as we begin to climb. I want them to laugh at us, to mock our efforts to scale this Rock. That is precisely what I want them to do, at least until they take a second look at us."

"And if they hold above us and wait, what do we do then?" he asked.

"Then we climb some more, we make whatever progress we can. And we must be convincing in our efforts if not in our progress. I doubt they have ever had anyone bother to assault their mountain, since all know it to be impossible." Invictus still looked confused.

"But why bother to attack in a way they know will fail? How could that help us?"

"Because Invictus, they don't know our minds, they only know their own. Neither do they know our capabilities. Men have never climbed this Rock, but men on gargoyles are a thing not seen everyday--and that novelty will draw their attention indeed. If we make any progress up the mountain at all we can create doubt in their minds as to whether we could actually pull it off. And that, my friend, is when they will show themselves. Rag-dan and Kae-san will be waiting and watching for that critical moment. So let your efforts be sincere and earnest, Invictus. They must be convinced that we are firm in our resolves to climb this Rock. The going will be at a snail's pace and it will be agonizing, I promise you. But every inch we gain will sow another seed of doubt in their wicked minds as they watch from above. And remember Invictus, wickedness, when pressed hard enough becomes cowardice every time. When the Mountain finally fears us, they will surely come out to drop on us from on high, thinking they can use that advantage to crush us. That is when the real fight begins. We will keep our gargoyle's wings concealed and hidden so they will believe they face only a land-bound Dreadlock. No better weapon is there to be had than the element of surprise, and when the time is just right, we will counter them, in the air! That should be just enough surprise to give us the advantage we crave."

Rag-dan and Kae-san remained concealed in the forest where they would await my signal. Invictus and I kicked our mounts to move out of the tree line, galloping beside the mountain's base.

The mountain itself, once beheld in all its glory, was more intimidating than even the evil ones who were said to defend it. Known as the Rock of the Ages, it is a solid eruption of hard, smooth stone thrust upward through the crust of the earth, two miles round at the base, peaking out a mile above with a stony point as sharp as the tip of a witch's hat.

Just below its pointed peak a cavern could be found, it is said, and that is where we hoped to find Ar-ric, guarded night and day, by the Blue Wings. The sides of the mountain are shear and mostly smooth, offering the climber slight hand and foothold. This is why it is called the Unclimbable Mountain. Until Ar-ric's ascent to its peak, carried their on the wings of his guardians, so we had heard, the top of this mountain was merely a habitation of birds.

Invictus and I rode on about the base, searching for a spot where we could begin to climb. We encountered no resistance and soon came to a place where a huge boulder, some two or three hundred feet high, leaned against the trunk of the mountain. The boulder formed an angled surface that could be mounted from the ground.

The boulder's surface rose steadily a great distance before making contact with the mountain proper. The angle looked almost climbable from our vantage point. I looked at Invictus and pointed to a good spot where we could hop up on the boulder. Seeing that he was game for it, I nudged my gargoyle carefully up and onto the rock surface, Invictus following.

We could sense the unease in our beasts, for the rock face was hard and smooth and offered little purchase. But the angle of the boulder was less steep than that of the mountain it leaned upon, yet steep enough to give us pause. We urged our gargoyles onward, and they at first tried to climb on hoofs alone, but beginning to slip, they extended their claws to gain a better hold on the stone surface.

The going was hard and slow, and progress was hard fought for, hindered by the many times our mounts' feet lost grip and began to slide backward before regaining traction.

After half an hour of fighting the boulder for every inch, we looked behind us to see that we had moved only some fifty feet across. We had at least another five to six hundred feet of surface to cross to where the boulder merged with the Rock of the Ages. The going would be unbelievably tough, but my greatest fear was that our gargoyles would slip off the boulder and, by force of instinct alone, attempt to extend their wings to fly. That would negate any surprise we might enjoy, for the watching enemy would then know we had the power of flight.

Precautions were taken to keep our mounts' wings concealed. Besides the heavy blankets draped over their backs, we had worked ropes around the beasts' middle to keep the wings tied down. In the past weeks of flying and training with their newfound wings, it had become a habit as natural as breathing for them to spread wings and jump into flight any time they felt off balance. It was all we could now do to keep them moving across the stone surface with wings held in-- to work them as land beasts only rather than land-air creatures. This tactic was confusing and unpleasant for both beast and rider, yet I saw no other way to carry out my plan to draw the enemy out.

On we struggled across the ramped surface of the boulder, our mounts pawing, scratching, sliding and bracing, muscles straining and rippling with intensity and fatigue. Twenty more feet we gained, then thirty more, then another fifty feet. Then we reached a small depression in the surface of the boulder that was invisible from the ground. It formed just enough of a pocket to hold us and our beasts. There we took repose, giving our tired muscles a much needed rest.

Even though Invictus and I had been riding on the backs of the gargoyles as they climbed the boulder, allowing them to do most of the work, we had been straining every second to stay aboard the beasts as we leaned into the angle and against nature's downward pull. Every slip of a gargoyle's hoof-claw sent alarms of terror through us, for we played a life and death game on this stone surface.

The dip in the stone was heaven sent, and tired as we were we could have rested there till nightfall, though the golden sun was still high in the sky above. Some fresh rainwater had collected in the depression and both man and beast drank deeply of the clear water. After almost an hour's rest, we prepared to remount and renew the climb. But before we started off, Invictus' face brightened with an idea.

"Scythe, we must find a way to let our beasts climb without our added weight, which is confusing their balance."

"I know that would be helpful for them Invictus, but what about us? We have neither hoof nor claw to help us. If we try to climb alone we will simply slide back down this boulder."

But what if we found a way to stay on the stone and not slide back? What if we could stick to the rock face?"

"Have you an idea as to how we could achieve that, Invictus?"

"Yes, I think I do. In my pack I have stored leaves I harvested from a vestal tree that I found near our camp last night. A wood-worker in my home village used to make a paste from these leaves that he would use to help fashion his tables and chairs. I think we can use it to get a grip on this boulder," he said, patting the mighty rock beneath us.

"Alright," I replied, "let's try it. But we can't take too long. I don't want to spend the night on this rock."

Invictus ruffled through his pack, pulling out a big handful of dark green leaves he had bundled tightly and bound with string. He lay then on the rock-face and, retrieving a flat piece of flint he kept for starting fires, he began to crush and grind the leaves. He skillfully added a handful of water from the small pool we had found in the depression. He worked for a few minutes more pounding and rubbing the leaves with the flint stone until a thick white paste was formed.

The young warrior took some of the past and applied it to our clothing at the knees and elbows and to our boots as well. Then we both coated our palms and fingers with the sticky substance. Out of the dip in the rock face we belly-crawled and began to make our way up the angle of the boulder, and instantly I knew Invictus' idea was working. The sticky paste held us on the angled surface of the rock face as we crawled, and our mounts found the going much easier without us on their backs. We were now making progress up the boulder at thrice the rate we were at first. And though we had barely begun our climb, I hoped someone on the mountain above was taking note--and beginning to doubt the reputation of this the mountain unclimbable.

SCYTHE

As we climbed and crawled across the bolder, I tried to come up with a plan as to what we would do if we failed to draw the enemy out of hiding before we reached the side of the Rock of the Ages. At our current pace, with no major slips or falls, we could scale the massive boulder and reach the shear side of the Rock in two more hours.

Would the enemy offer battle before then? It was impossible to say, but if we were attacked, we would have to free our mounts to fly by releasing their wings. If Ar-ric sent the Blue Winged demons to sweep down on us, to sweep us off this stone, we could not afford to await their attack. We must see them coming, and meet them as they came, flying up to engage them in mid air.

Invictus and I kept going on our bellies, like two crippled snakes crawling and wiggling up the surface of the boulder. The angle of the boulder began to grow sharper, but the day was cool and a light breeze kept our sweat knocked down. The sunlight reflected brightly off the rock-face, hurting our eyes, but it also warmed and dried the stone underneath us, helping us to stick to the surface. Ever closer we crept toward the mountain-proper.

Afternoon had come round and though nightfall was still hours away, I wanted the confrontation to come to a head with plenty of daylight left in which to get the job done. Our gargoyles were doing well, setting a good pace. As risky as it was to dismount them, the risk seemed to be paying off. They were maintaining a more sure traction on the slippery-smooth stone without us on their backs.

So on we went, making progress up the angle of boulder. As it often is in life, all we could do was to carry on with our task and not worry about that which we could not control. We could attempt to draw the enemy out, but we were in a position of weakness and could not force their hand.

Invictus and I refused to focus on the top of the mountain, lest we grow discouraged. For hours wecontinued, working the stone, glancing up occasionally to check for enemies, then focusing again on the climb as the sun made its slow track across the blue dome. But we were getting tired and our progress was slowing.

And when the sun was but three hours from falling into the west, I began to fear that nightfall might catch us exposed on the face of the boulder. But we drank some water from skins and were refreshed. Soon enough I looked up, surprised to see that we were not far from the shear side of the mountain.

SCYTHE

Even though I had no idea what we would do when we reached it, I figured that at least the mountain's wall would give us protection for our backs, as well as something to lean and rest upon. It took another hour of hard crawl-climbing up the slab, but finally we reached the place where the boulder touched the side of the mighty mountain, the Rock of the Ages.

Ages of water cascading off the Rock onto the boulder had formed a flat area where the two met. The slow but steady erosion of time and the elements had taken its toll on the boulder at this point, yet as I reached out to touch the Rock for the first time it seemed this mountain might be immune from nature's pull, for the feel of it was the very essence of immovable solidity.

As I removed my gloves and put two bare hands on her, the mountain seemed to hum with density, as if rooted to the very core of the earth, reaching down through all time and every earthy layer to attach itself to the earth's core, as the roots of a jaw tooth welded to bone. Invictus joined me and we sat together leaning on the cool side of the mountain. Our muscles ached from the torture of the climb, but the pain of that was almost overwhelmed by the pure pleasure of rest. Again we found small pools of water in crevices, and the clean coolness of it refreshed and energized us once again.

"Scythe, how did you know there would be water on this rock?"

"I didn't know."

"Then what did you plan to drink after our water skins ran dry?"

My answer was to nod at our gargoyles.

"The beasts? What, you planned to get milk from them? I didn't notice any utters on them."

"Not milk, lad--blood. We could tap a vein, as the men of old used to do with their ponies, and fill our bellies with their warm blood." Invictus looked again at the gargoyles, one of which was tending to its claws by extending them and licking them with a foot-long forked tongue.

Invictus frowned.

"I'd rather stay thirsty than wrestle that one for a drink of its blood."

We searched our packs for some meat we had dried and salted. I knew it would increase our thirst, but after the day's climb we needed something solid on our stomachs. A few strips were left over and were tossed to the gargoyles, who went after the dry slips of beef as if they were steaks. The smallness of the gargoyles' meal did not worry us though, for Rag-dan believed the beasts had more than one stomach and could draw from them at any time, thereby carrying a week's supply of food with them everywhere they traveled. With that many stomachs to fill or empty at will, these beasts could be either voracious or scant eaters at any given time.

After the small meal we reclined against the mountainside, wondering what move the enemy might make. Surely they had seen our progress. Surely, I thought, they would not allow us to work the Rock of the Ages unmolested much longer. But the enemy was clever and I was not sure what they might do. Ar-ric could just as well wait us out, laughing at our attempts to get at him.

Invictus volunteered to take the first watch while I took some rest. Evening was upon us, but there was still some time before nightfall. Though the Rock might hold hellish things ready to rip us apart, fatigue overcame anxiety and I, with my weapons laid our around me, was able to drift into a tense semi-sleep much needed by my body. But not for long.

Something shook me awake. Not a hand, but a whirl in the air, a force of whistling noise and violent vibration.

I rubbed my eyes, looking out over the forest we had climbed out of. Something was in the air over the trees, moving towards us quickly. Coming to my feet, I rubbed my eyes again, realizing now that the flying thing was Rag-dan, riding his mount in full and furious flight towards us.

Anger filled me. This was not part of the plan--there was to be no airborne attack until my signal. Rag-dan was close enough now that I could see his face, wide eyed and full of fear. Something was wrong, very wrong. The whistling noise was not coming from Rag-dan.

I looked above me. And there it was, falling towards me like a streaking, brilliant blue star. It drew closer, close enough I could make out the eyes. Yes, eyes, but no discernable head. I saw talons outstretched toward me, instruments of torture reaching down to bring pain first, then death upon the mountainside. I wanted to move but those eyes had me, and I could not look away. New fear took me, that paralyzing fear one can only know when looking into the eyes of a demon you have never seen before. I had never even imagined something like this could exist. My mistake was to stare into its eyes, for they had a power of their own.

But the Blue Wing also erred. It was so focused on me, so intent on splitting me open with its beak and fangs and talons that it never saw

Rag-dan. And at full speed Rag-dan's beast collided with the Blue Wing, t-boning into it a hundred feet above us, smashing the demon into the shear, hard mountainside with a mighty thump and explosion of force.

With frozen stares we gazed above us, Invictus and me, startled and dazed with no thought of what to do next. We had never been attacked from the air and the newness of the experience made us pause in dangerous inaction.

Rag-dan's gargoyle had its huge jaws clamped around the snake-like neck of the Blue Wing. Both were flapping massive wings but locked together as the two were, the wings caught no air and they were plunging towards us in a mass of falling and tangled claws, fangs, blood, scales and blue feathers. I had to move or be crushed, but the only level place on the boulder was about to be buried under tons of raging flesh and bone.

All I could do was dive towards my mount, hoping it would keep me from sliding down the boulder-face. Diving head first, I was able to grasp the pack I had tied to my mount, but my gargoyle had been spooked already and had lost its footing as well. I felt the beast lose its footing and begin to slide downward, headlong, dragging me with it. The slide was arrow-quick, doubling speed in split seconds. With an effort that required all my remaining strength I was able to pull myself onto my mount's back. The beast was struggling to get a grip on the slippery stone, and had extended claws fully to slow us, but it was no use, the momentum was already too great.

Now was the time, if ever, for the beast to extend its wings and lift us off the surface of the boulder, but the beast was panicked and seemed unable now to realize what it needed to do. The ropes still bound its wings, but as I reached for a blade to cut them I realized my weapons had been left on the small shelf above us. I had nothing with which to cut the ropes that held the wings bound.

So hard we had worked to release those wings from inside the beasts, and now realized that we had tied the wings down to our own doom! At the rate we were speeding down the sharp face of the boulder, neither I nor my mount would survive the crash at the end. At least, I hoped, my three fellow Dreadknaughts would survive to finish this battle of the Rock of the Ages.

But just as that thought ripped through my mind, something caught my eye. I looked in horror to see young Invictus holding onto his gargoyle, sliding out of control down the boulder just as I was. No sword was in his hand and I knew he was in the same predicament that I was in. No weapons, nothing to do but slide and wait for the end. I looked down and saw sparks flying off the feet of my mount, and smelt the burning hoofs as the friction of the slide began to melt them away. It was the smell of death.

Then something unexpected happened. Though I could not sever the ropes that tied the gargoyle's wings down, the gargoyle itself decided that it could. Without warning, the beast rolled onto its side, nearly throwing me off in the process.

At first I was angered, but then realized what the beast was attempting. The gargoyle was pressing its left side against the boulder-face. It was going to let the stone and friction burn the ropes off! And though I smelt its hide burning away with the rope, the beast shifted all its massive weight downward, pressing the rope into the stone. It took only a few seconds more for the rope to fray and then snap.

As the rope snapped, the gargoyle's left wing spring open, but the right wing did not. It was still tied down by a separate rope that had not made good contact with the surface of the boulder. The free wing was out, but now acted as a drag, and pulled us hard to the left, right into Invictus and his mount. I braced for the collision as best I could, and when we crashed into them I felt myself lift off the gargoyle, landing on Invictus. But the young man was strong and I swear he threw me backwards, and back onto my mount as we continued to slide down the boulder.

Then my mount began to scream, a scream I could barely hear through the fear and rush of air whipping around my ears as we fell. But Invictus' mount did hear and must have understood because it then shifted its weight onto its side as my gargoyle had done, imitating the move that would burn through the rope. In seconds it had one wing free, its right wing.

Now, there we were, two men on two gargoyles speeding uncontrollably down the angle of the boulder-face, each with one free wing. Each gargoyle now had one wing free and one still bound, neither being able to take flight.

Then the idea entered my mind like a star-burst. If neither gargoyle could fly on its own, maybe they could fly if locked together as one, each using one wing to lift us off the stone! But to make it work we had to exchange places--my mount with the free left wing had to be on the left side of the formation while Invictus' mount, with the free right wing, had to be on the right side. Only then could we lock together and form for flight with a free wing on either side.

We were sliding down side by side, but I knew I had to let Invictus pass me--I had to get behind and around him so we could rejoin for flight. I knew of only one way. Still holding on to the boney saddle of my mount's back, I swung both my legs over the left side of my mount, pushing my booted feet down hard onto the surface of the stone. Though the soles of my boots began to smoke instantly from the friction, it was our only chance. The extra drag I was creating began to slow us, allowing Invictus to pass. Invictus saw what I was doing and was at first puzzled. But the young Dreadknaught was always a quick study and when he was far enough ahead of me, I saw him throw his feet over the right side of his mount, creating drag on that side by pressing his boots to the boulder and moving his mount to the right. Now behind him and to his left, I jumped back astride my mount, allowing for more speed to catch up to him. Regaining his side, I reached out a hand that he grasped and we pulled ourselves and mounts together, still sliding all this time at an incredible speed, with the edge of the boulder drawing nearer. In seconds we would careen off the edge to be impaled on the thick trees of the waiting forest.

Our mounts sensed now what we were attempting and the two, each with one wing free, began to work in unison, reaching out to the passing air, allowing it to flow under their outstretched wings. They were searching instinctively for the perfect wing angle to create lift, and when they found it I felt us lift off the boulder-face as one and begin to rise. Off the boulder we lifted and into the air, the gargoyles each flapping a massive wing in perfect unison to give us lift.

Relief flooded my soul! I looked around for a place to make a soft landing, but there was nothing but rock and trees to be seen. Our gargoyles were doing well, but I knew they could not stay airborne for long on the power of only two wings. We were going to come down, and if we hit either boulder or tree, it would mean the end of us all.

A shodow crossed us, drawing my gaze upward. I could not understand what I was seeing, for my comrade Kae-san, mounted on his flying gargoyle, was headed straight for us. Why? What did he mean? He was going to smash into us, breaking us apart and bringing us crashing to our deaths below! He was but fifty feet away now and moving fast towards us. And I saw him draw double swords with a look battle rage upon his face, and his eyes flashed as he bore into us. Our gargoyles saw it to and were confused, and in their confusion they lost their union and I felt the separation. I looked to Invictus and his face was pale with fear for he knew we would both fall like stones dropped into a well, a freefall into what waited below.

Then I heard Kae-san yelling "move" and he flew between us swinging razor sharp blades along the sides of our mounts, and Invictus and I both pulled our legs away just in time as his blades sliced into our gargoyles. And time seemed to slow to a crawl as I wondered why Kae-san had betrayed us to our deaths...why he had joined Ar-ric and the darkness when we needed him so much in the light. Kae-san's mount had pulled both its wings in tight to its sides in order to fit between Invictus and I, and he was close enough I could see his expression for a split second...and it was laughter on his face.

Laughter? Not just laughter, but the laughter of one brother who had pulled the ultimate trick on another. And I realized what the trick was when the remaining rope fell from my gargoyle and its now free right wing flapped and caught the air. Kae-san's true blade had cut just deep enough to sever the remaining rope without spilling my mount's insides onto the boulder below. His other sword had done the same for Invictus, whose mount now also extended both wings, fighting the air for flight. We both regained steady flight, and rising high, wheeled back around towards the mountrain. Kae-san, I'm certain, was laughing all the while but I could not see his face for he did not turn towards us. He made straight for Rag-dan, who was involved in a bloody fight with the Blue Wing he had slammed into moments before, thus beginning the Battle of the Rock of the Ages.

Rag-dan and the Blue Wing had crashed down onto the flat shelf of the boulder where Invictus and I had earlier rested. Just before the pair had made contact, Rag-dan had somehow rolled with his mount over and atop the winged demon, forcing it to take the brunt of the punishment as the battle-locked mass crashed to the waiting boulder. As I wheeled about to face what was happening I was able to size things up in my mind. The impact had flung Rag-dan and his mount away from the Blue Wing and now both had regained the air and had clashed again, jaws and beak snapping, claws and talons ripping at each other. It was a desperate fight.

This whole thing was moving at a rapid pace--lifeblood would be spilt soon, I knew. The Blue Wing was clearly larger yet more air-agile than the gargoyle it faced, and with its long flexible neck and dangerously sharp beak it could rip into the gargoyle with a striking motion, a motion much like the strike of a rattle snake but a thousand times more deadly.

Faced off like they were in hovering flight, it would not take long for the Blue Wing to wear the gargoyle down. The demon used swift, darting attacks that seemed bodily impossible for even one whose wing flaps quickened to a buzz when hovering, a wing action almost like that of a humming bird despite its huge size. It used these unique powers of flight to zip about through the air and could force the gargoyle into defensive maneuvers which also forced it to expend much strength, thereby wearing it down. The only thing prolonging the fight was the fact that Rag-dan was quick enough with his sword to punish the Blue Wing with a cut when it came near. Yet, with Kae-san now closing in to help, the Blue Wing would find itself pressed from both sides, making that fight more evenly matched.

I motioned to Invictus to fly to Rag-dan's aid as well. Three on one should be more than even odds. And, I thought gladly, after we slaughtered this Blue Wing, we would search this mountain for Ar-ric. But no, something was wrong; it couldn't be as easy as that. I tilted my head back, lifting mine eyes to the mountain top, from whence something was coming, but nothing good. Though the sun was about to set in the west and the distance incredible, my vision was just sharp enough to reach the peak of the Rock of the Ages, and it was with a feeling of dread that I watched as five more winged figures separated from the peak.

The five circled briefly before beginning their descent towards us. They would be on us in seconds and, counting the one we already had engaged, it would now be six of them to the four of us, impossible odds for the Dreadlock. Something had to give and I was the one who had to make it happen, and fast. But I had not even recovered my weapons yet.

Things were not looking good for the Dreadlock.

Not only had Ar-ric been guarded by at least six Blue Wings, he had been willing to sacrifice the first one he sent down in order to *draw us* out of hiding. He had reversed our plan against us! I had no idea of what to do, yet I knew that it is at times like these that fortune most favors the bold. So I let instinct take my mind and body to become something Other. And instinct told me I needed a scythe in my hands.

I kicked the sides of my gargoyle and we flew in the direction of my blades, and the ongoing airborne battle. The three Dreadknaughts now had the Blue Wing backed so close to the shear side of the Rock that its serpent-headed tail almost touched the stone as it now hovered in a defensive position.

As I flew towards the action, an object gleamed on the boulder below the Blue Wing. I recognized the blade of my scythe, lying there with the point reaching skyward toward the belly of the hovering demon above. Instinct made me pull hard on the reigns of my mount and kick it in the ribs, and we rose higher and faster, and with powerful strokes of its quick beating wings it carried us quickly to the Rock. I wanted to get above the single enemy.

My three comrades had not yet seen the on-coming threat of five more Blue Wings, so they were taking their time in dispatching the first one, yet we had no time to lose. As I reached the side of the mountain, I looked down on the Blue Wing hovering about a hundred feet below me.

I had my mount pull both its wings in and we stalled, and then dropped like a rock falling off the mountain, much as the Blue Wing had attacked us at first. Downward we fell, and my gargoyle and I were but a blur to the eyes of the three astonished Dreadknaughts when I crashed into the Blue Wing's back, hitting it square between the wings, ramming it down onto the boulder below.

As we hit the boulder, I heard the Blue Wing scream, then go quiet and still, its long neck and beak flopping against the boulder.

Looking up, I saw that my men had, finally, seen the new threat from above. Meanwhile, my mount kicked and clawed the lifeless demon until it rolled over and I found what I knew I would find, my scythe blade buried full into its underbelly.

Gripping the oak handle with two fists I yanked, and with a wet, sucking sound the now bloody blade came free. The blood on the blade was black and thick as ground-oil, and I knew the tip of the blade had punctured the demon's heart, killing instantly. I let the gargoyle kick the body of the dead Blue Wing down the steep slope of the boulder, trailing a smear of nightblood as it went. No time to celebrate, I collected my hand sickles and remounted, taking to the air again.

Airborne, I looked around to take stock of the situation. The balance of the Dreadlock had acted wisely. All three had backed hovering towards the shear side of the Rock, swords all thrust outward to receive the attack from on high. That tactic, coupled with the sight of the limp body of the dead Blue Wing sliding on a blood-slick down the boulder, gave the attackers pause and interrupted the neatness of their diving formation.

I watched as fear and confusion stalled their attack and the five were forced to swing away from us. But they quickly fell into a smooth sweeping movement and again formed up to come at us straight on. Now they were screaming. High-pitched, blood curdling demon-screams filled the air and added to the confusion. I tried to make a plan, but Instinct locked my mind and all I managed to do was fill my hands with weapons. Killing the first Blue Wing was big for us because a new and unknown enemy is a mystery, and mysteries have power precisely because they are an unknown.

We didn't know if they could be killed until we did it. And with the new arrivals it was now five rather than six on four, better odds than before, just, but still a great disadvantage for the Dreadlock. If it took four of us to kill the first one, how would the same four of us manage to kill five of them? I was afraid, not so much for myself I think, but for my men. I didn't want to see them slashed to death on this mountainside.

I called out the only tactic that came to mind, hoping someone would hear it above the din of beating wing and screaming, onrushing demons.

"Stay together! Stay together and don't let them separate us! We must fight as one!" The Dreadlock heard and responded to my direction and I joined the formation. Now the four of us were all hovering, treading air, with our backs close to the mountainside. Our gargoyles whipped their tales about, slapping at the mountainside behind us to gauge the distance from the Rock. It was a tall order to take on five Blue Wings, especially in their own element, the air.

Though our gargoyles loved their new powers of flight, they were winglings indeed compared to these demons, which moved through the air like sharks through seawater. If we could but take them to ground, our gargoyles could use all of their leg strength to leverage, but the only thing below us was the steep decline of the boulder on which two of us had almost died already.

With one final raging scream the four ripped through the air, closing on us. This would be a difficult fight for us to win, maybe impossible. But all we could do was to answer the challenge as best we could, and die like men if called to it.

The Blue Wings were not slowing up and the impact would come in seconds. I looked over to check on the men and to make sure our battle formation was sound. Invictus was restless, and I called out to him to calm him. But I was chilled when he looked my way, for in his eyes were a wild look that I recognized, and I knew he was about to break ranks and do something rash and dangerous. I watched him as he backed his hovering gargoyle all the way to the wall, so that his mount could press its hind hooves firmly against the wall of the Rock. I tried again to yell to him, to order him not to leave the formation, but there was no holding him. He had to go.

He held my gaze as he launched, his mount pushing off the wall behind us with hind legs while beating the air hard with its wide, strong wings. Into the sky above us they shot, Invictus and his gargoyle, at a steep, ambitious angle. I turned again to the oncoming Blue Wings and saw three of them peel off the formation to pursue Invictus and I knew that was what he had wanted, to draw a few of them after him and away from us, but I could see tragedy playing out before my eyes.

Now we had the two remaining and inbound Blue Wings outnumbered, but Invictus was outnumbered as well and his gargoyle could not out-fly the Blue Wings--they would catch and give death to him within moments. The remaining two would be able to occupy us as the other three disposed of Invictus. Then those three would return to help finish us. Invictus' decision was a terrible one, I was thinking, recklessly brave and undisciplined. But he had made his own decision and, as foolhardy as it was on his part, I could not worry about him now for I had to defend myself from what was coming.

The two demons came on hard, hoping to knock us out of the air. But I was looking for such an attack and as the first one came at me I had my mount drop its head and duck under, then pull itself back up into the attacker, allowing the Blue Wing's own momentum to carry it towards the wall behind us.

I also swung my scythe blade at the Blue Wing, making a good slicing contact on the demon's wing, causing it to pull the wing in. But it flung its other wing at me. This caused the demon to roll in the air, loosing its air-balance and it dashed hard into the wall of the Rock at near full speed, beak first, and I saw its long beak shatter, falling in a bloody dribble to the boulder below. I heard the crack of bone on stone as the rest of its body met the unforgiving Rock wall, and I knew this Blue Wing was either dead or near enough to death that I could dismiss it for the time being.

SCYTHE

But I looked over to see that my comrades had not fared as well with the other Blue Wing. Rag-dan had attempted a duck-under move similar to what I had done, but the Blue Wing had dropped even lower and Rag-dan and his mount had taken the demon's full weight in a collision that had knocked the gargoyle spinning in the air, Rag-dan holding on for life like a rag doll. But Kae-san had seized the moment and sicked his mount on the Blue Wing's flank, fangs and claws tearing at the thing. Rag-dan had somehow recovered from the blow he had taken and was bringing his gargoyle back to the fight. He and Kae-san now were in a standoff with the demon and I was moving to join them, but I chanced a glimpse heavenward to see what was happening with Invictus.

He was far above and away now, having pushed his gargoyle hard and high, and his mount responded by climbing the sky, wings pulling harder and harder against an updraft that had blown in at just the right time. Yet I could hear the pursuing Blue Wings' hungry screams, screams that seemed to say that they would enjoy nothing more than taking man-prey and destroying it. Their wings moved at a far quicker beat than did those of Invictus' mount.

They would catch him, the three Blue Wings would, I knew, catch him from behind and pull him down to a death so young. And though he knew the likely outcome he flew on, higher, with the demons closing on him every second. Invictus was moving fast but could not reach the peak of the Rock, if that was even his goal, before they caught him.

It took only a few more seconds and the Blue Wing closest to him was harassing his gargoyle's flank, striking at it with its razor sharp beak. And they were so high and far away that I doubted my eyes when I thought I saw the young Dreadlock Invictus turn and leap from his mount, but that was precisely what I was seeing. With sword drawn high, he dove backwards off his gargoyle and *onto the Blue Wing* that was close by, surprising even the demon, with such audacity.

The Blue Wing had obviously never been mounted before and suddenly lost its momentum, the cadence of its wings being interrupted by the sudden attack. Just like that, the Blue Wing was in a fight for its life with this crazed man-thing.

With a slashing sharp blade of cold steel, the man-thing was on its back, having jumped unexpectedly backwards and onto the pursuer. Invictus wrapped his legs around the body of the blue wing and, with one hand full of scale-feathers, was hacking his sword down hard with the other hand.

The Blue Wing went into a hover-spin as it tried to whip its beak around to knock the man-thing off, but the man seemed to be welded to its back. The man-thing was our Invictus and he now reversed his sword, point down, and with a two handed thrust began to stab down into the demon's back. The other two pursuing demons hovered near but could not get a beak or talon on Invictus because of the buzzing, thrashing wings of the Blue Wing he was riding.

Invictus somehow stayed on the demon, who must have felt like a bucking bull underneath him, and he kept stabbing his sword point-downward.

Then it happened. The Blue Wing seized up, its long neck stiffening straight out, its wings doing the same from base to tip, wings fully extended as if to glide on the wind. Invictus' sword had found a sweet spot, that one spot on a Blue Wing unprotected by the hard, bone-like shell that lies just underneath its scale-feathered skin. His sword sank deeply, all the way to the cross-hilt, slicing through flesh and tissue, all the way to the Blue Wing's black heart.

Nearby, Invictus' now rider-less gargoyle turned in midair to attack one of the two remaining Blue Wings. Invictus saw the move and the distraction it caused, and again he leaped screaming, battle-mad, yelling, jumping through the air, this time from a dead Blue Wing to one still alive.

Familiar now with the Blue Wing's weak spot, Invictus went to work plunging the tip of his sword downward in probing stabs, and it took only a second longer to find the spot that allowed the sword tip to enter, plunging again all the way to the heart.

Just as before, this Blue Wing seized up, its wings shooting out as straight and stiff as if made-through of solid oak. The gargoyle took one more bite into the Blue Wing but recoiled as the black, poison vile blood of the demon filled its mouth. Like gall it repulsed the gargoyle, making it gag so hard it nearly threw-up one of its own stomachs. So fouled, Invictus' gargoyle fell down and away through the air, trying to recover its senses.

Invictus did not notice his mount, he only felt the incomparable joy and elation at having killed two of his pursuers. In celebration he lifted his arms and clinched fists high above his head. As he did, he winced as something jerk at his body. A new sensation ran through his shoulders. He had told me that once, as a boy, he had been playing in a green meadow when a storm cloud covered the field, overshadowing him, and his hair had stood tingly on end, followed by a bolt of lightning into a nearby tree.

Invictus probably didn't understand why he was feeling a similar sensation now, but when he lowered his right arm, all he pulled down was a bone-jagged stump of arm that spray blood all into his face. Stunned, appalled, Invictus noticed he could still 'feel' his right hand clinched into a fist, though the severed hand and forearm was now falling away to smash to earth somewhere below.

Instinct alone made the still-stunned and one-armed Dreadknaught duck to avoid the sweep of another Blue Wing's talon, a sweep that would have taken his head clean off to fall to the ground as his arm had done. One-armed Invictus found himself on the back of the second dead Blue Wing with stiffened wings, a dead-glider on the wind moving earthward. The flow of cool air in his face brought Invictus back to his senses and he realized what had happened.

Looking around, he saw that the Blue Wing that had snapped his arm off had turned about and was now flying towards him, to finish him off. Full in control of his senses, the smile of a doomed man formed on his lips. With his left hand he grasp the handle of his sword which was still stuck deeply into the dead beast's back. What instinct told him to twist the sword, I do not know. But in twisting it he made the body of the dead Blue Wing wince, its still active nerves reacting to the movement of steel in its heart.

Again he twisted the sword and again the wings moved, the rear flap-edge of the massive pair of wings dropping to catch the air. This pulled the whole dead-demon body out of its downward glide and shot it back upwards into a climb into the strong current of wind. Invictus had ingeniously discovered, with audacious bravery, a way to both kill and then from its dead back, steer a Blue Wing demon!

As Invictus rose higher, the pursuing Blue Wing dove underneath him, seeking to sweep back up and into Invictus for the kill. But Invictus' face reflected nothing save the wildness of man as he pulled the sword from the demon's back and, holding it in his only hand, lay back until his own back was sliding headfirst down the dead demon's back towards the serpent tail, a tail that had died with the rest of the demon. Along the length of the Blue Wing's back Invictus slid head first until his head and shoulders and the rest of his body slid off and away from the dead demon. Invictus then pulled his legs up close to his body and began to tumble, feet over head through the air, like some circus performer.

Then I realized his end game. Coming out of the tumble, he extended his body and sword, shaft-straight, and plunged towards the open beak of the pursuing Blue Wing. The Blue Wing seemed at a loss for what to do except to accelerate into the flying man-thing, but that only helped Invictus' cause. I watched as the tip of Invictus' sword plunged into the open beak. I did not see what happened next because something hit me hard across my head as I heard Rag-dan call out a warning, too late.

I was drawn back into my own fight by the shock of the blow, and I looked around in time to see the serpent tale of a Blue Wing snapping at my throat. A demon was facing away from me, Kae-san offering it battle in front while its serpent tail menaced me. I whipped my scythe around as it struck, the blade catching it clean, slicing off the serpent-head cleanly. The Blue Wing gave a screech of pain and fury, and spun around towards me. It would have overwhelmed me in its wrath, I am certain, had not Kae-san with zero hesitation pushed his mount forward to merge with the demon as it turned. Hacking away with his heavy sword, Kae-san drew black blood and forced the Blue Wing to defend two fronts, his sword cutting from one direction and my scythe slicing from the other. Both of us worked furiously, our gargoyles attacking along with us, ripping with both fang and claw.

Our attack was furious, yet so quick were the movements of the Blue Wing, so tough its protective coat of scale-feathers, coupled with long-necked strikes of its razor beak and talons, that this one demon was more than a match for Kae-san and I. And so we were both bleeding from multiple wounds, our strength nearly spent, when Rag-dan re-entered the fray with a flying dash into the Blue Wing's blind side.

Shaken by this third attack, the demon looked for an escape route, but none was to be found as the three of us closed in, tightening the ring of blades around it. It fought on with the wrath of the hellion it was, but thick black liquid flowed freely from a hundred cuts to its body and Rag-dan had taken one of its talons off with his sword. Finally the thing wilted before us as a cut flower in a harsh sun, sinking away on broken wings to die on the boulder below us. It slid down the angle to leave another bloody streak as a twin to the one already cutting a black gash down the stone face of the boulder.

SCYTHE

Catching my breath now I looked all around but could see a trace of neither Invictus nor the Blue Wing he was last seen attacking. Neither Rag-dan nor Kae-san had seen what had happened to him, but we knew there was no time to search now. Our business was far from finished.

"We will have to find Invictus later. Let us finish what we came to do. Fly to the Peak of this Rock!" And the three of us turned our mounts to the heavens and urged them up and onward. Their wings found new strength and we began to rise on a stiff breeze that was our reward for a thus-far victory. It took what seemed an age of hard flight into air that grew thinner and colder by the second to reach Peak level. With an index finger I drew a circle in the air above my head to signal the other two to fly round the Peak of the Rock and find out what we were up against. When they returned we hovered together on icy air, the glassy crystals now forming on the leading edges of our gargoyles' wings.

"There are three openings into this mountain peak, Scythe, including the one visible there," said Rag-dan, pointing to a spot. "That one there and two more on the back side."

"We must cover all three," I replied, "though it means we have to separate to do it. A gamble indeed, yet we cannot risk Ar-ric's escape."

"What makes you think he is still in there?" replied Kae-san.

"I do not know for certain, but my guess is that with at least six Blue Wing's guarding him, Ar-ric feels quite safe. If you were guarded by such, wouldn't you?"

"I see your point," Kae-san said with a shrug, "but we have proven that we can kill them."

"Yes we have, but we don't know if that is enough to frighten Ar-ric. I think we will find him in there," I said, pointing to the Peak, "though I know not what we will find in there with him."

With icy smiles, knowing and grim, my two Dreadknaught brothers turned their mounts and flew away, one to the left side of the Peak, one to the right side. Each of us would enter one of the three openings on the mountain's peak.

I checked my weapons, making sure my scythe was strapped securely to my gargoyle mount, unsheathed with the blade naked and thrust forward, so that if anything attacked us, the exposed blade would be the first thing it made contact with. Then, taking a deep breath of cold air, I dug my heels into the gargoyle's ribs and the beast took us flying towards the cave-mouth that seemed now to yawn in dark anticipation of us.

The opening was a few hundred feet below the actual tip-point of the Rock of the Ages. Because we had hovered at Peak level, I was now flying downward, gravity my friend, and in seconds we were approaching the opening, which now seemed a gaping black hole in the mountainside. The jagged whole in the mountain had a snow-covered, flat shelf of rock that one would pass over first before entering the opening itself.

My mount and I descended quickly towards the cave mouth and I could now see that the opening was about forty feet wide. That was just enough room to fly my mount right into the cave. And why not, why not make a flying entrance grand enough to impress my former friend residing inside this mountain top fortress? But that old friend was clever, I remembered, and he was bound to have a last trick or two for me.

So, just as my mount was about to sweep through the cave entrance I slid from its back, sliding down the length of its outstretched left wing. Rolling off the wing tip as it swept near the ground, I dove for a snow drift that had collected around some scrub brush that somehow cling to the rocky shelf in front of the opening. The snow broke my fall nicely as I roll over it and back to my feet. I had left my scythe strapped to my beast but I still had my hand sickles on me. These I drew, and rushed forward into the cave behind my winged friend who would serve to block the way of whatever surprises Ar-ric had waiting for me.

I ran hard across the crunching snow to close on my mount, which had already entered the mouth of the cave. As I entered the cave I sensed something massive moving, tumbling towards me. I dove quickly to my left and felt the razor hair of a demon brush across my face, slicing the skin of my cheek enough to draw blood. The tumbling, struggling mass rolled on past me and out of the cave entrance.

It took a moment to catch my breath. Then I realized what I had seen. Two ferocious beasts had locked up in a rolling death match that had nearly crushed me. One of the beasts was my mount, the other a Blue Wing.

The Blue Wing had been waiting inside the cave and had jumped the gargoyle as it entered. It was their death grasp that tumbled past and nearly over me. I wanted to follow and lend a hand to my mount, but at that moment my eye caught a glimmer of a blade on the cave floor and I recognized it as my scythe. It had been knocked loose in the melee, and the sight of it reminded me that my duty lie inside this cave.

The gargoyle would have to fend for itself, for I had business was with Ar-ric. Scooping up my scythe by the oak handle I made my way into the heart of the cave at a steady but cautious jaunt. I did not have to go far, for the cave soon opened up into a large room that was well lit by multiple fires and wall-lanterns.

There, looking back at me in the middle of this cave-room, stood Ar-ric. I was surprised to see him dressed in what looked like bed clothes, a long white night gown covered by a red satin robe. A stone fire-pit smoked before him with what looked like a dressed rabbit skewered and roasting over the fire. He held a wine glass in one hand, while a wispy trail of smoke drifted from the end of a long cigar held between the fingers of his other hand. Very much at ease, he spoke first in an almost casual tone.

"What took you so long, old friend?" There was a distance of some forty feet separating us. I held my weapon firmly in hand, checking every crack and corner of the cavern visible to my eyes for any hint of another ambush. I did not trust the man before me, though he seemed quite disarmed at the time. I moved closer.

"Please come into my home, such as it is. Of course, I had hoped the personal protector assigned me could have relieved me of you, but that having failed, I see no reason we can't make the best of whatever unpleasantness you have in mind. Come, sit down," said Ar-ric with pretended courteousy.

"I'll stand if you don't mind." I eased nearer to him as he took his seat in an arm chair at the center of the huge cave-room. Ar-ric was the kind of man whose manner made you want to trust him even while you knew it would be wise not to, therefore my scythe remained ready in hand for the time being. Neither of us knew how my mount had fared in the one-on-one combat with the Blue Wing, neither did I know what my two comrades had encountered on the other side of the mountain.

Ar-ric's casual, unworried demeanor concerned me. Did he know something I didn't? My own worries aside, the situation as it was felt somehow natural, expected, as if a part of some greater design. Why should it not come down to Ar-ric and me, one on one, just as it had been all those times when we trained against one another as youngsters? That feeling helped me to relax, if just a bit.

"I see that you are living rather large up here," I said to him. "Your benefactors are taking care of their own." As a traitor to his original cause, I was sure Ar-ric felt the edge of accusation in my words, yet his voice remained calm.

"Yes, I am kept up with at least the basic needs of life." He took a deep draw on the cigar, tilting his head back to exhale rings of smoke that roll back neatly into themselves. "Somehow I manage to get by." I noticed that the sofa near his armchair was covered with a thick mink throw, and the cave floor beneath it was smooth, polished stone, cut with articulate designs.

"I think you are more than getting by," I replied. "You have powerful friends, doomed though they are. They help you now, but only for as long as they find you useful." I saw his eyes flash a little then, but he kept his calm.

"I see that you and your so-called Dreadlock finally discovered the treasure hidden in the bellies of your beasts. I've known of it for sometime, and marvel that it took you so long to discover."

"Now is no time for lies between old friends, Ar-ric. You could not have known of their secret wings--suspected perhaps, a whisper from hell maybe, but you did not know for certain. Even Rag-dan was unsure."

"Rag-dan? Is he still alive? Only met him once. A dense little fellow I recall."

"You can tell him that yourself. He will be along in a few moments." I noticed for the first time that the room was decorated with swords and armor hanging on the walls all around.

"Are you so quick to gamble with the lives of your men? Rather ignoble of you I would say."

"Gamble? A match between you and Rag-dan would be a fair one. Indeed, I think I would really enjoy the contest."

"Are you so confident now--now that you are known as Scythe? I remember when they called you John. Yes, 'dull little John' we called you behind your back. You were more likable then, I think, though just as dishonest."

"Dishonest, Ar-ric? And when was I dishonest with you?"

"So soon we forget," he said, no longer able to smother his anger with false civility. "Do you not remember telling me that you had no love for--for Pristine?" It seemed to pain him just to say her name, yet he continued. "It is just like your hypocritical order of Hunters, little slaves of Jonasius, teehee, pretending to be so holy, yet all the while as deceiving as the devils you chase about the world."

"Do you still think of Pristine? That was over a decade ago, when neither of us had even seen our seventeenth summer. I told you back then that I chose not to love her. The part you couldn't stomach was that she continued to love me even though I moved on to my duties."

He bristled at my mention of Pristine's love for me, for he knew it to be true by an experience all too real. He had loved her as much as I had, and after I had left and was out of their lives he had fully confessed his love for her. But her feelings for me would not cool. It was this unrequited love for Pristine, daughter of our Hunt-Master, that drove him towards the darkness. Deep in the woods he had met an emissary of the Dark Prince, who had sent one of his own personal favorites to recruit Ar-ric, seeing much potential in the conversion as well as in the convert.

Ar-ric spoke again, gazing now into the fire with a faraway look in his eyes.

"I loved her, but she loved you. And what did you do with her love but kick it away from you, right back into her beautiful face! And she could think of nothing else for months. I know--I watched her over seasons, waiting for her to change, waiting for her broken heart to mend, but after what you did to her she could love no other." He looked up at me with hate-etched eyes. "Only a scoundrel would treat a girl like you treated her!"

"I had my duty before me. I had my calling. I did not go to the Hunt-Master to win his daughter, but to sharpen skill and blade for the Holy Cause to which I am called--to which we were both called!"

"And that is just the thing John, that is your problem," he said with an evil chuckle, rising from the chair, laying aside his cigar. "You never learned to see it all as a game. You have such an epic mindset, John. You think you must see everything in life through the rosy lens of 'honour' and 'service' and the 'struggle' between good and evil, right and wrong." He waved his arms about as he spoke. "Don't you know all that lofty talk is as thin as the cold air that surrounds this mountain?"

"I have lost much for the Cause, Ar-ric. Yes, I even had to deny the thing I wanted most, the one I loved the most, the girl we both loved." I saw him cringe at that, but I continued. "Yet I have learned to die daily on the way to my goal. Self denial is a way of life for me now. What have you learned on your way, old friend?"

"I have learned..." He paused, his voice trailing off to a bitter hiss. "I have learned that pleasure is to be taken before so-called honour. I have learned that people are to be used and disposed of as no more than objects. I have learned that only fools believe that Heaven anymore represents good than does Hell. There is no good, and there is no evil, John. There is only time, and I chose to enjoy the time I have on earth, not to waste it camping with fools like you in the woods."

"You once believed in a Cause that was good, Ar-ric. What changed your mind? What changed your heart?"

"My heart has been stone since the Bower Green," he said grimly, turning to face me. "My heart has been stone since Pristine."

"Could a Heaven of Love not still move even a heart of stone?" I offered. Even Ar-ric deserved one last extension of mercy, but he would have none of it.

"Heaven is not love, John, it is only a House of Power. Just like Hell." He said this as he began to move over to a wall-mount that held a coat of mail and a battle sword, apparently his favorites for they both glinted with a fresh polish.

"Two Houses of Power arrayed against one another for eternity. It is not a question of which one is good and which one evil. It is only a question of which one is stronger, which the more ruthless, which one will end up on top." As he spoke he was discarding his night gown and slipping a coat of mail over his shoulders. I did not hinder him as he armed himself. "I chose to go with the one who would not weigh down my mind with silly ideas of guilt and sin, right and wrong, honour and justice." He lifted the shinny battle sword from its cradle, its heft resting gently in his hand. The rippled muscles of his arm and shoulder bulged beneath the skin.

"What about love for a girl, Ar-ric, and hate for me? Is your mind also free of them?" Ar-ric grinned slightly, replying,

"Love is just a feeling John, nothing more. Love can confuse and make one weak. And hate--hate is a feeling as well, but also a fire that can keep a man warm on top of a mountain."

"And so you live here in this mountain with the fires of your hatred, and that is all you want out of life?"

SCYTHE

"I want pleasure now, nothing more. And nothing would give me more pleasure than to spill your entrails all over this cave floor. Oh no, John, I *will* go into the long night, but not quietly will I go."

He swept the sword through the air in quick, hard strokes, showing that his more than ample skills were extant still.

"John—Scythe, I mean, it seems that your friends are late, and I was never impressed with that farmer's tool you fight with!"

His feet moved quickly and his blade flashed. I pulled my scythe up just in time to parry. Around he spun, swinging his sword blade for my throat, and again I caught it with my scythe blade, but with his free hand he grabbed the handle of my weapon and pulled himself close to me, landing a glancing blow across my face with the hilt of his sword. We pushed each other away. He was fighting with a confidence I could not deny.

"I see you've kept up your skills," I complemented, rubbing my freshly bruised cheekbone that was already swelling.

"Not much else to do in a cave on top of a mountain," he replied, circling me now. "Besides, I knew this day would come...we both knew it would come." He paused. "Oh yes, almost forgot to invite everyone to the party." He put two fingers to his lips and blew a loud, piercing whistle.

To the rear of the cavern was a small opening. Little clicking noises were coming from the opening along with high pitched and evil giggling sounds. Out trotted three little Minions. I had heard of them but until that moment had never seen one. Tiny demons that resembled pigs with cat-like heads, walking upright on two hind legs with split-hoofed feet that clicked as they cobbled across the floor. They had wings also, but the wings looked shrunken and deformed, unfeathered and useless.

Always either giggling with evil delight or else squealing in cowardly terror for their lives, these Minions were known to be harmless, unless armed as these now were with tiny bows. These little bows they could barely manage to string with six inch arrows.

The arrows were small and ill aimed, but made of wood and tipped with iron points which could fly flat and fast from the bowstring. The arrows were short of shaft and could hardly penetrate armor but were very dangerous if they found flesh. I would have to watch for the arrows as I fought Ar-ric because without hesitation the three giggling little devils pulled back arrows and let fly in our direction. But Ar-ric and I both had to duck to avoid the flying darts as they sailed just over our heads. He yelled angrily, pointing his finger at them and then me,

"Curse ye little devil-stinkers, don't shoot towards me! Move around behind him!"

But the Minions had broken into a fit of even louder giggles after they fired their little arrows, dancing a jig now in clicking little circles arm-n-arm with one another, and were much too skittish to draw closer to the fight.

They were known to be easily frightened, so I grabbed a nearby lantern from a wall-hanger and flung it across the cavern. It crashed on the stone wall above their heads, sending all three squealing and scrambling for their lives back into their hiding place. Ar-ric turned his attention back to me, starting to circle me once again. I kept my feet moving as well, circling with him, locked together now in a dance of death.

My boots were wet from the snow outside and I was trying to gain purchase on the polished floor. Ar-ric was bare footed, which gave him a better foothold, but also gave me an idea.

"You say you knew this day would come--but I never thought of you, you never much crossed my mind," I said, just before lunging at his face with my scythe. He easily dodged the blow, but failed to see my free hand slip down and pull a hand sickle, which I flicked at his feet. The razor sharp sickle blade rotated across the toe-end of his left foot, slicing through skin and bone before bouncing back into the air, boomerang-like, and back into my hand.

Ar-ric backed away quickly, looking down at his bloody foot from which three of the toes dangled, held on by mere shreds of skin.

"Now that may sting a little in the morning, if you live to see it," I taunted.

"John, you fight like a girl, scratching with little kitty claws!"

"Whatever works, old friend."

"No problem really, you only got the three middle ones," he replied. "I don't really need those."

And he swept his sword tip down and across the toes, severing the skin that held them on. He then kicked the loose toes across the marble floor.

"A nice little appetizer for my blue winged friend, before he sups on you as the main course." I winced at his act of toughness, admiring it. Yet blood now flowed steadily from his foot, and would be slippery on the floor surface.

SCYTHE

I feinted a charge and he moved to brace for it, and almost slipped down on the bloody marble. I chuckled, making him angry, and I thought it a good time to remind him of something else that might draw anger.

"You are angry, Ar-ric. You were always such an angry lad. Pristine told me once, when we were alone, how ugly she found you to be when you grew angry. I think she was right."

And we kept circling one another, looking for a weakness, for an opportunity to strike. I kept up the mind-pressure.

"She said you had the look of a swollen frog, and she refused to kiss a frog-boy. She held out for a face she could love, a face like mine." His eyes flashed with rage, and he came rushing at me. I let a sword swing pass then brought the oak handle of my weapon up and into his rib cage. The chain mail tunic could not soften such a blow, and I felt the ribs give way. One must have broken and punctured a lung, for it was just a few seconds before I saw blood trickle from his mouth, his breathing belabored. I kept up the pressure.

"Why let one mention of Pristine draw blood? Now you'll have to finish this fight sucking air with one lung, coughing and spitting blood all the while." We circled. "All for a girl who never loved you." His eyes were still intense with anger, yet he smiled through bloody lips, savoring the release of his most cruel blow.

"No, she never loved me, but she'll stop loving everyone tonight. When I first saw you and your fools at the base of my mountain, I dispatched a Blue Wing to destroy her and the old man. Yes, I know where they live, and their bodies will be well digested and discarded in the drought by now." His words had frozen me. "No man will have my head *and* my lost love, not even you, John."

I was stunned, as stunned as if a giant claw had probed me to the very quick of my soul. I barely sensed his movement, and I reacted just late enough to take the tip of his sword into the flesh of my right shoulder, splitting it open. I could not know if he really had sent an assassin to kill Pristine, but I had to assume he was telling the truth. He loved her still, I knew, yet might sacrifice her to heal the one he loved the most--himself. As long as Pristine lived, he would have no peace.

My coming to The Rock may have been the spur he needed to order it done. Now I needed to finish the fight and race back to her. Yet he had the advantage on me now. His wounded foot hobbled him a little, but my split shoulder hurt badly. Sensing his opportunity, on he came with a barrage of sharp and heavy sword swings and sweeps, from the right, the left, upper cuts and from on high the blows came with dazzling speed.

It was all I could do to block and parry and defend myself. Though the underlying bones and tendons in my shoulder had suffered no damage, skin and muscle were mangled and to use my right arm was the essence of pain now. Blood flow freely from the wound, down my arm and onto the handle of my weapon, making it hard to keep a grip. Backing away from his onslaught, I somehow managed to evade his double edged sword for the moment. Yet if he continued to bring the fight to me, it could go his way in a hurry.

But he slowed suddenly, for something was hurt inside him. I watched him spasm, sucking wind, and cough up a chunk of something thick and deeply red. When I sensed his pause, I used my slippery grip against him by thrusting the scythe blade directly towards him and allowing the long wooden handle to slip through my hand, extending the weapon's reach. It was a move he hadn't looked for and the sharp edge of the blade caught him under his chin, opening a shallow gash in his neck. He backed off quickly, clutching at his wind pipe to make sure it hadn't been punctured. I saw his relief when he discovered it was a surface wound only.

"What's wrong Ar-ric, are you afraid to die? Worried that your hellish friends won't be so careful with your feelings when you end up in Hell with them?" He had backed off some fifteen feet, bending at the waist and breathing heavily with a gristly, gurgling breath, trying to rest for the next round. Between deep breaths he replied,

"John, my dull little believer, haven't you guessed it yet? I've made a deal with them. A covenant. I won't face an eternity of their company, or that of any others. I have chosen annihilation. At my death, I will simply cease to exist. That is my reward for turning. That was my bargain with them in the night."

"And it all ends, just like that? No justice, no judgment. Sounds like wishful thinking to me, Ar-ric. What makes you think Hell even has the power to annihilate? That kind of power is reserved!"

"John, John, Johnny my boy...what a fool you have always been. You still think Heaven holds more power than Hell? Why do Hunters and Demons still strive on this earth if that is true? No, the powers are equal, and you have no guarantee of victory!"

"And what guarantee of victory have you?"

SCYTHE

"My victory is simply an end. An end John, a ceasing of my very existence, a ceasing of the very soul. Eternal sleep--that will be victory enough for me, along with the death of those who have tormented me from my youth, you--and her."

He took his long sword in both hands again, and crept towards me. Clicking little hoofs again echoed across the floor and behind him I saw the Minions come from hiding and draw back, then release three more little arrows towards us. I dropped quickly to the floor to avoid the volley as the three burst into a fit of giggles again.

Ar-ric saw my reaction and ducked as well, though one of the arrows fluffed his hair as it passed close by him. He pulled a dagger from under the mail tunic and turned, letting fly a wild throw at the Minions that clanged on the stone floor near them. The three jumped and squealed again in terror, scampering back into their hide. I enjoyed a quick laugh at the Minions, who for all their evil intentions were very amusing. Ar-ric had turned to face me again, and I reflected on what he had said about the ending of his soul.

"Yes Ar-ric, I am a believer, but so are you. It must take at least a little dark faith for you to accept Hell's promise of an end," I said as I prepared to receive his next attack. "At least you still have the capacity to believe in something." This thought seemed to enrage him, as was my intention, for anger usually clogs the judgment with rashness.

"Nothing!" he yelled, charging now, "Nothing! I believe in nothing but death!" He came in with a straight thrust for my throat. I ducked under and blocked up with my scythe handle, guarding against the downward cut. He pulled back again for an overhand hack at me, and holding my scythe in my right hand, I reached for my hand-sickle and pulled it up in time to catch his sword blade in the sickle's curvature while whipping my long scythe blade around behind his legs and pulling back towards me.

I keep both edges of the scythe blade razor sharp, and the inner edge cut deeply into his calf muscles as I pulled, causing him to growl in pain. He tripped backwards over the blade, sprawling on the bloody floor, though he made it back to his feet before I could rush him. It would be hard for him to finish the fight so gashed in the legs.

Kicking at my blade, he moved away from me in obvious pain, blood running down the backs of his legs. The loss of blood slowed his movements, and from the look on his face, he knew he was in trouble. Worry verily dripped from him now that he was hobbled and bleeding in this a match to the death.

Ar-ric had said he was ready to die, ready for an ending, and thought all was prepared. It seemed that life without Pristine was a life not worth living, and so he would welcome the end. Yet what man really yearns for death, to embrace the cold hand and wade into the deep river of mystery? Ar-ric seemed to have doubts now about his near future, all contracts with Hell aside.

As for me, I was looking for a way to end the fight, for there is also a time in the death match that the stronger one knows he can strike the death blow and finish it. I took my next step with that very thought in mind. In a flash I saw how it would be, the first thrust of my scythe as I moved in on my wounded prey, then the likely reaction and counter strike by Ar-ric, my own second and third moves, all setting up the one killer slice that would come high and hard and irresistible, leaving my enemy's head lying bodyless at my feet. It was time.

I moved within striking distance and punched at his face with my weapon. When he moved to block my thrust, I sliced the blade across his arm, drawing fresh crimson to the surface. And I punched again at his face and he was late to block it and my weapon landed on his nose, breaking it with the sound of crunching gristle that could be heard across the room. His eyes were blurred now from the blow to his face and I whipped a round-house swing of my scythe at head-level and he managed to pull his sword up to block it. But the force was more than he counted on and his own blade was pushed flatly upside his head, knocking him to the floor.

I closed quickly, raising my scythe high, wanting to bring it down with all my strength to cleave Ar-ric in half. The scene of Ar-ric's harsh death flashed through my mind, I could see it happening and my scythe was raised high in the air to make it happen. But something dark and blue and terrible screamed sweeping above me, a cold draft of air chilling me as it came. My ears nearly burst at the high-pitched screech and I felt an impact, and the color of intense blue, a blue brighter than any other I have seen, filled my vision.

My heart sank from my chest as I realized the Blue Wing had returned. The impact I felt was this flying menace snapping my scythe handle with its beak, and suddenly I held only half an oak handle with a broken, jagged end where the blade once had been attached. The impact had knocked me down as well, and I saw the blade of my scythe lying on the floor a few feet away. But where was my winged mount? If the Blue Wing had survived the fight, my mount was likely dead.

I looked up and watched the Blue Wing fly and rise almost as high as the ceiling of the cavern we were in. As it reached the ceiling it banked slowly to its right and turned on me once again. I knew it would swoop in for the kill this time, and I now had no long-weapon to protect myself with. I checked Ar-ric, who was taking this chance to hold a cloth to his freshly cut legs, trying to stop the bleeding.

He looked pale now and couldn't afford to lose any more blood. I looked again at the flying demon which had started its descent now from on high. And from that height it would build tremendous force and speed as it dropped hundreds of feet in a near free-fall to crush me. I knew it would be more weight and force than I could withstand, but if I was to die, I resigned myself to die facing my foe and not running away.

I stood to my feet, pulled my hand sickles and braced for the attack as best I could. I could not worry about Ar-ric now, for the Blue Wing had pulled its wings tight to its sides in a death-dive. It meant to settle the issue, to drop upon me with irresistible force. On it came, seeming to grow larger and more ferocious as it came, screaming, and I could hardly admit it was happening, but I did not move. And just before it hit me, another object slid through the air at such speed that to blink was to miss it.

It was my mount, still alive and in the fight, and it hit the Blue Wing broadside in an explosion of tremendous force and blue scale-feathers. The cracking sound of wing bones snapping was unmistakable, and I knew I could not watch that match but must turn back to Ar-ric. His sword was already slicing air when I turned to him. Just able I was to catch his blade with my curved hand sickle, but I failed to guard low and he made me pay for that mistake with a foot kicked hard into my gut. It sent me sprawling across the hard marble floor. But I had cut him deeply earlier and his legs now buckled beneath him. The gargoyle was dominating the winged demon now, finishing its own death dance with the Blue Wing as they tumbled and crashed about the walls and floor of the cavern.

My breath had been kicked out of me. As I struggled to catch up my breathing, I looked over to Ar-ric. He could not stand, but with a bitter, wrath driven look on his face he was crawling, dragging himself towards me, sword in hand, leaving a glimmering trail of blood behind.

My hand sickle was nowhere to be seen, and Ar-ric was almost on me now. But something felt wrong--something was underneath me. I had fallen on some object. I realized what it was just as Ar-ric reached for me with his free hand. Though his legs were spent, the strength of his arm was unnatural with hate, and I allowed myself to be jerked towards him.

His sword was raised to strike me but it did not fall. His eyes were wide with disbelief, realizing now that something long and sharp and steely cold had punctured him underneath his chain mail tunic, passing through his lungs and exiting near his spine.

Ar-ric looked me in the eyes. His hand slowly released the sword and it clanged loudly against the bloody stone.

There we were on the cave floor, both knelling, face of face. Oddly enough, his face was no longer pale but was more lifelike now that his life was pouring forth from his wounds. He leaned to fall forward and I caught him, holding him upright. On the other side of the cavern, the gargoyle had worn down the broken Blue Wing and was ripping the last mournful breaths out of the thing.

Ar-ric tried to speak but could not, his pride and his hate and any good left within him all wrestling for control of his will. A long stream of blood dribbled from the edge of his mouth, running crimson down his polished silver chain mail.

We both knew that his end had come, and though he would have had me dying in his stead, I yet felt a pang of sorrow for a former comrade who had gone to the bad. I looked into his eyes and they were glassy, the light fast fading from them. Ar-ric looked back at me but said nothing. Something within told me that even a man such as this should not pass without a word being said. I could not apologize for defending myself, but I could express regret for the end he had come to, and whatever part I played in it.

"Ar-ric, I'm sor-". He cut me off, grabbing my shoulder and shaking his head 'no.' And a dying man has the right to determine what is allowed to mark his passing, so I obeyed. Not another word was uttered until he died trembling, kneeling with me there on the floor of a cave at the peak of the Mountain Unclimbable, where Ar-ric of the Rock twice discovered that Hell could not save him.

SCYTHE

Rag-dan and Kae-san had encountered no resistance upon their entry of the mountain, and when they had finally found their way to the central cavernous room they found me, kneeling and somber, beside Ar-ric's collapsed form. All was reverent silence for a time for they knew Ar-ric and I had once been the best of friends. At last, Kae-san broke the moment with a hand on my shoulder.

"Scythe, you've won a great victory here. Perhaps now is a time to celebrate it rather than mourn."

"Yes my friend, there will be a time to celebrate, but that time is not now. Ar-ric had gone to the bad long ago, I know, and that grievously. But that fact made his passing all the more sad to me, not less so. And what kind of man would I be," I continued, looking up at my two comrades, "if I could not mourn at least for what he had once been, if not for what he had become?"

Rag-dan retrieved a blanket off the couch and I used it to wrap Ar-ric's body in. His body could not stay there, it had to come with us.

Now that our present foes were destroyed, I shared with my fellows the threat Ar-ric had made against the life of Pristine and her father. I wanted to fly immediately to her, to protect her, but neither man nor mount were in any shape to fly anywhere--without food and rest we wouldn't last ten miles.

While we waited on some food to cook over one of the fires, there was something else we could do in the meantime, a dreadful task that had to be done sooner or later. We had to find Invictus. And just the thought of what we might find brought a great lump into my throat. But the Dreadlock takes care of its own without hesitation, no matter how painful or inconvenient that task may be. Invictus himself had proven that beyond doubt.

And so it was with a measure of dread that we went back out into the cold wind, taking flight on our gargoyles and gliding back down to the base of the mountain and the boulder that lean upon it. Invictus' body was not difficult to find, even by the light of the torches we each carried. We simply looked for the enemy dead, and there he was in their midst.

Never had I seen a face so delicate and gentle on a man I knew to be as fierce as they come. His golden-blond hair was streaked with blood, some his own and some that of the enemy's, some red and some black. One arm was but a bloody stump with bone protruding. The other arm was buried to the shoulder into the beak of the third and last Blue Wing he had killed. His hand still gripped his sword, though we only knew that because the point of his sword was sticking out of the Blue Wing's back.

Judging from the way the beast's twelve inch talons were buried into Invictus' body, it was not hard to guess how Invictus' young life had come to an end. The last I had seen of him was the flying sword thrust. That thrust had apparently carried the sword through the open break of the Blue Wing, cutting a hole clean through its body, killing the thing instantly. And the demon was no doubt as good as dead when its talons thrust forward by nerve and nature, puncturing Invictus' body in a dozen places.

Chapter Twenty
Honour the Brave Dead

In a rage Kae-san now began to whack away at the Blue Wing that had killed our fellow Dreadknaught, though we all knew it was long dead. We helped Kae-san regain himself, and then separated Invictus from the demon carcass. It was about that time when we heard Invictus' gargoyle come trotting up through the underbrush.

It had its master's severed arm in its mouth, having retrieved it from when it had fallen in the trees. The gargoyle tossed the arm playfully near the body of its former rider, as if to make it whole again.

We gathered the severed arm and tied it to Invictus' body, then tied his body to his mount. The four of us took flight again, one last ride for this Dreadlock. Up we flew into a sky almost black now with the coming night, lit only by moon and stars. Back to the Peak we flew, four gargoyles rising, three with Dreadknaughts sitting in bone saddles, one with a Dreadknaught draped over it, bearing the pall.

We took Invictus' body into the mighty cavern, for that is where he would rest in honour, on eternal patrol. Invictus' mother, who had been so proud of her son despite the seminary thing, had passed away since he had joined our band of brothers, and there were no other family members to take him home to.

The Dreadlock agreed that the Peak was the highest point in the lands known to us, and it alone was worthy to bear the remains of one who died in such a brave and selfless last act of battle glory. The funeral would held right there, and be carried out with the ceremony worthy of a fallen Dreadknaught.

First we located the crevice where the Minions were hiding. We thought we had them cornered for the kill, but they knew the labyrinth better than we and found their way to one of the entry points. We watched all three jump off the mountain, doing their best to fly into the cold thin air, though they seemed to be having a hard time of it. But our strength was spent and we did not pursue.

Next, we gathered what furnishings Ar-ric had about the place, set it on fire, and tossed it over the side of the mountain as well. We watched it burn as it fell, fireballs falling in the darkness. It would be ash long before it hit the ground.

Now that the place was cleaned and prepared, we took Invictus' body off the gargoyle, replacing it with Ar-ric's body. Rag-dan brought in pales of snow which we melted over the fire to clean the blood from the Invictus' corpse. His sword was cleaned with snow, polished with sand. We took fresh, clean clothing from Invictus' knapsack and dressed him in it, smoothing out the wrinkles with care.

We tied a noble looking cape around his shoulders, put his severed arm into the empty sleeve on the clean shirt. Then the four of us, each taking a corner of the cape, lifted his body gently and walked over to the center of the mighty room. We lay the body down quietly on the clean stone floor, then lay his freshly polished sword upon his chest, point down, and brought his cold hands up to grasp the handle. Having completed this task, we each took a torch in hand, and standing around the fallen brother, said our last farewells. After each man gave a personal remembrance, we joined our voices as one to recite the Last Rites of the Dreadlock.

THE CALLED, THE FEW, THE CHOSEN,
MEN OF HONOUR, BESTOWED BY GRACE,
CALLED TO A PURPOSE BEYOND OURSELVES,
CALLED FROM WITHIN THE HOLY RACE.

VESSELS OF WRATH, KEEPERS OF FLAME,
GIVING OUR ALL, FROM SWORD TO HELM,
FALLEN IN BATTLE, RESTING IN PEACE,
WATCH O'RE THIS SERVANT,
O LORD OF THE REALM

Many say that these farewells to the dead benefit the living, those who must continue on in this present cruel world, more than they help those who have passed. Yet I cannot help but believe that somewhere Invictus was listening, hearing, feeling the honour that we spread and spoke over him at this, his noble end. His life was young and brief, yet he died more than well, a sacrificial death so that others might live. What better way is there to die than that?

As we closed out this Dreadlock hymn to our Brave Dead, something caught my eye on the ceiling towards the other side of this cavern room. I had not noticed it before, but on a mantle of rock that jutted out from the ceiling there was something carved in the stone. It glittered in the firelight of our torches though we could not make out what it pictured.

Rag-dan walked closer to it, holding up his torch, and said that it appeared to be a likeness of a person's face. Ar-ric! I thought. Was your pride so consuming that you had to carve an image of yourself on the ceiling--your own icon that could worship you, its eyes following you about your stone fortress? Then Rag-dan noticed a shelf of rock formed on the cave wall.

"That shelf hangs almost directly underneath the image," Kae-san observed. "It must have been on that shelf that the stonemason stood when hewing the image." Kae-san dipped his torch low behind him, and then flung it up through the air and onto the shelf. Other debris must have been left on the shelf, and dry, for the fire jumped up and crackled higher when his torch landed there.

The three of us backed off to behold the image, amazed. No icon of Ar-ric the Betrayer looked down on us. Rag-dan voiced what we all felt, though none left alive in that cavern could feel what I was feeling.

"She's the most beautiful girl I've ever seen," said Rag-dan.

"Incredible," added Kae-san.

"Pristine," I explained, and in the twinkle of an eye all my worries for her safety vanished from my mind. Ar-ric had left me one last message, though he thought I would never see it.

"It is Pristine, gentlemen," I said, still gazing upon her image. "Pristine of the Bower Green, daughter of the Hunt-Master Ell-ory that trained both Ar-ric and I. Pristine was the one I loved, but duty took me from her. The same girl that Ar-ric loved but was rejected by. And now I know that she is safe, Ar-ric's threat was as empty as his soul."

"The stonework is exquisite--I've never seen it equaled. I wonder what mason was flown to this place to accomplish such craftsmanship?" wondered Rag-dan.

"It had to be him, Rag-dan, it had to be Ar-ric who carved that face," I answered.

"How can you be sure, Scythe?"

"Because it is perfect--utterly perfect. From the curve of the cheekbone to the hair-framed brow it is an utterly perfect likeness, in stone. And, unless another has taken her heart, I know of only three who have hearts emblazoned with the beauty of that face. The first is her loving father, the second would be me, and the third Ar-ric. This was Ar-ric's home for years, and only he could have carved that stone. Look at how he cut each angle, each feature to perfectly catch the light of a flame. This mountain must be formed of some uncommon substance, lending it both extra density as well as reflective qualities when sculpted. I can just picture Ar-ric in my mind, sitting on his sofa here as Pristine's face, cut with just the trace of a smile, looked down on him, watching over him through the lonely night."

"It must have taken years of tedious chisel-work...look at the detail," admired Kae-san.

"Not much else to do alone at the top of a mountain," I replied, echoing Ar-ric's own words.

"He must have loved her very much," Rag-dan mentioned.

"He loved her very much," I replied, "so much he could never have hurt her as he falsely told me. This," I continued, pointing to the hewn image, "is Ar-ric's soul bearing witness now to my own. She is safe, I know it. His love, though unreturned, has kept her safe, even from Ar-ric himself."

"You took his life in self-defense," said Kae-san, still looking up to Pristine. "We know what you did was right. He would have gladly taken your life and fed you to those Minions. Yet looking at the perfection of this lady-likeness, carved by love, I can't help but wonder if there was some good left in him--a drop only perhaps, but some at least?"

"I don't blame you for wondering, but you ask the wrong man," I replied. "I have no more judgments to make upon his soul. How easily could our places have been reversed back there in the house of the Hunt-Master, with me becoming the dark and bitter one! But for grace, I could have been the one dwelling alone up here for these long years."

It was time to seal the cavern which we had transformed into a crypt for our fallen brother Invictus. Rag-dan, who had some skill in stonework, knew just where to cut the stone above each entryway to weaken it. He did so with our help. And aided by the strength of our gargoyles and some heavy chains Ar-ric had stored, it was not long before we had collapsed tons of stone over the three entries into the Peak. The tomb was sealed now, and Invictus' earthly body would lay entombed in honour there for all time, with the face of that most beautiful girl watching over him. Somewhere, I am certain, his soul looked down and smiled upon the scene.

Chapter Twenty-One
The Long Way Home

The morning light had barely kissed the sky as we departed the Rock of the Ages. We had a long journey before us, and we were still weary from battle. But we could not stay on the Rock and, in truth, I needed to put some distance between myself and that place.

My feelings, as well as that of Rag-dan and Kae-san, were a crude mix of sorrow and joy, of pain and relief, of grief and hope. We had won a great battle, but paid for it with the life of our young brother Invictus.

Our mounts must have felt what flowed from us, for their flight echoed our feelings. Low they would drop, their bellies almost sweeping the black treetops, and then, regaining strength, they would soar into the heights, through the clouds and into the purple heavens, their wings lit by the stars. Then, slowly, they would sink again back towards the earth.

Despite this erratic flight pattern, we did not stop them, but allowed them to fly as they pleased.

Being the leader of the hunt-pack magnified my feelings, both the good and the bad ones. The guilt over having lived while Invictus had died was overwhelming at times. At other times, my soul was overtaken with the dizzy elations of our most important victory in the history of the Dreadlock, perhaps one of the greatest in the history of the whole Order.

Against all odds we had won a victory that could clean our names so wrongly soiled. It was a victory of which the news would spread quickly. Only two months had passed since we were accused at the Council, so the issue would still be fresh on the minds of all. The timing was well nigh perfect for this win, I figured, as an answer to the charges of treachery, and my mind would thrill at these thoughts as my mount lifted me higher.

But after a while the beast would level off its flight, then begin to sink earthward, through and then below the clouds. The earth-air, made dusty from all that goes on there, was thicker in my lungs than that air above the clouds.

At the low points I would remember the young man entombed within the cold stone, forever young, but lifeless. He had been under my care, and I had led him to his death. Sure, he made his choice to die, but in dying he had done the impossible and taken out three Blue Wings, and that was certainly the act that spurred us to victory.

His death had been ridiculously brave and noble, but there were still questions to be answered. Had I led him to his end for reasons as noble as his last act? Or had I led the men to the Rock so that my reputation might be saved?

I knew there was more to it than that. Surely when I led them there I was thinking also of the Cause, the wider war, Ar-ric's ability to hurt our friends if left unchecked. My motives were as muddy and unclear as a bog. Had I let Invictus die for some higher purpose, or for my own reputation? How could I know my own heart at the moment? How could I judge these things? Who could help me sort it all out? Jonasius? Ell-ory? The Dreadknaughts? No, all of them were good men and brave, but what I needed right then was a girl-- *the* girl.

But could I call her my own yet? What made her mine, words spoken far and away on the sand by a sea? There was but one way to answer that question, and it would be found in no gathering of brave Huntsmen, no Council of Elders. It could be found only in her arms.

I needed to get back to Pristine. I could scarcely believe that she had waited through lonely years for me. How could she have known I would break my vow and return? How could she have known I would find her? Was there some unspoken bond of love made between our hearts that my mind remained ignorant of? I know much of battle, I decided, but perhaps I know little of love, or of the fairer sex.

On we flew. It took days of flying over virgin forests just to regain the lands of men. Then we first delivered Ar-ric's remains to the village of Fog Castle. It was a known Hunt-Order stronghold, visited by hunters of every stripe year round. We had a coffin nailed together. We sent word to Jonasius that the body of his would-be assassin could be picked up there, a message sure to get Jonasius' attention. Making sure that the body would be handled with reverence was important to me. Ar-ric had once been a Hunter, and though he went to the bad, his remains deserved to be treated with the respect fitting any Son of Adam.

Taking leave from Fog Castle, we gave our beasts' wings a rest, taking a slow land route to a place called Will Boatright's Lagoon. The central feature of that place was a large freshwater lagoon, teeming with fish and eel. It was considered a safe haven for men like us, a place to recoup and refresh, with less bustle and movement than Fog Castle.

Those who knew of it knew it was a place where a hunter could rest after battle, recuperating from injuries, rearming, and if need be, recruiting. A man could sleep in his own tent, unarmed and unworried. Bellies were filled with solid food and sweet fruit from local orchards. And the fish and eel caught daily were cleaned and fried over open fires every evening, along with potatoes and green tomatoes rolled in flour, and garden vegetables we steamed over hot coals. All of this was then dumped on a long wooden table.

Men would smell the food, bringing their appetites to the table, raking great portions onto their plates. Other men would simply move along the edge of the table, grazing on the delicacies. The atmosphere was light and relaxing, far from the worries of war and battle, and it was just what my men and I needed at that point in our journey. The recent events had taken a physical toll on us, especially on me. Ar-ric had wounded me deeply enough to weaken my blood, but good food was restoring my strength.

While we relaxed at supper one evening, a thin little man, a servant from the village, was sweeping up around us. He had thin black hair that was pasted about a boney head. I noticed that he kept looking at me out of the corner of his eye as he worked, and he had an irritated look on his pale colored face.

"Is there anything wrong, friend," I said to him.

"Wrong with what?"

"With anything?"

He shook his head side to side, continuing to watch me as he worked the broom. His voice was high pitched, squeaky and feminine.

"I'm not your friend, and there is nothing wrong here, not with me. I do my honest work and say little. I keep to myself and leave things as they are. No need for me to touch the bloody business. No need for me to stir up evil, your kind takes care of that."

He said all this while working his broom in short, jerky movements. I looked at him a moment, chewing my food slowly, before making a reply. He kept his shirt buttoned all the way to his neck. His pants were pulled up almost above his naval, giving him an odd look.

"Friend," I said, "I have no problem saying your work is honest. But perhaps you have a problem saying that about mine. You do not appreciate the Hunters, I take it?"

SCYTHE

"What is there to appreciate? Some can't leave evil alone, some must stir the pot. Claim to hunt down evil, claim to do some good, but methinks it's just to get glory for oneself. Why not just leave things be! There is evil in the world and you can't change that. Bad things happen and that's that. I say stirring up evil only begets more evil!" His squeaky voice grew louder as he spoke, and I could tell he had brooded over his opinion for some time.

"When a man finds evil in this world," I questioned in reply, "should he not oppose it. Should he not destroy it if possible? What kind of man would not try to make a better world?"

"Don't paint yourself a hero, Mister, don't drape bloody deeds with holy cloth. An honest man does an honest day's labor. He lives cleanly and minds his own business. I've worked in this village my whole life, cooking and cleaning up for those who run about the woods shedding blood." He continued to jerk his little broom about without looking down, his shoulders hunched. "I go along with whatever I'm given, that's what a man should do. Leave the world to run itself. Running to extremes is just a way to get out of real work."

"I must disagree with you, friend. In fact, you couldn't be more wrong," I said calmly.

The little man stopped sweeping, his face twisting now into a scour.

"Are you saying I'm evil," he hissed at me, "are you saying my life doesn't count?!"

"It's not that you're evil, it's just that you never give evil any worries. I will harass evil till my death while you will live at peace with it till yours. Now which would you say is the more extreme position?" He looked at me with a hateful eye for a moment, and said no more as he stomped away.

Chapter Twenty-Two
Bring the Pain

We tarried in that place for a few days, and word of our victory on the Rock began to come in. Strangers whispered our names, pointing. The bolder ones sought us out at our tents, curious for information about the battle. What were the Blue Wings like? How could you have scaled Mount Unclimbable? How bravely had the fallen young warrior fought? The questions came quickly around the night camp-fires, and we answered them as best as our tired, worn minds could manage.

It was rumored that the Baptines passed through while we were at the Lagoon, though we never laid eyes on them. If they did come through, they were sure to have heard of our recent adventure. We hoped Jonasius had heard as well. Nothing of importance ever escaped him, we were always told.

After a few more days, having had our fill of the kind of rest only to be had on stomachs full of savory-rich food and drink, we gathered our things, said our goodbyes, and struck out. Our strength gathered, it was my plan to return at once to the islands where a beautiful young lady walked lonely beaches thinking, I hoped, of me. She would be waiting there for me, I felt sure. Whether her father would welcome the sight of my return I could not say. Little did I know that a higher authority would change my fragile plans.

We had been airborn for nearly eight hours when we spotted a town below. It had become our usual custom to land in clearings of the forest where we were unlikely to encounter any bystanders, since the sight of our gargoyles descending from on high was bound to frighten the average villager. We made land in just such a clearing and the men and I made our way into the village on foot.

The first hint of trouble came as we entered the town to find the local tavern. As we walked down the main street that cut through the town's center, we began to pass other Hunters. None of them recognized us, but we recognized faces from the Lionloff gathering.

We could tell that something was very wrong. The men looked worn, not the worn weariness that comes to all who attempt hard work, but the kind that is deeper, a kind of fatigue of the soul. It is specially seen in the eyes. The men looked discouraged and defeated. Not only that, but we noticed that some wore blood-stained tunics, and had wounds fresh and still draining. They were armed, but

carried their weapons like heavy weights, having no spring in their
step at all.

Worst of all, there was fear on their faces. A Hunter can remain
effective after many a cut and blow, but if he lose his nerve, he is
likely done.

Finding a tavern, the Dreadlock entered through a swinging
double-door. There we saw another small group of our kind, demon
Hunters for sure, but in the same condition as those we passed in the
street outside, covered in blood, dust and sorrow. They were sitting
at a corner table with their backs to the wall, trying not to look like
Demon Hunters but doing a poor job of blending in.

"Everywhere we look," I said to my men, "there are wounded
Hunters, men who look defeated. Something has happened, some
event, near this place." A part of me wanted to ignore the business of
others, to follow my own concerns, to follow my desire back to that
island where Pristine walked the beaches, waiting for me. But a
stronger part of me called 'duty' made war on my desires, forcing me
to know, to find out what was going on amongst my bloodied
brethren. 'Duty' had become a heavy burden upon me. Yet I asked
myself, could a man honour-bound do more than his duty? Would he
ever dare to do less? I knew what must be done.

Walking over to their table, I introduced myself and my men. Two
of them would not raise their heads, judging our intentions by
watching the movement of our feet only. One did raise his head,
looking at me with large eyes that stared from under the brim of a felt
hat. That one saw something familiar in me and spoke.

"I know you--or at least know of you. I saw you at the Council.
You are called by the name of your chosen weapon, a farmer's
implement that you slay demons with--I think they call you 'Hoe,' he
said sincerely.

"Scythe," I quickly corrected. "I am called Scythe, and with these
men I form the Dreadlock. We are Hunters, as are you."

The men at the table looked embarrassingly at one another and
then around the room, realizing their cover was thin indeed. We
joined them at their table and began to inquire as to what had
happened to them.

Sometimes Hunters can be very aloof, keeping their business to
themselves, which is almost never a bad idea. When these at first did
not answer my questions I thought they might just want to be left
alone. Clearly these men were shaken, so jaded by some trauma that

they would hardly speak. Finally, the one who had recognized me began to tell the tale we needed to hear.

Looking from me to his mug of dark brown coffee he began to describe a terrible scene. His hunt-group had been called to a regional meeting of Hunters. When they arrived at the grove of elms in which the meeting was to take place, they saw that a few score of Hunters were already there, waiting, with more arriving by the moment. Yet not one seemed to know why the meeting had been called.

"Suddenly," the Hunter detailed, "the tree tops began to rustle as dark clouds blotted out the sun." Horses had spooked. A strong wind kicked up quickly, carrying a strange, unearthly sound to their ears. What happened next was unclear. The noise grew as loud as to almost burst their ears, he claimed.

One of the men said that he saw some of the elm trees being uprooted, though no visible cause for it was seen. The uprooted trees were tossed rolling over the gathered Hunters. Bodies of men and horses were crushed amidst cries of pain and alarm. Men were impaled with jagged limbs.

Then something passed overhead, blotting out the remaining light. Darkness suddenly took the forest, with the rolling, splintered trees and the howling, deafening wind bringing chaos and confusion. An evil presence seemed to fill the very air, choking the life from man and beast alike. Flashes of blue were seen even in the darkness, tearing through the men, the headless bodies of Hunters flipping in the air as it passed. One man claimed to have seen a hollow face, huge and bodyless, hovering over the scene of destruction. Nearly a hundred hunters had come to that grove, but fewer than fifteen had left there alive. Most of what survived we had passed as they straggled through the village.

We learned all we could from the three. Their personal hunt-team had numbered sixteen as they arrived at the elm grove, but this few were all that survived of it. I called over the Master of the Tavern, a squat little man with a full mustache and but little hair above his ears. Shaking his hand, I pressed an unseen but heavy gold coin into it, and spoke to him quietly.

"Sir, I want you to put these men up for the night. Give them the warm rooms, the ones with fire-hearths. I want them to have clean water, soap and towels. Before they sleep, serve them a meal of fresh bread, meat and cheese. Make sure they are not disturbed. All the comforts this coin affords will be shown them." The man took the coin, examined it, felt its heft, and finally bit into it. Then he smiled.

"Yes sir, it will be precisely as you have asked," replied the Tavern Master as he clapped his hands together thrice in a quick burst. Hearing the claps, two young boys appeared out of nowhere and came running to receive their orders. The boys then hurried up a set of stairs leading to the second floor where the sleeping rooms were located. The little man turned back to me.

"Shall I prepare rooms for you and your men as well, sir?"

"No, I think not. I cannot sleep until I find out what I need to know. Please prepare four packs of food that we may take with us as we go. How much more do I owe you for that?" I asked as I reached back into my pocket for more coin. But the little fellow grabbed my arm, not allowing me to bring out the more.

"No more," he said, "Your gold has cared for these men--my silver will care for yours. If you are who I think you are, I owe you much more than a few packs of food. All will be ready soon." With that the man walked away, back into the kitchen that sat behind the bar.

This man was acting as if he knew me, but how could he? Or did he merely mistake me for someone else? Puzzling, but that was a question for another time. I had more pressing matters that called for my attention.

While we waited for the food to be prepared, I gathered the Dreadlock outside to talk, away from the noise of the tavern now crowded with hungry and thirsty villagers. But before I could speak, the men began to question me.

"Scythe," asked Kae-san, "what do you make of all this?"

"It is impossible to say yet, but clearly something major has taken place. I can't say for sure what exactly took place in that elm grove, but it smells of an ambush. I don't know what it all means, but I don't mind telling you the mention of the blue demons sent a chill down me."

"I had the same stirrings, Scythe. I doubt not that the events just related to us inside that tavern could even be connected to our adventures at the Rock, and to Ar-ric's death," added Rag-dan.

"How could that be," questioned Kae-san, "so little time has passed since the Rock, and we left none alive to tell the tale? How could word have spread so fast?"

"Mysterious, yes," I replied, "but in these times the mysterious has become the normal. Until I learn otherwise, I will assume that these things are all connected. It is the only safe assumption to make. Therefore, we cannot return just yet to the isle of Ell-ory." Surprisingly, Rag-dan objected.

"But Scythe, will not Pristine be worried and will she not be looking for you? It would be wrong of you to leave her in a limbo of doubt," he said firmly.

"You are right old friend, I must send her word of our victory, and of my personal safety. The question is how? Would you go to her, Rag-dan, if I asked it?"

"Ask anything, Scythe, and it is done," replied faithful Rag-dan.

"Then I will send you with a message to Pristine and her father. That message will include not only news of our victory, and of Invictus' tragic death, but of the events of the elm grove just related to us. Rag-dan," I said, putting a hand on his shoulder, "talk it all over with Ell-ory. He is a hard man but fair, and his heart has always been with the Cause. Assure him that every enemy at the Rock was taken down, none were left alive to cause us future trouble. That will take some convincing, so you must relate to him every detail of what happened there. Then let him talk. Listen to his words, and gather his wisdom. See what he makes of the event at the elm grove. There is much we can glean from his experience. While you are away, Kae-san and I will find out more about the events at the elm grove. We will learn all we can."

"And what about Pristine, any message for her?" Rag-dan was grinning.

"Yes, tell her that my heart is hers forever, and that only business of the most urgent kind has kept me from her side. Tell her I will be returning to her just as soon as possible, and tell her that I said that all the power of Hell itself cannot keep me from seeing her again."

The three of us made our way back to our gargoyles, remounted, and kicked our beasts skyward. The faithful creatures responded with powerful wing strokes that whipped the tree limbs and stirred the grass.

We rose in the air about ten tree lengths high, then we bid Rag-dan farewell on his journey to take my message back to Pristine and her father. Rag-dan turned the nose of his mount due-east and headed out. He had not made a thousand yards from us when suddenly, the sky, just blue, began to turn blood red.

A harsh hot wind scattered the clouds, pushing our winged mounts through the air so that they had to fight with all their might just to remain aright. A loud buzzing noise filled the air around us, so loud it seemed meant to deafen us. I felt my hair standing on end, presaging the lightning bolts that began to fall across the garnet sky with a crack.

The wind gale stronger, rolling us now through the air, and we could not stay airborn. We were forced to make land as best we could, yet we made it to the ground below and, as if by miracle, no one was hurt. We found ourselves in a field green with short rye grass.

Rag-dan had been wind-pushed back towards us and was there as well. Almost immediately, all of nature's aberrations ceased: the red canopy of sky dissolved into a sea of clear blue, not another lightning bolt fell, the winds ceased. As quickly as it had started it fell to nothing. And there in the middle of that rye field amongst us sat a man on a white horse. The man was hooded and cloaked, and though he was yet to show his square jaw and golden hair, I recognized Jonasius' messenger.

"Lukas, what manner of greeting is this? I was nearly thrown from my mount." The man folded the hood back, showing us the same face we had seen in that cellar of the village inn on the night the horseman was stumped by Crokow.

"Jonasius the Whiteheart sends greetings. My master also sends congratulations on your splendid victory at the Rock of the Ages. The deeds of the Dreadlock are being praised, even feasted, in Jonasius' own halls. My master knows that Blue Wings die hard."

"I don't recall being invited to any feasts in our honour," Kae-san pointed out. Lukas, the ever solemn messenger, heard the smart remark but made no acknowledgement of it.

"Jonasius further acknowledges the loss of one of your Dreadknaughts, and has offered prayers for that man's soul." I was interested to know that Jonasius already had knowledge of our work at the Rock, and of Invictus' death. Yet I knew that 'congratulations' was not the only reason for Lukas' appearance amidst such audacious natural phenomena. There was more to hear.

"Thank your master for his recognition and sympathy. Now, we would hear the rest of it." Lukas did not hesitate.

"The Dreadlock is being called to a gathering."

"Another Council, so soon?" asked Rag-dan.

"Not a Council, a gathering of warriors, but not for talking." I then realized the seriousness of what the messenger was saying.

"Lukas," I asked, "are you calling us to join battle with you?"

"Yes Scythe, a great battle is coming, it will take place soon. Both sides are gathering forces. We expect to meet our gathered foe somewhere near the Basin of Zanzinthrall. Our scouts tell us *that* is where the enemy is collecting. Jonasius would strike them there before they can organize for battle. That means a double-timed sprint to the Basin will be required to execute my master's stratagem and catch our enemy off guard."

"What can you tell us about the happenings at the elm grove not far from here? Something terrible happened there," said I.

"That was an ambush, probably set up by the Guillelocks posing as Hunters, leading our friends into a trap," replied Lukas. The Guilelocks were men, evil spies, humans who were in league with Hell and the demons. Ar-ric had been of that class, though once a soldier of the Light. Lukas continued, "The attack at the elm grove was the enemy's first major offensive in the new battlefront that is now taking shape. Jonasius thinks it was a retaliatory strike."

"Retaliation for what?" I asked. Lukas paused before answering.

"Retaliation for Ar-ric's death, and for all that you wrought at the Rock of the Ages. The enemy considered Ar-ric and the Rock as its privileged possession. No other Hunter had ever dreamed of attacking that fortress. The enemy did not take the loss lightly." This statement made Kae-san bristle.

"Are you saying the Dreadlock is held in blame for killing Ar-ric and his Blue guardians? That we were somehow wrong in what we did?" But Lukas turned sternly on Kae-san.

"I am giving you no opinion, only the confirmed facts. I can tell you that some that sit at my master's side thought it a foolhardy move to attack the Rock. They would have let Ar-ric stay there with his guardians, virtually out of the war, rather than provoke the enemy."

"Sounds like the false wisdom of a Baptine!" snapped Kae-san.

"It might be pointed out to your Master's advisors that Ar-ric and his guardians are indeed out of the war, permanently out," added Rag-dan, taking up the argument. "The Dreadlock cares not whether the enemy be provoked, for we will see the enemy dead!"

The messenger Lukas kept his face cold, refusing to be baited to anger by my men, men who were naturally frustrated at knowing those advisors to Jonasius had cast aspersions upon our work at the Rock. His reply was stern but calmly measured.

"Jonasius, though cautious, has always favored a more aggressive stratagem than those advising him. Your victory at the Rock of the

Ages brought him joy. Whether it provoked the enemy or not is debatable. But that debate can wait until for another time. All that matters right now is that Soldiers of the Light must quickly gather at the Basin of Zanzinthrall to face the gathering Darkness." But Kae-san had one last jab.

"Are you saying, messenger boy, that the honour of the Dreadlock is still in question, even after the Rock? What is our standing?" But Lukas snapped back with his final word, and it was a powerful one.

"Your standing, Dreadknaught, may depend on your response to this call to battle. But know this; you have not fought your last Blue Wing--we believe that Blue Wings will lead the demon army that we meet at Zanzinthrall. The Dreadlock may be the only Hunters who have faced them in battle and lived to tell it. Oh no, Dreadlock, you will be no rear guard in this action. It is you, the Dreadlock, who have been chosen to be the tip of our Holy Spear! The Basin of Zanzinthrall is where Jonasius bids you fly--and to make all haste!" With that, Lukas mounted and galloped off, and just as he entered the tree line, a blaze of white light flashed, engulfing him, and he vanished.

The men gathered to me in a tight circle of three, taking stock of the new situation.

"Well," Rag-dan said, looking at me.

"Well," I replied and began to chuckle for some involuntary reason. Rag-dan and Kae-san caught my chuckle and began to laugh with me. The seriousness of the situation was no laughing matter, but, perhaps, our souls just needed to laugh, as all souls sometimes do.

"And so, gentlemen," I said, "we will live to see a major pitched battle of gathered host, a titanic match between Light and Darkness."

"Not only that, Scythe, he even said we would play an important role in this battle," said Kae-san.

"Aye, the tip of the spear," added Rag-dan.

Kae-san folded his arms and said,

"That would be the pointy end." We looked at him and burst into laughter again. I put a gloved hand on each man's shoulder.

"Let us mount-up and make our way to the Basin of Zanzinthrall. I want to get a look at this army of rag-tags Jonasius is putting together for this adventure. My message to Pristine will have to wait."

"Whatever army Jonasius has assembled to join us, I think there is one thing for certain--the tip of the spear is going to bring the pain," said Rag-dan with a glimmer of fresh battle-joy in his eye.

SCYTHE

Chapter Twenty-Three
A New Recruit?

We called our gargoyles to us and mounted the three. All eyes fell on Invictus' mount, which was looking very lonely at the moment, its big bright eyes lost in sadness.

"That gargoyle," said Rag-dan, pointing at the bare-backed beast, "really needs a rider."

"Yea, how long will this trio fight before we return to a quartet?" asked Kae-san.

"It is my sense of things, men, that we should consider a new recruit immediately, though be in no rush to choose one. That gargoyle needs a rider to keep it at its full potential and skill, as well as to carry a blade into battle," I pointed out. "But until we find one willing, able and suited to the ways of the Dreadlock, Invictus' beast will serve as a pack animal when we travel, and it will attack alongside us in battle, riderless if necessary. It will likely be months or even years until we find a man with guts enough to ride it, let alone fly it into a fray. Few men of Invictus' quality walk the earth. He will not be easily replaced."

All nodded their heads in hardy agreement and we took to the air. We set out on a north-westerly course, straight for the Basin of Zanzinthrall, a thousand mile trek as the gargoyle flies.

As we winged our way towards our destination, we passed over landscape that almost took my breath in its beauty. How can a world so full of dark things yet contain something so awesomely beautiful?

We saw crystal flowing rivers with jeweled bottoms winding through valleys lush and green. Over the plains we witnessed enormous herds of wild antelope grazing in seas of wavy tall grass. And then the plains would give way to rolling hills, and the hills would grow into a range of mountains, and now and then a snow covered peak would appear above the clouds, forcing us to fly a bit higher into the cold air.

Those icy peaks never failed to remind me of The Rock of the Ages, and of Invictus, and how he died so bravely. Our long flight gave me time to think. That battle at the Rock of the Ages was only the beginning of vindication for the Dreadlock. We would have to prove ourselves again as leaders of an attack in this coming battle. Would Jonasius send us on a suicide mission just to prove our faithfulness?

SCYTHE

I did not know the answer to that question, I only knew that we were going to battle and that no one's survival was promised.

It was several hours into our flight that Kae-san, our sharp eyed tracker, edged his mount close enough to me that I could hear him yell.

"Don't look now, Scythe, but we have someone, or some thing, following us."

Astonished, I tried to sneak a look backwards without alerting whatever it was that Kae-san had seen. It took several tries before I spotted it flying a mile or so behind. The thing was keeping its distance, and its color seemed to be shifting to match whatever landscape it was crossing over. I would not have noticed it had Kae-san not pointed it out to me, and how *he* spotted it I do not know.

But there was no doubt that something was following us. Best I could tell, the thing was larger than any bird, but not nearly as large as one of our gargoyles. With its reflective quality, small size and ability to fly, it occurred instantly to me that it was perfectly designed to trail us! It had a long, outstretched neck with a smooth, egg-shaped head at the end. Its body was like a larger version of the head, egg shaped and smooth. I saw no feet, only a long, flat tail acting as a rudder in the wind, and featherless wings that waved in the air as if many-jointed. Its feet, I figured, were tucked underneath the thing as it flew. I wanted to know as much about it as possible, for I had already decided we were going to catch it if possible.

I instructed Kae-san to duck down behind the next ridge, wait for it to pass over and get behind the thing. Kae-san carried out the move with perfect patience, first getting ahead of us. He did not hurry his descent but took it slowly before disappearing behind a rising hillock.

Rag-dan and I, along with the extra gargoyle, flew on for several miles, giving Kae-san ample time to make his move. Our timing would have to be impeccable, for it wouldn't take the thing long to figure out that one of our number had doubled back and gotten behind it.

When I thought the time was right, I signaled Rag-dan and we turned our winged mounts quickly and sharply, flying back now towards the creature. We flew fast and bore down hard, but the thing following us had kept its distance and therefore had plenty of time to see us coming back at it.

I had hoped it would at least turn around and back-trail, running directly into the trap Kae-san would spring. But whatever it was, it

was clever enough to suspect a trap and instead of turning around
when it spotted us, it simply went to ground, punching down into the
forest that we were over-passing. Kae-san saw it make its move, so he
landed in the forest somewhere behind the creature while we went to
ground in front of it, and spread about.

We now had our enemy between us, enclosed in a triangle of
Dreadknaughts, and we had but to reduce the size of the triangle by
moving inward. We would have to watch the gaps between us to
guard against the creature's escape. Yet we found that the things
ability to take on the color of its surrounding was a big advantage for
it. We drew our weapons, ready to attack, though I wanted the thing
taken alive if possible so we might study it for some clue as to who
sent it and why.

The woods we were in were not as thick as some we had been in
before. The underbrush had been knocked down, probably by
lightning induced fire the summer before. This improved visibility
and worked to our advantage. When we had closed our triangle to
about half its original size we dismounted our gargoyles, sending
them out in either direction. This would help us close any gaps in our
lines, changing the triangle now into a circle. With their keen senses
of smell and sight, our gargoyles would be hard to get past unnoticed.
Tighter we drew the net as we moved cautiously but anxiously
towards the center of our kill radius.

Suddenly, Kae-san came barreling through the trees towards me.
Seeing me he called out,

"Did you see it? It must have ran right by you!" In truth I had seen
nothing, but then heard a loud rustling in the woods behind me. And
there it was, running on four legs. The thing had slipped past me
unnoticed. Kae-san was mounted, chasing after it. I fell in behind
him, calling to Rag-dan and our mounts all the while. On we chased
the thing through the woods. Rag-dan and our mounts caught up
with me and soon all three dreadlocks were mounted and gaining
ground on the thing.

We drew closer to the thing, and we knew it was a demon-servant
of some type. It had two long fangs projecting downward from its
thin mouth and it made an evil, snake-like hissing noise as it ran. Our
mounts covered the ground well, remembering that they were land
beasts years before discovering their wings. Kae-san was closest to
the thing and I saw him pull an arrow on his bow-string. He loosed
the arrow, and we watched it fly true to the target, making solid

contact with the creature's back. But the thing had a protective hard-shell at that spot and Kae-san's shaft bounced harmlessly away.

Again Kae-san drew and loosed an arrow, again the bodkin hit the mark squarely but bounced off again, failing to penetrate. Kae-san was frustrated but determined to bring the thing down. Finally Kae-san drew closer yet to the fleeing enemy, and was drawing back an arrow on his bow-string. But before he loosed the shaft, another arrow came streaking in from our front-left, hitting the little demon-servant in its side as it was jumping over a fallen log.

The creature's hard-shell protective plate covered its sides as well, but it did not matter. The mighty shaft that bore into it was longer, heavier and faster moving than any arrow I had ever seen before or since. It looked more like a small spear than an arrow. The iron tipped projectile penetrated the demon's hide and shell with such force that it pierced clean through the thing, spiking it off the ground, nailing it cleanly to the truck of a nearby tree. Kae-san was stunned at the sight, looking around to see which Dreadknaught had so bested his archery skills. But he could see by the looks on our faces that neither Rag-dan nor I had made the shot. Someone else was in the forest.

We heard that someone as he ran towards his kill, his boots crunching into the leaf covered forest floor. A huge fern-covered embankment hid us from his vantage point, and the mystery archer did not see us as he came up at full trot to examine his prey. Still not seeing us, he was looking over the shaft-impaled thing stuck to the tree.

"Nice shot," I said loudly. Startled, the archer turned quickly on us. His hands, I noticed, moved so fast that he had another dangerous shaft knocked and the string pulled all the way to his ear as he turned to aim at us. No one moved.

"Easy there, fellow," I said, careful not to make any sudden moves. "All on the same side here." He had the arrow aimed right at me, which made me nervous considering what I had just witnessed with the now impaled beast hanging limply on the long, bloody shaft. I noticed that the archer's right arm and shoulder, the ones he used to pull the bow-strong back with, were nearly twice the size of those on his left side. I have seen many archers, some raised with a bow in their hands, but I'd never seen such over-development as this. This had to be an inborn trait handed down from his fathers, which gave me a hint to the man's history.

Kae-san, still smarting from being out-shot, was less patient.

"Lower that bow, boy. We mean you no harm!" Kae-san's voice was loud and angry. But the young man's only reaction was to shift his aim from my chest to that of Kae-san.

"You mean *me* no harm?" spoke the archer, mocking Kae-san's threat. "You live only as long as I can hold this string back. And who are you calling 'boy'?" Kae-san, for his part, showed no fear at all, his pride driving him on in a test of will and nerve, though he kept his hands off his weapons.

"I am calling you 'boy', boy! And the last person to aim a shaft at me ended up eating it, point first. Put the arrow down!" Kae-san ordered manfully.

"Well," said the undaunted archer with a chuckle, arrow still drawn to ear, "I would like to see you make me eat this one." Kae-san's pride now overcame his good sense and his hand fell to his sword. At Kae-san's first flinch the archer released, and the black feathered shaft jumped with amazing speed from the bow. I had no idea Kae-san could match the arrow's speed, but by the time the shaft made it to Kae-san, he had pulled his sword blade into the arrow as he shifted his body sideways. The sword-blade cut the shaft in two, but not quite in time, for the arrows' iron tip ripped through the skin of Kae-san's right shoulder as it passed by. The wound was not serious, but by the time Kae-san had recovered his balance, the young archer already had another shaft notched and drawn.

"Nice move, very quick you are--but the next one takes your heart!" said the archer.

Kae-san simply sheathed his sword and smiled through the pain burning now in his shoulder. The young man with the bow was puzzled.

"What, not even going to try this time? Fine, then die like a gentle she-dog." But Kae-san merely laughed at the young man.

"Laughter is it? Dieing, like a laughing, bleeding she-dog! You laugh, demon rider, but I will have the last laugh!" The archer must have thought our gargoyles to be from hell, though not the first one to make that mistake. But he waited too long and never released the arrow. He heard Kae-san say,

"This is no demon I ride, boy, and this one is not the only one." It was at that precise second that Invictus' gargoyle burst forth from where it had been stalking the young archer. The young man's face was pure terror as the gargoyle came roaring over and on top of him.

The bow and the arrow were dropped and forgotten as the archer fought for his life, though there was no use in fighting. The gargoyle had him pinned to the forest floor and was baring its fangs to sink into the young man's ribcage when I thrust my scythe into the small space between the beast's dripping fangs and his new-found prey. The gargoyle realized I was asking that the archer be spared, and let out a roar in protest before turning and trotting away.

I turned and looked at the young man on the ground, who took a moment to convince himself that he was still alive. Extending a hand to the archer, I pulled him off the ground and helped brush his clothes of debris.

"What's your name, archer?" I asked.

"Name's none of your business," he replied with an attitude. Kae-san had dismounted and made his way over to us.

"What are these creature's you people are riding? They must be from hell!"

"They are called gargoyle," replied Kae-san, "and they know the difference between "sick 'em" and "go get 'em.

"If that thing comes near me again I will drive a shaft in its gizzard!" said the archer. However, his bravado aside, I was anxious to know who he was and how much he knew.

"Do you know what it was that you just killed?" I asked him.

"Ofcourse, it was an Iskarit-devil, handy as a spy and hard to spot. And you fools nearly fouled the only shot I was likely to have," said the brassy youngster.

"You seem mighty unappreciative of the men that just spared your life, boy," Kae-san said in a voice heavy with challenge.

"What are you people doing in these woods? We are far from any road or village," said the archer, ignoring Kae-san for the moment. I spoke up before Kae-san had a chance to.

"We were flying over these woods, but had to come to ground to pursue the little demon that had been following us. I wanted to catch it alive, but your excellent archery skills have ended any chance of that."

"Flying eh?" he said, narrowing his sharp eyes to study the wings of our mounts. "Now *that is* useful! Turning back to me he then asked, "So why would you want an Iskarit any way but dead? What man wants a demon to live one second longer than necessary, except one in league with hell?"

SCYTHE

"Knowledge of the enemy is useful in building strategy," I replied, "You will learn this if you hunt long enough. How long have you been hunting hellions?"

"Since I could weild a man's bow. First of my line and young with no Hunt-Master. My father taught me how to track, my brother how to shoot, and the War in the Red Lands made me hard for the fight. I've got no taste for Lords and their bickerings, so I entered the Hunt."

"The Red Lands were your home? Then you've seen as much blood as any man. So what exactly were you doing in these woods? There is no way you could have known this thing was going to drop down here," I said, pointing to the arrow-stuck carcass.

"Wasn't hunting Iskarit--was hunting Ogdognal. Heard there were some strange creatures spotted around here and so I came to have a look."

It was obvious to me now that this young man was seasoned in the Hunt, particularly for his age, and was fairly versed in demon-lore as well.

"I heard rumor that Crokow was seen stalking about this way. Hoped to find a crew willing to hunt that cur daown, but so far I've found nothing but boys with swords that fancy themselves Hunters."

Kae-san stirred to shoot down the boy's ambition but I raised a hand to cut him short. Now thoroughly interested in our new acquaintance, I probed him further.

"Crokow is no trifle, yet you planned to take him by yourself, if necessary?"

"Every man who crosses Crokow knows its danger. I met it once when riding with a group of eight that called themselves the Free-Riders. They were my friends, but few of them came out of that meeting with their lives. If I could find ten willing swords, I would gladly repay that hell-lunger in kind. But to answer your question, yes, I will take Crokow on alone if need be." I decided to break the news to him.

"I'm afraid you won't get the chance my friend. My brothers and I dispatched Crokow and two of his horde a few months ago."

"You lot?" he replied suspiciously. "Many a man would be quick to claim such a kill, but claim so falsely!"

Seeing his disbelief I reached for my proof. In a weather-worn saddle bag I dpet some token of some kills, and from it I retrieved a broken claw taken from Crokow's carcass. A Hunter needs proof of a kill from time to time, if not for others then most certainly for himself. Holding it again, I felt in its heft weeks of hard riding, sleepless nights, and empty stomachs when there was no time to stop for a meal. If not for the taste of victory it left, I would rather not have its memory. I tossed the heavy claw to the young archer for his inspection. He turned it over in his hands carefully, nodded his satisfaction, and tossed it back to me.

"Perhaps I misjudged you three. How many others were with you when you took Crokow?

There was another band of Hunters involved in the fight, Baptines, but they proved more nuisance than use," replied Rag-dan.

"Nusiance," quipped the archer, "sounds like the Baptine I met one time." Even Kae-san had to smile at the jab.

"And the fourth...gargoyle, the one that attacked me," he asked, pointing after Invictus' former mount. "It's rider was in this fight as well?"

The raw pain of our lost brother still lay heavy on us. The archer must have sensed this, for he looked away uncomfortably.

"Yes," I said. "His name was Invictus, and he lost his life in the Battle at the Rock of the Ages not long after helping us kill Crokow.

"He died like a warrior-ture," added Kae-san proudly. "Send three Blue Wings back to the pit as he fell."

"Three Blue Wings! Unbelievable!" said the archer, astonished.

We have spoken true, archer," I replied. "Whether you believe the truth or not is your choice. We have no more time to waste here. There is a summons upon us to join with a host that Jonasius himself is gathering for battle at Zanainthrall." I started to turn my mount but the archer shouted after me.

"Wait! Let me go with you," he said with what sounded like relish for the fight. "I do not know the way to Zanzinthrall, but I am strong and can deep up any pace you set. I have a good horse tied not far from here."

"Does this good horse have wings?" said Kae-san. "We are not traveling by land, as we already told you! Besides, this will be a battle for veterans. Why should we be responsible for the death of an unproven lad like you!" The young archer bristled at Kae-san's dig.

"In one minute of close combat I could prove all that you need to know!" replied the angry young man as his hand rose to the long-bladed axe sheathed across his back. I doubted the young man a sword-match for Kae-san, though I certainly admired his sand. He seemed fearless enough, and I had already judged his skill level with a bow to be almost frighteningly extraordinary. A bowman such as this could be very useful in the coming battle.

There was, however, one little obstacle to the young man's request to come with us, that being his ability to accept a flying gargoyle mount, as well as the creature's willingness to accept a new rider. I looked around to conclude that the beast must have meandered off in the woods, but then my ears caught the sound of beating wings.

A large stand of wild blueberry grew nearby, bunching high against some trees, blocking my view of the sky. Pulling back the bushes, I looked back at the archer, jerking my head for him to come have a look. Walking over, he looked through the bush I had separated and saw the airborn gargoyle hovering over the treetops.

About that time the beast spotted us and growled, twisting its fanged mouth into a snarl, further showing its fierce and dangerous nature by extending its claws. I looked at the archer, gauging his reaction. His face bore the look that comes to everyone upon their first sight of the Ferocious in flight. His face was a reflection of fear, mixed with confusion and awe, all at once. I gave him a moment to try to come to terms with flying such a beast.

"I think I can fly it," he said finally.

"I'll have your name first." I said, allowing the moment to humble him a notch. He certainly needed some humilty.

"My name is Dallion, Dallion son of Graycott. My father, and all our fathers before him, were archers. It is in our very blood."

"Alright, Dallion, son of Graycott. That," I said, referring to the hovering beast, "is a Gargoyle. It is both a tracker and a mount, and it can cover ground either on land by hoof-claws or through the air by wings, whichever is preferred. We ride these creatures across land and sea--and into battle. From the look on your face," I added, "you may not be ready to approach such a thing." But Dallion did not want to seem afraid, though clearly he was, and should have been.

"No...no, if you all can ride them, Dallion can ride them as well."

"We shall see. If the other men agree, I want to invite you to join our band, at least on a trial basis," said I to him and looked to Rag-dan and Kae-san for their reactions. Rag-dan nodded agreement. Kae-san, still bitter from the earlier confrontation with the young archer, said nothing as he turned away. I took that as a definite 'maybe.'

"I want in, as a trial," said the young archer with obvious satisfaction.

"Alright Dallion, let's get you mounted and ready to fly," I said as I called for the mount that had been ridden by Invictus. The beast came to us, sniffed about the young archer, and seemed ready to allow the man to ride on his back.

The beast seemed to warm to the new rider well enough, and Dallion took handily to the reigns, at least while walking about on the ground. When the archer felt comfortable enough, Kae-san volunteered to introduce him to flight. Kae-san kicked his mount into the air and called Dallion's beast to follow, which it did, with relish. Up through the trees and into the clouds Kae-san led, the archer's mount following and matching wing-beat for wing-beat. Kae-san had them climb high, stall, and then dash towards the earth at harrowing speeds. Dallion the archer was ghost-white pale when the gargoyle returned to dump him unceremoniously into the grass, at our feet.

"Perhaps you two will grow to be friends," I said to Dallion. "It is much better to be friends with a beast than to be its enemy."

"I thought I had already made friends with it," said Dallion, still breathless and grasping two clumps of grass in his fists as if to hold himself forever to the ground.

"I wasn't speaking of the gargoyle," I replied while looking chidingly at Kae-san, who only grinned in return.

Dallion stood up and, with slight reluctance, climbed back aboard the gargoyle. I looked about at our newly whole Dreadlock, and with nodding approval said,

"Enough delay! We must hurry and not be late to the battlefield. Generations have passed since such a thing has been seen and I'll be dead before I let a Baptine ride ahead of the Dreadlock!"

"I'm sure Theologus would be sore if you didn't show," added Ragdan, smiling.

"We'll be sore if he does," Kae-san said, laughing.

"Blue Wings to our front and Baptines to our rear...what could be more fun than that?" Our mounts leapt skyward as we laughed together, rising on strong wings and a strong wind that would carry us to Zanzinthrall, and battle.

The End...
Of Book One

SCYTHE

VOCABULARY DEVELOPMENT

What is the meaning of each of the following words as used in its context?

Acidic (found on page 2)
Vengeance p.5
Emboldened p.6
Harmlessly p.8
Stoic p.11
Unmistakable p.13
Reunited p.18
Inn p.19
Glimmer p.22
Certain p.24
Hope p.27
Hideous p.27
Amiss p.27
Penultimate p.32
Specie p.33
Score p.36
Mischievous p.44
Encumbered p.45
Massive p.48
Impenetrable p.55
Sardonic p.55
Liberties p.55
Baffled p.56
Tantamount p.56
Quartet p.56
Over-reach p.57
Conclusion p.57
Antagonist p.58
Variety p.62
Obedient p.63
Suspicious p.65
Woods craft p.77
Cogent p.83
Volunteer p.91
Rummaged p.102
Skillfully p.107
Betrayed p.112
Impossible p.113
Hovering p.113
Screech p.118
Design p.121
Deceiving p.121
Parry p.123
Retaliation p.140
Glimmer p.142
Fray p.143
Survival p.143
Bested p.145
Protective p.145
Patient p.145

SCYTHE

10 Questions for Discussion:

1. What was the official name of the group of Hunters lead by Scythe? What ideas and/or feelings do you think bonded these men together?
2. What was the name of the leader of the Baptines who disliked Scythe and his men? Did he have a good reason to dislike Scythe? Why or why not?
3. Who was the youngest member of Scythe's group? What kind of personality did he have? Did you like this character? Why or why not?
4. What kind of creatures were utilized by Scythe and his men that gave them an advantage over others? What member of the group discovered these creatures? How did the use of these creatures change the group?
5. What structure stood in the way of Scythe and his men when they were on the way to the Council? What painful lesson did one of the men learn when investigating this structure? What was the one painful lesson you have had that you will never forget?
6. What kind of place was the Great Hall Lionloff? What were some strange things you noticed about that place? How would you feel if you ever visited such a place?
7. Who was the girl that Scythe cared for very much? Why had Scythe had to leave her when he was a younger man? How did the girl feel about Scythe when he found her walking on the beach? How would you like that part of the story to turn out?
8. The girl in question seven had a father. What was his name and what did he do for the Order? What kind of relationship did he have with Scythe? Do you think he wants Scythe and his daughter to get back together? Why or why not?
9. In fifty to sixty words, describe the character named Ar-ric and the role he plays in the story.
10. What is the difference between fantasy and reality? Why do people need to read fantasy literature? Which do you enjoy the most, fantasy based stories or historical, reality based stories? Name some other well-known fantasy stories, books or films?